THE LIBRARY AT THE EDGE OF THE WOOD

LIZ DELTON

The Library at the Edge of the Wood
Copyright © 2026 Liz Delton
All rights reserved.
Paperback ISBN: 978-1-954663-33-6
Hardcover ISBN: 978-1-954663-32-9

This book was proudly produced by humans:
Map and Deluxe Cover Design by Liz Delton
Trade Cover Illustration by Amy Marchant
Cottage Exterior and Character Art by Amber Finnegan
Cottage Interior Art by J.P. Misslecrow
Black & White Character Art by Mirela Pilko
Edited by Sara Lawson
Formatted by M. H. Woodscourt

Tourmaline & Quartz Publishing LLC
P.O. Box 193, North Granby, CT 06060 USA
www.LizDelton.com

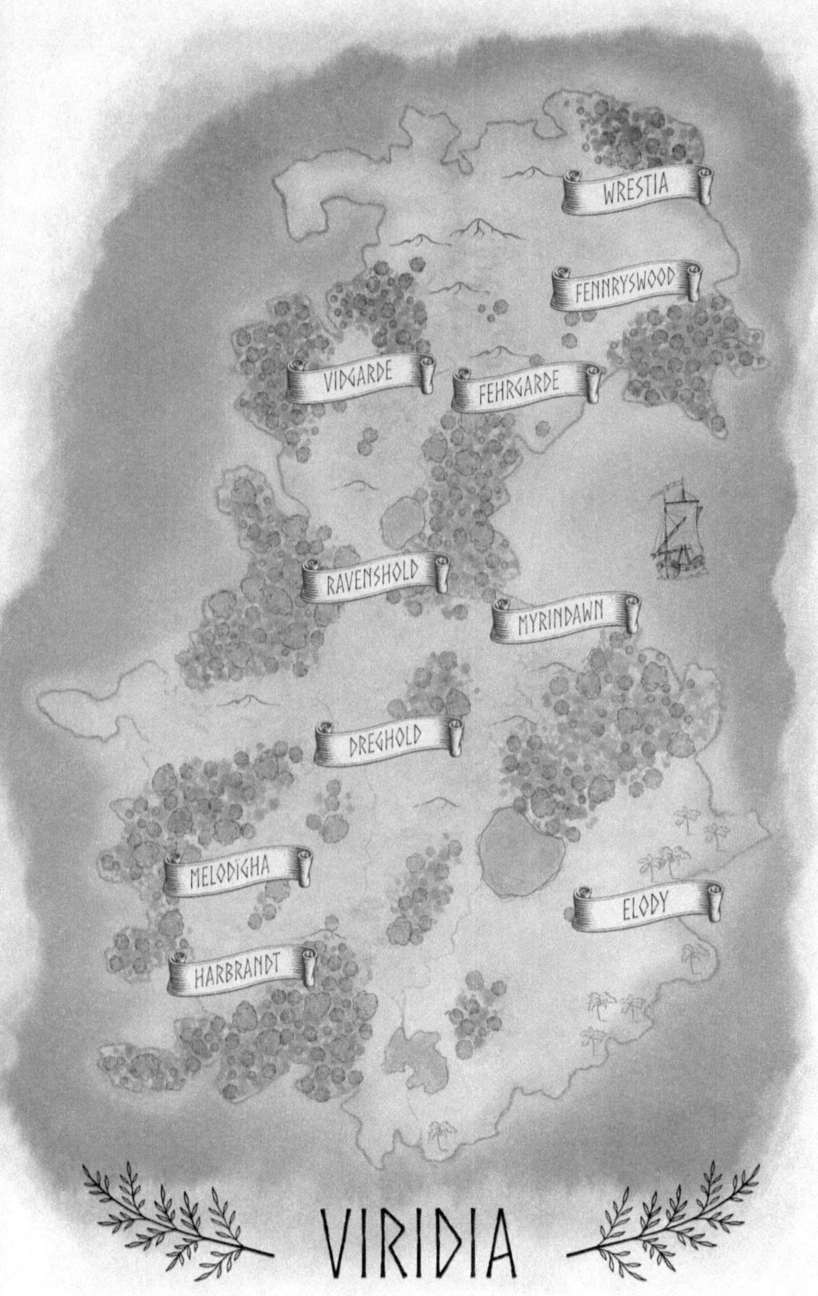

WRESTIA
FENNRYSWOOD
VIDGARDE
FEHRGARDE
RAVENSHOLD
MYRINDAWN
DREGHOLD
MELODIGHA
ELODY
HARBRANDT
VIRIDIA

ACT I

Fierce snow pelted Everson Wrestin as he trudged back home, winds from Mount Wreya battling down at him as if to dissuade him from returning. But he'd finished with his deliveries for the day, and all he could think of was curling up with a cup of tea and a book.

By all the gods and Omens, he didn't want to be out here—trekking through the snow. And his small flat back in Wrestia wouldn't be much warmer, since he'd been gone all day, but at least he'd be out of the wind and snow. Once he got the fire going, it would take a few hours to warm the drafty place up. But it was all he could afford while he saved up to attend Ravenshold University.

Everson sighed, his breath clouding before him only to be whisked away by the next gust of wind. He pulled his hat lower and shivered. He wished he had a warm cozy place to call his own. If he went back to the palace and asked his stepbrother, he'd be able to live in his old quarters again.

That was the last thing he wanted to do.

Stuffing his hands farther into his coat pockets, he trudged on. Then he glanced up. Something strange had appeared at the corner of his vision. A cottage at the edge of the wood. He made deliveries to the outskirts of Wrestia every week—how had he never noticed it before?

It looked a little run down, but smoke came from the chimney. A gust of wind bowled into Everson, sending shivers down his back. Perhaps he could seek refuge with whoever lived there until the winds died down. They had a fire; he could warm up before heading home. He turned toward the cottage, feet numb with cold as they sank into the foot-deep snow.

When he reached the cottage porch, he stomped the snow off his feet. The door hung from a single hinge, giving the place an aura of abandonment. But the aroma of smoke was real—someone must be nearby.

He knocked, the sound muffled by his threadbare gloves. "Hello?" The wind howled at his back and pelted him with snow.

No answer came from inside. He gave a shout, competing with the winds. "Hello? Can I come in and wait out the storm?"

Cold air stung his lungs, and he shivered violently. He wasn't cut out for delivery work, but it was the only job he'd been able to hold down since leaving his step-family's palace. He'd spent most of his early years indoors, never one to enjoy the year-round chill of the northernmost city of Viridia. At first, he'd stayed indoors because he preferred his books and the warmth of his childhood home, but when his mother had married a noble, Everson had had to keep to his new rooms out of necessity, lest he accidentally divulge his secret to his new family.

Everson had wanted to escape from Wrestia after his mother and stepfather died. He'd had his heart set on Ravenshold University, where he could devote himself to his studies instead of hiding in his rooms. But he refused to take any of the money his stepbrother had offered him when he'd left the palace and struck out on his own. *And look how far I've gotten*, he thought bitterly. *A delivery boy, freezing his limbs off in a snowstorm.*

He banged his fist on the door once more, harder this time. The wonky door shifted a little, and Everson could see the firelight flickering inside. "Hello? Can I come in please?" he asked through chattering teeth.

From all the children's stories he'd read of witches and evil faerŭn, he wasn't sure if it was a particularly bright idea to enter someone's woodside cottage without permission, but he knew some things in those fairytales he'd read as a child weren't true—like the legend that all faerŭn were evil witches.

He was certain of it, in fact, because *he* had been born with the silver hair and slightly pointy ears of the faerŭn-touched—and he didn't think himself particularly evil.

His mother had known, of course, but would never speak of it—except the day she'd married Vastion the First of Wrestia. That day, she'd pulled him out of his reading nook in the palace nursery where he'd been deposited early that morning while his mother dressed for her special day.

At age seven, Everson hadn't minded his mother marrying a noble, especially if that meant he could explore the palace and the ice gardens, and—even better—the large library tucked in the east wing. That is, until she'd drawn him aside that morning.

"Everson," she'd said, her hands behind her back as she paced the nursery, looking like the most beautiful princess in her gown with her blonde hair sculpted into braids. "Today is an important day. And you must know that I love you and accept you as you are. But the world can be a cruel place. You know that silver hair of yours marks you as faerŭn, don't you, my love?"

Everson nodded. Since he could remember, his mother had made him wear caps, even indoors, to cover both his stark silver hair and slightly pointy ears. Neither his mother nor his birth father had passed him such a thing. He'd read the stories. Faerŭn traveled from their own realm to steal babies and swap them with their own sickly kind.

He didn't believe the tales. But after he'd seen a traveling faerŭn chased from Wrestia by a mob carrying torches when he was five, he knew others *did* believe them.

Eyes swimming in unshed tears, she paced over to him and sank down, her beautiful ice-blue wedding dress pooling around her. She took his little hands in hers.

"Vastion is a kind man, but Wrestia is not a tolerant place. I hope...someday I can speak to him about it. But until then, keep your secret, all right?"

The noble had a son as well and had grown lonely as a widower. He'd met Everson's mother by chance at the winter solstice celebration, and even seven-year-old Everson could clearly see that the two of them had fallen in love.

Everson nodded again, tugging at his cap. It was a new one, which the haberdasher had crafted particularly for the big day. It was a little big—to accommodate the coverage needed for his ears—but Everson didn't like them too tight, anyway. His soon-to-be stepbrother, Vastion the Second, had already taunted him about wearing hats indoors, then skipped away down the halls of the ice-colored palace singing a naughty refrain.

Now standing on the doorstep of the cottage at the edge of the wood, Everson tugged at his cap in reassurance. This cap was a far cry from the riches he'd had while he lived in the palace, but after his mother and stepfather had both passed away from the Fen flu, Everson couldn't stand having to keep to his rooms to avoid scrutiny, no matter how many books he'd squirrel away from the vast library or pastries he'd pilfer from the kitchen. With his mother gone, he no longer felt welcome there, and Vastion's "joking" remarks to the same end didn't help. Everson still didn't know if his mother had ever brought up his faerŭn heritage to his stepfather.

Everson huffed and pushed on the door. "Hello?" he tried one last time. Still no response. The crooked door swung open. The cottage was completely empty. But a cheerful fire was roaring in the hearth to his right, and he rushed to stand in front of it, holding his palms out as he looked around. A passing traveler must have lit the fire and then left, because grime and dust coated the place like it had been abandoned for years. Only a lingering scent of tea, roses, and something else he couldn't identify remained. It reminded him of his mother and her teas. He smiled.

He turned around to warm his back, surveying the cottage. An empty loft sat above a kitchen nook that appeared just as barren. There was nothing else to the interior of the cottage besides a few windows blurred with age, their sills coated in a thick layer of dust. The window closest to the fireplace was tucked in a corner, cozy enough to read by, should he choose to delay his return home. A few chapters, maybe. He just wished there was somewhere he could sit down and relax.

If he hadn't been staring directly at the empty corner by the window, he wasn't sure he'd have believed it when a red and gold chaise lounge winked into existence right in front of him. He swallowed, taking a hasty step back.

Everson yelped as heat seared him. Then he scrambled away from the hearth, turning to make sure he hadn't caught fire. He must have only been the victim of a stray spark. Once he finished checking his coat for the third time, he had to wrestle with the fact that he'd just watched a piece of furniture appear out of nowhere.

He shook his head. No, he'd been reading too much, imagining something like that. But when he lifted his gaze, the thing was still there. He crept toward it, filled to the brim with the need to know for certain if it was real.

He inched closer and closer, his hand extended. The wind outside howled, and he flinched, fingertips finally meeting the smooth material. It *was* real. Or as real as a magical piece of furniture could be.

Was it some magical chaise that only appeared when you needed it? Indeed, it sounded like something from one of his fairytale books. He gave it a poke, but it didn't feel particularly magical. The desperately logical part of his brain was still trying to bring up the idea that maybe he simply hadn't noticed it when he first came in—but he shut that thought down. He had seen it appear.

Tossing fears of cursed faerŭn couches to the wind, he flung himself down to sit with a hysterical chuckle. He *had* been looking for somewhere to sit, after all.

He only wished he had a new book to read—the only one he'd brought with him was a spare novel he kept in his satchel for downtime at the courier's. That book had been thumbed through so many times, its binding was in danger of falling apart.

When he leaned over to retrieve his satchel, he saw a black leatherbound book sitting on the end of the chaise, which definitely *hadn't* been there before. Like magic.

"What in the name of the Omens?" Everson muttered, mouth hanging wide as he stared at the hardcover.

He shot to his feet, looking around frantically. "What is going on?" he demanded of no one in particular—or perhaps the cottage itself, because it couldn't be... It *couldn't be* magic.

Could it?

He stripped off his damp, threadbare gloves and tossed them on the floor near the hearth. Then, he picked up the book. Covered in black leather with gold foil designs stamped onto the cover, he couldn't resist running his fingers over the indentations. He shivered, but that was more likely from the dampness that had seeped into his clothes, so he brought the book over by the roaring fire, careful to keep it a safe distance from possible stray sparks. He sank down to sit cross-legged on the floor and positioned the book before him. Dozens of questions rattled his mind. Where had it come from? Had it really appeared because he had wished for it?

But most importantly... What was the book about?

He lifted the front cover and gasped when he saw the title page. It was *Turn of the Tides,* the newest installment of Vindo Jeffryson's epic *Whirl of the World* saga!

"How in all the Omens...? This book hasn't made it to Wrestia with the traveling tinkers yet!"

He flipped through the pages, eyes scanning the text, then slammed it shut. No. He didn't want to spoil it for himself! He had to sit down and read this book properly! And *now* certainly wasn't the time...

The hairs on the back of his neck stood up, and he looked around the cottage once more. "What is this place?" he whispered.

He had only noticed the cottage when hoping for somewhere warm to wait out the storm, and then a fire had roared in the hearth as if waiting for him. When he'd wanted somewhere to curl up by the window, the chaise had appeared. And the book—he'd wished for a *new* book to read.

By the Omens, this was probably the newest book on the continent.

He shivered again and stripped off his boots, socks, scarf, and finally his hat and coat to lay out to dry beside his gloves now that he was starting to warm up.

The socks he'd removed were full of holes, and even more threadbare than his gloves. *I really wish I had some thicker socks*, he thought idly. He gasped when a fluffy pair of wool socks appeared on the floor before him, and he hastily stuffed his feet into them. He let out a pleased sigh, his eyes wide. As much as this felt like a fairytale, it was becoming increasingly clear that whatever he wished for, the cottage provided. Unless the snowstorm had addled his brain.

What else could he wish for to test his theory?

First things first, he wished for new, warmer clothes. His heart pounded when they appeared, and in a daze he promptly put them on, laying the wet ones by the hearth to dry. The soft, thick fabrics caressed his skin like a warm bath after battling the storm.

"I wish I had a cup of tea," he wished next, and one appeared in a large mug with a handle, exactly the way he liked it. He took a hasty sip and burned his tongue a little, but held onto the cup just the same, the heat warming his fingers. He couldn't believe this.

Next...

His gaze landed on the book. He tugged on his chin as he thought. Sure, it *looked* like the book it claimed to be, but how did he know that the cottage had provided an accurate copy?

"Or are you taking them from elsewhere?" he mused aloud, looking up at the empty rafters. The wind howled outside as if in response, and Everson felt even more grateful that he'd found this cottage. But the book...

He wanted to summon more, but first, he needed to know.

He dragged the chaise in front of the hearth, causing it to scrape loudly along the wooden floor and pulling it back and forth until it was just right. Then, he retrieved the old book from his satchel. A few pages made valiant attempts to fall out as he carefully cradled the old thing. It was Gren Vi's *Exploration of Villikry*, an account of the famous explorer documenting his journey across the country and its faerŭn roots. It'd been one of Everson's favorites since he was little—knowing that the faerŭn were once celebrated had always made him feel less...alone.

"I wish I had a copy of Gren Vi's *Exploration of Villikry*," he said, looking up at the rafters expectantly. When he looked down, a slim green hardcover sat beside him on the chaise. He swallowed.

When he idly wished he had a table to compare the two, one appeared before him, a low table just in front of his knees. He let out a hurrah, starting to feel light-headed. This felt like a dream—one he never wished to wake from. He stood up, sat back down again, then moved both books over to the table, laying them out next to each other.

His well-loved copy was made of ancient black leather, the embossed words on the cover faded from years of use. Pages stuck out at angles, coming loose from the glue binding them. The new one had bright gold foil announcing the title on green leather and hard gold edge protectors on the corners. The pages were lined up pristine and precise, beckoning his fingers to reach out and delve into them.

He remembered his abandoned cup of tea on the

floor and retrieved it before beginning his examination. It was all well and magical that the cottage granted his every wish, but he was making a valiant attempt to reserve judgment on the books. Sure, it *looked* like a beautiful copy of the book, but what of its contents?

Taking a sip of the now perfectly cooled tea, he sat down to work, opening both books and flipping through the pages side by side. Of course, he'd read *Exploration of Villikry* dozens upon dozens of times, and could probably recite it word for word, but he skimmed both pages for accuracy's sake.

As he flipped each page, excitement bloomed in his chest. Between hasty sips of tea, he leafed through the books, finally and joyfully coming to the conclusion that they were indeed identical.

The cottage could make books.

The cottage could make books!

His head swam, and he put his tea down on the table lest he spill it before leaning back upon the chaise.

After staring up at the rafters for a few minutes—or a few hours, he wasn't really sure—he finally straightened. His thoughts raced, book titles surfacing in his mind, and before he knew it, volumes were appearing in his hands. He set each one on the table, running his fingertips over their glorious covers.

Book after book. Heavy hardcovers, slim novelettes, a large blue leather-bound hardcover with silver foil, a set of paperbacks with symbols on the covers, and more. One after the other. His fingers ran over spine hubs, across ribbon bookmarks, along soft indentations of foil lettering, down gilt edges, and around smooth paperback covers.

Soon, he was practically buried in stacks of books. Tears welled in his eyes. It was almost too much.

He'd always suspected magic existed. And now he'd found it here, in the cottage at the edge of the wood.

The storm rattled the shutters on the little cottage, and Everson glanced around at the piles of books he'd summoned. He'd exhausted his mental list of favorite books, which were now piled in great stacks around the cottage. The new Jeffryson book still sitting on the low table called to him. He navigated around one of the chest-high piles of books and picked up the prized volume, eager to enter its pages.

He had to move a few stacks off the chaise and wished for a few more logs for the fire, which he tossed on the blaze, earning a few sparks that flickered up the chimney. Stomach growling, he asked for another cup of tea and a plateful of biscuits. The tea appeared...and nothing else.

He groaned. "Sandwiches?" he asked hopefully. Nothing. He tugged on his chin. So the cottage had limitations after all. Even though his stomach was grumbling, he couldn't resist the Jeffryson book much longer and opened the first page. Besides, the tea should hold him over until...

Until he went home? He frowned. Home was a rundown flat, the best he could afford while he saved for the university. Even if the snowstorm wasn't still raging outside, he couldn't imagine returning home now that he'd discovered this place. It had been abandoned when he'd found it, after all.

He wished for a warm blanket—then another two—and settled in to read.

Neverending books, cozy blankets, and tea? He was never, ever leaving this cottage.

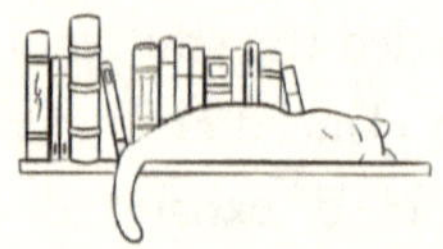

Everson awoke when the book slipped out of his hand and landed on the floor with a *bang*, which made him lurch upright. He had to get to work, had to...

He glanced around the cottage, remembering last night and where he was.

Daylight had begun its weary battle against the snowbound countryside, the sun hardly daring to peek its head over the horizon. It was no surprise to Everson that he'd fallen asleep reading—that was how he always fell asleep—but to awake here...

He stood, a smile bursting across his face as he took in the results of last night's furious book summonings. Dozens of stacks now illuminated by daylight made the cottage hard to navigate, but he made his way to the crooked front door to peek outside. When he wrenched it open, he was greeted by an icy chill. He wasn't surprised to see the snow had gathered in a drift as high as his knees in front of the door. Clear dawn presided over the fallen snow, and ice crystals twinkled over the landscape and every tree branch in sight. He inhaled, the familiar and sharp scent of snow biting his nostrils, and turned to shut the door. It gave him a fight once more, and he couldn't get it to close quite all the way.

His stomach growled, and he frowned. With the daylight—and the very real prospect of losing his job at the courier's should he not show up, Everson realized that he did, indeed, have to leave the cottage. He needed to eat at the very least, and to eat, he needed the money he'd get from his job.

Or did he?

It didn't take long to discover another of the cottage's limitations when he asked for coin and none appeared. Even if he couldn't summon food or money, the books and everything else were worth it.

A plan brewed in his mind, and he asked the cottage for more layers of clothing, a cloak with a hood, a new pair of boots, and some snowshoes. Then he asked for a new hat, a warm knit cap that he pulled firmly over his ears. Finally, he tucked the new Jeffryson book in his satchel along with the new and old copies of *Exploration of Villikry* and made his way out into the snow.

The trek back to Wrestia was even more difficult than ever. Normally, it was because he had his dreams set on moving to Ravenshold, enrolling in the university, and delving into their famed library. But now...now he had his own refuge, and he was loath to leave it.

He made it to the courier's office just in time. His

boss Filgaria handed him a stack of envelopes and one small package, eyeing his new clothes.

"Those are nice, eh?" the gnome said as she leaned a magenta-tinted elbow on her low desk. "Will be nice and tidy for delivering that package."

Everson, still daydreaming of the cottage, looked down at the mail in his hands with a frown.

The package was addressed to Vastion Wrestin.

His eyes bulged, and he opened his mouth. "Can't someone else…?"

"Sorcha's already been in, and Franz is off today."

"But—"

"Hand to hand," Filgaria warned in a singsong tone, pointing at the sign hanging outside the shop window— Hand to Hand Couriers. She'd painted the wooden sign herself, magenta lettering highlighting the letters carved into the wood.

Suppressing a groan, Everson signed off on Filgaria's clipboard and headed back into the cold. Whatever luck of the Omens that had rubbed off on him when he discovered the cottage was wearing off. With every fiber of his being, he longed to return there now, but he needed to keep his job.

He flipped through the rest of the heavy envelopes, memorizing the locations and mentally mapping his route before stuffing everything into his satchel. His brand-new gloves bumped against his new books, and he gave himself a small smile as he headed toward his flat on the way to the palace.

As he passed Beautemps Bakery, he inhaled wistfully, salivating as he looked through the window at all the pastries lining the front counter and the soup tureens lining the back. Perhaps he could spare a couple coins now that he wouldn't need any of his budgeted money to buy new books...

But his pockets were empty, and he had food at home anyway. He trudged past Ragnan Square and down Munin Street, stomach rumbling something fierce as he headed for his flat. Up two flights of stairs that somehow always smelled like wet dog—even though no one in the building owned one—he let himself into his flat with his tiny brass key. His modest bookshelf greeted him when he entered, but he headed straight for his kitchen cupboards. He didn't have the patience to build a fire, so he ate some cheese and day-old bread. *I wish I had a cup of tea*, he thought, then he barked a laugh. He'd already grown spoiled with the magic of the cottage!

Part of him had wondered if he'd suddenly developed his own magic, but now he knew for certain: it was indeed a magical cottage.

"I'd better get going," he muttered to himself. The sooner he could return to the edge of the wood, the better.

Everson couldn't bear to let the leftover bread and cheese go to waste, so he wrapped what was left in a waxed cloth and tucked it in his satchel. He stalked over to the bookshelf and pulled a slim wooden box from between two books, then inserted a key in the lock. Inside were his meager savings—still nowhere near enough to enroll at Ravenshold University what with the rent on his flat and his small food and book allowances. But he could cut out *two* of those expenses in one go by moving to the cottage. He shoved the little black box into his satchel, its contents bulging so much that he had to do the clasps to keep it shut.

Before leaving, he pulled a sheaf of paper from a stack on his bookcase with his nerves jumping madly and penned a letter to his landlord.

I, Everson Wrestin, hereby declare my notice of departure from flat 3B. I have found other living quarters and am paid up until the end of the month.

Heart soaring in excitement, he slipped the letter under his landlord's door on his way out and headed back into the brisk morning.

As much as he didn't want to deliver the parcel to his stepbrother, he thought he'd best get it over with. The sooner he was done with his deliveries, the better.

However, the longer he walked down the frozen streets, and the longer he was away from the cottage, the more it began to feel like the whole thing was a dream. Doubt crept in, and he wondered whether it might have been a little *too* hasty to give his landlord notice so soon. He kept patting the books in his bag to reassure himself. They were still there, as were his clothes and boots, so the cottage and the magic *must* have been real. But what if someone else came along and claimed the cottage while he wasn't there?

He hastened down Vastgar Street, past the ice gardens. A cursory glance through the large open gate revealed some of the ice sculptures: a magnificent ice dragon swirling around a frozen fountain with jets of ice spiraling out of the fountain as the main attraction. The dragon was surrounded by dozens of other sculptures—from nine-tailed foxes to massive flowers, to more beasts of myth and legend. He'd toured the ice gardens with his mother nearly every day before she'd married Vastion the First and they'd moved into the palace. Once she'd become a nobleman's wife, she'd been too busy for daily walks, and Everson had been lucky to get her to come with him once a season.

The excitement of the morning had melted into a black pool of dread in his chest as he spotted the palace. He clutched his bag like the books were the last bit of warmth in a raging blizzard.

What was it that made returning home so difficult? The memories not yet painted with rose-colored hues, which still twisted like a knife in a wound? The terrible need for acceptance that always rested just out of reach?

Digging out the parcel addressed to Vastion, Everson let himself in through the servant's entrance. The guard stationed there recognized him and gave him a nod.

"Hand to hand," Everson muttered to himself, shaking off the cold as he found himself enclosed in the warm, dark servants' corridors. He took the familiar path to the main receiving chambers, encountering no one on the way, which made things easier.

Spilling into the receiving chambers, he caught his breath at the sight of the empty thrones at the head of the room. His eyes were immediately drawn to his mother's chair, slightly smaller than the other but equally as elegant, carved marble with swirls reminiscent of the ice sculptures. His eyes stung, and he looked away from the thrones, cursing Vastion for not being in the proper location. These were public calling hours, weren't they? Annoyed, Everson glanced at the ornate clock on the far wall. They were.

Sighing, he stalked through the room, heading for the doors the public would normally enter through. They were flung wide, but no petitioners stood waiting. It *was* early, he supposed, but where was Vastion?

As he strode through the open doors into the main entry of the palace, he almost ran into a large orc. Thanking the Omens he'd caught himself in time, Everson stepped back, an unwitting smile bursting over his face. Halmund Fraumine, the massive orc in charge of the palace's servants and guard, would have knocked Everson senseless if they'd collided. Halmund's leaf-green face broke into a toothy grin, lips stretching over his protruding fangs.

"Evers, my boy!" he roared.

Everson braced himself as Halmund threw an arm around him in a rib-cracking hug, and he gave the orc a feeble pat on the back. "It's nice to see you, Halmund," he croaked, breathless.

"Likewise, likewise!" Halmund pulled away and looked Everson over. "You're looking well! Met someone, have you?"

"W-what? No, I—"

Halmund tapped the side of his nose knowingly. "Sorry. Had that euphoric look about you."

"Oh, I suppose—new books—" Everson struggled.

"Ah! Of course. Our scholar! Any word on the university?"

"Not yet," Everson said, but was he pleased he didn't sound as morose as he normally did when people brought it up.

"Of course. Vastion's out this morning, touring the ice gardens with his betrothed, but he should be back soon."

"B-Betrothed?" Everson demanded. *"Vastion?"*

"Aye, he's taken to walking the ice gardens with her every morning to get to know her better."

Irritation burbled into Everson's throat, as he remembered the walks with his mother that had been taken from him by this very palace. He frowned, his jaw clenching involuntarily.

"Ah, there he is," Halmund boomed.

Everson started, his arms crossing tightly over his chest. Vastion was alone, striding down the corridor toward them, raven-black hair cutting sharp angles in conjunction with his jawline and cheekbones. A smirk brought up the corner of his mouth as he hailed him. "Brother! So nice of you to come by. To what do we owe the pleasure?"

By the way Vastion was eyeing Everson's satchel, Everson frowned, crossing his arms even tighter. "I think you know, Vastion. I've a parcel for you."

"Well? Hand to Hand, isn't it?"

Everson's scowl deepened. "You did this on purpose," he said, tugging at the parcel to retrieve it from his bag. But in his haste, he dislodged one of the bulging books and sent the new copy of *Exploration of*

Villikry flying. It hit the floor between them with a *slap*.

Vastion bent over with a flourish to pick it up. "You're not still reading this, are you? Though I see you've invested in a new copy, at least."

Everson yanked it out of his hand and held out the parcel instead.

Vastion didn't take it. Instead, he turned his back and strolled into the receiving room, clearly expecting Everson to follow—which he had to do in order to deliver the Omens-cursed parcel.

After exchanging a look with Halmund, Everson followed, safely tucking his book back in his satchel and redoing the clasps.

Vastion paused at a side table to pour himself a tiny glass of sherry, holding the decanter expectantly over another empty glass.

Everson shook his head and kept frowning. "I've got other things to deliver," he said curtly. Not to mention he wanted to make haste in getting back to the cottage. If it had all been a dream born of the snowy madness of the storm, perhaps he still had time to catch his landlord before he made any other arrangements. But the new clothes he'd summoned and the books in his satchel were a solid reassurance against the hysteria. His desire to return was beginning to ache something fierce. How was he supposed to concentrate on work with the promise of such a place awaiting him?

Vastion sniffed the sherry and sipped it, eyeing Everson. "Fine, give it here."

Relief flooding his limbs, Everson handed the parcel

to Vastion, then turned his back and headed toward the door.

"You might want to see what it is," Vastion called.

"I doubt it," Everson said, retreating as quickly as he could.

"It's for you, actually."

Everson halted in his tracks and pinched the bridge of his nose. "It's for…" Turning on his heel, he spun to see Vastion pulling a brand-new hat from the packaging, even higher quality than the new one he'd summoned from the cottage. "So you tricked me into coming here."

"Worked, didn't it?" Vastion tossed the hat to Everson, who chose not to catch it, letting it fall to the floor in front of him.

Everson turned back to the door, shaking his head as a sour feeling filled his stomach. Vastion had always been full of tricks.

"Look, I would have sent you a letter if I thought you'd open it—"

"Omens, and why wouldn't I?" Everson shot sarcastically over his shoulder as he continued to leave.

"How else was I supposed to invite you to the wedding?"

Everson's steps slowed.

"And introduce you to my betrothed," Vastion hurried on, his voice growing closer as he pursued Everson. "Look, I need you there for the ceremony. I *want* you there. Please. I'm sorry I've always been a total prick."

Finally, Everson stopped, his throat swelling. Vastion *never* apologized. What had gotten into him?

"Ah, here she is now," Vastion said, coming up beside him.

A woman entered the receiving room, dark skin wrapped in an ice-blue gown that was all the fashion with Wrestia's upper class these days, with a tight bodice and fur-lined shoulders sweeping out like decorative pauldrons. Her skirts were long and lined with fur to offset Wrestia's unforgiving climate. Her black hair was coiled tightly in braids that were woven into a bun and gave her an elegant bearing from the tip of her head down to her smooth jawline. And her face...it was one Everson knew well.

"At last, we meet again!" Druida called, holding out her arms as if she might embrace Everson. He stepped back to avoid any such thing.

"*Druida Glace* is your betrothed?" Everson whispered, his heart hammering painfully in his chest.

"Of course!" Vastion said with a grin. "Once she saw past my prickly exterior, we became quite smitten."

Druida clucked her tongue. "*Or* our prickly exteriors clashed for so long growing up that they finally melted away like snowflakes in the south."

She came to join elbows with Vastion, and he said, "Clever, isn't she? I keep telling her she should write a book of poetry. Bet you'd read it, eh, Everson?"

"I-I—" Everson stammered. "I have to go. Congratulations." As soon as he'd blurted out the words, he turned heel and ran.

By all the gods, what were the chances that the woman his brother chose to marry was the one person who knew Everson was faerŭn?

LIZ DELTON

LIZ DELTON

Everson's knees wobbled when he spotted the cottage, half buried beneath yesterday's snowfall. Not a hint of smoke came from the chimney. But it was *there*. He wiped his suddenly damp eyes and staggered forward, heading straight for the crooked door.

"Thank the Omens," he breathed as he entered. The place was just as he'd left it, though the fire had gone out. A smile warmed his face at the books stacked throughout the cottage and the cozy chaise by the hearth. He did his best to close the door, but it still wouldn't shut all the way. It wasn't drafty enough to be a problem, just mildly irritating.

He set his bags down on the floor, and went over to the hearth, where he discovered a few coals still had life in them, so he quickly got to work building the fire back up. Elation was filling him up like a balloon—particularly after his harrowing jaunt to the palace.

After he'd left his brother, he'd completed his deliveries and stopped at Beautemps for a quick bite of soup. And to purchase a bursting bag of pastries. The baggy-eyed baker had hoisted extras on him, since it was near the end of the day and they wouldn't keep, which was why Everson had gone there last.

As he warmed himself before the roaring fire and nibbled on a cranberry scone, Everson thought, *I wish I had a cup of tea*. When it appeared on the low table, aromatic steam rising to meet him, he groaned in delight. "I don't think I'll ever get tired of this," he whispered to himself. He made quick work of the scone now that he had tea to wash it down.

Tomorrow was his day off, and on his walk he'd thought out detailed plans for what he wanted to do with the cottage. But he wasn't going to wait until tomorrow to get started. He brushed crumbs from his fingers and stood, adjusting his vest. *I wish I had a large oak bookcase.*

Everson leapt back as one appeared directly in front of him, blocking the hearth. "Omens!" he cursed, running a panicked hand through his hair. The bookcase towered over him, solid oak polished with a dark finish and subtle ornamentation on the top corners. He leaned over to peer behind it. It wasn't in danger of getting burned, but this couldn't stay here...

Placing one hand on either side of the gargantuan thing, he maneuvered it to the nearest wall beside the hearth, sliding, scooting, scraping, and shoving it into position. By the time he got it into place, he was sweating, so he took off his coat and laid it over the back of the chaise, staring up at the magnificent bookcase. It was nothing like the cheap pine one back at his flat, which Everson himself had fixed more times than he could count—since the middle shelf kept collapsing under the weight of his books. Everson ran a hand over the shelves, the grain of the wood telling a story beneath his fingertips. Grinning, he went to the nearest stack of books and started placing them on the shelves.

There was no order to it. For now, he just wanted to get the books off the floor so he could summon more shelves—and eventually more books. *Next time, I'll ask for it closer to the wall*, he thought to himself with a snort.

He couldn't help but study the books as he shelved them, internally cataloguing their titles and trying to memorize their covers. He was in awe of the blessing from the Omens that he'd found this cottage. He supposed his brother marrying Druida was the Omens' way of evening out his luck. He frowned, wondering if Druida had already told Vastion his secret or if it was only a matter of time before his brother found out he was faerŭn.

But Everson had already prepared for that outcome. He hadn't taken any Wrestin money nor even the inheritance his mother had left him. He didn't want any of it. Everson had wanted to make it all on his own. So if Vastion found out, the only thing Everson would lose was a stepbrother who had always been "a total prick"— even in his own words. He shook his head, not wanting to think about that right now. No, right now he had a magical cottage to experiment with.

The shelf towered over him, and he gave it an experimental push. He would need to secure the furniture to the wall, unless he wanted it crushing him with the weight of all his new books.

Though if I had to choose a way to go... he thought

wryly. Then he snorted and asked the cottage for a hammer, a heavy-duty leather strap, some nails, and a stool. He'd done the same for the bookcase in his flat, so he had a general idea of how to do it. He cringed as he hammered one end of the strap into the beautiful book-case, but it was at the top where no one would ever see it. Then he maneuvered the other end of the strap flat on the wall, where he secured it before getting down to study his handiwork.

Half of the books he'd summoned last night fit on the new bookshelf, and he had plenty of room for more shelves. Standing with his hands on his hips, he surveyed the darker side of the cottage, where the firelight barely touched. A few carefully worded wishes rewarded him with a beautiful black candelabra hanging from the ceil-ing, its candles alight.

He stared up in awe before settling his gaze on the floor, where the dust was now even more evident. Everson frowned. He couldn't very well put all his new books into such a dusty place.

Just as he was wondering the best way to clean the cottage, he heard a soft mewling outside. The winds had picked up; he heard them howling through the crack in the door, so he went over to peek outside. Darkness had settled over the snows. It was much later than he'd thought. He *had* spent quite some time looking at the books as he'd put them away...

Shivering on the porch, in one of the footprints he'd left, sat a gray cat, his ears pressed back as if to warm them against his fur.

Everson gasped. "You poor thing!" He wrenched

open the door, and the cat strode inside without hesitation, snow-covered paws padding prints over the floor as it slunk toward the fire. Everson stared at it. It didn't look wild, from the way it had confidently entered the dwelling, but there weren't any houses nearby it could belong to, either. It must have traveled a long way, he concluded, casting about among his bags for something to give the cat.

He pulled out the bread and cheese he'd packed for himself, but that wouldn't do, so he dug in the pastry bag from Beautemps. Toward the bottom he found two sausages, wrapped in baked dough. He quickly discarded the dough, tossing the sausages onto the floor by the hearth.

The cat seized upon them with gusto, gobbling the sausages faster than Everson could have imagined.

"Well, then," Everson said. "I guess I have another mouth to feed. Too bad I have to keep working at the courier's to do so..." he added in an undertone.

The cat ignored him and flopped onto his side by the fire, so Everson went back to his task with a small smile on his face, glad for the company.

"I wish the cottage was clean," he sighed.

As he blinked, the dust disappeared from the cottage as if it had never existed. Even the stacks of books had tidied themselves up, their spines lining up into neat towers. Everson stared wide-eyed around the cottage— even the wet cat-prints were gone, and the gray, spent coals in the hearth had disappeared. He was grateful he hadn't spent any time actually cleaning.

"That does make things easier," he breathed. Now

that the cat was here, it was nice to know he wasn't talking to himself so much anymore.

He yawned, glancing at his satchel where the Jeffryson book still sat. But he wasn't ready to read and sleep just yet; he still wanted to try something else. He went over to the wall behind the door and positioned himself just right before repeating his request for a bookshelf.

Another one appeared, identical to the first, and only a hand-span from his nose. He quickly stepped back to admire it. Since he'd been standing close to the wall, this shelf had lined up perfectly and didn't require any moving about. He retrieved the stool and asked the cottage for a dozen more leather straps, then got to work securing the new shelf to the wall with a content grin on his face.

He sighed in relief when he was back to the floor. Then he stepped to the side to repeat the process. Shelf after shelf, the cottage provided.

Eventually, the whole cottage was lined in shelves— anywhere he could fit them that wasn't blocking a window, or the kitchen nook. Everson grinned like a maniac at the new space he'd created and the promise the shelves would hold. The stories they would keep.

The chandelier cast a respectable amount of light over the space—enough to read by, but nothing intrusive. The dark shelves gave the cottage a great sense of presence, much like the library at Ravenshold, which he'd never seen, but heard stories of from the traveling tinkers. Ravenshold Library was a private institution, one he'd have to pay for, enrolling in the university to even access it. But now...now he had his own library. Or he would soon anyway, once he summoned more books.

A yawn interrupted his musings, yanking his face into submission while his belly growled. He'd completely missed dinner, and though he didn't have a timepiece, the late hour was evident. He scarfed down the bread and cheese he'd packed at his old flat and went over to the chaise for another perfect night with a cup of tea, cozy blankets, and his brand-new book.

A knock awoke him just as dawn was peering in through the windows. Everson threw the blankets off and hastened to his feet, finding his hat and quickly jamming it on his head before answering the door.

An old dwarf stood at ease on the porch, admiring the sunlight as it sparkled through the snow-draped trees that hung over the cottage. A rogue cloud was sifting snow down on them, and Everson couldn't help but smile.

"Excuse me," the old dwarf said, stroking his gray braided beard, which was covered in frost. "But I'm weary of travel and looking for the city of Wrestia. Might you help an old man and point him in the right direction?"

"Oh, of course," Everson said. "Would you like to come in first?"

"That would be most welcome," the dwarf answered with a shiver.

The door gave a little difficulty as usual, but Everson got it closed most of the way before pulling out the bag of pastries and offering it to the stranger. "Come, warm yourself by the fire, if you like. You're not far from Wrestia. I suspect the passing snow was blocking your view, but it's a straight shot north from here."

"I thank you most kindly," the dwarf said, selecting a thickly iced cinnamon bun from the top of the bag, "for the directions, and for the tasty treat. I say, you have a nice place here. Are you opening a bookstore?"

Everson's mouth opened with an audible pop, and he quickly turned toward the kitchen nook to cover the awkward moment. "Can I offer you a cup of tea?" he asked. Then he froze. He couldn't ask the cottage for anything in front of the dwarf!

"That would be even more welcome than this pastry, my boy. Do you happen to have any jasmine?"

"Um, let me look," Everson muttered, turning his back firmly to the dwarf to hide his movements at the empty kitchen counter. He opened a bottom cupboard and asked the cottage for the things he would need, which, just as quickly, he pulled from the cupboard. A teapot, which was conveniently already filled with hot water, two cups, and a tin of jasmine tea. He set them all on the counter, moving them about and preparing the tea, hoping his slim frame had done a good enough job of hiding the magic from the stranger.

"Here we are," Everson said cheerfully a moment later, with a gesture toward the arrangement.

The stranger had already polished off the cinnamon roll and eagerly approached the counter as Everson poured them both cups of fragrant tea. The smell reminded him of his mother, and he smiled.

"Forgive me," the stranger said. "You've invited me in and given me the finest hospitality I've had since leaving Ravenshold, and I haven't even introduced myself. I'm Nod. I'm visiting my brother and nephew in Wrestia."

"Oh, I'm Everson. Pleased to meet you."

"Excellent. Now it's not two strangers sharing tea, but two friends. And this is your bookstore, did you say?" Nod asked, picking up his cup.

"Erm—no," Everson said, seizing his own cup. The thought had crossed his mind when he'd realized he still needed to make money, but he couldn't possibly *sell* these books. The cottage had given them to him; they were a gift.

As he thought of the private library in Ravenshold—where only the most elite were allowed to utilize the stacks—and the joy the little cottage had already brought him, he blurted, "It's going to be a library. A free library."

LIZ DELTON

After a second cup of tea, Nod began looking over the books stacked around the cottage with keen interest.

"I don't suppose you'd lend me a book, young man? My brother needs help opening his shop, so I'll be in the city for a few weeks, building shelves and counters and the like—I'm a carpenter by trade—but I didn't want to carry any reading materials, what with my tools already weighing me down."

"Of course!" Everson nearly shouted. "I'd be delighted to lend you one—my first patron."

Nod tugged on his beard and gave Everson a warm smile, then sifted through the books on top of the nearest stack. "This will do nicely," he said after a short minute of perusing. He held up a slim leatherbound novella: *Interpretation of Myth*.

"That's a good one," Everson said. "Return it whenever you come back through, then."

"It's a deal."

Nod left for his final leg of the journey, novella

tucked securely in his pack, and Everson paced the cottage, his head swimming in the possibilities of turning this place into his own free public library.

Not many would trek this far outside of Wrestia just for books. But still, he'd enjoyed Nod's visit, and Everson was happy to share the wealth the cottage had granted him. A few patrons now and then to share his love for books wouldn't be too bothersome. Even if people took books and didn't return them...he could always wish for another. What could go wrong?

Everson finished off the rest of the tea while he asked the cottage for more books with a renewed vigor—saying the words aloud to Nod had made the idea real—and now he had a public library to fill, not just with books he'd already read. The cat had to relocate to the small loft as the stacks grew, and Everson experimented with his wishes.

"I wish I had some books about Wrestia," he said, knowing he was being vague and not confident the wish would work. He was rewarded by a stack of five books that appeared on the low table in front of the chaise. He sat down and studied their titles. He'd seen *The Noble History of Wrestia* in his stepfather's library, but the rest were new to him. He was excited with the way the cottage didn't need a specific title request, like a personal magical librarian.

Next he tried, "I wish I had a couple of books about running a library." His expectant smile grew as he watched two books appear next to his teacup. He moved the empty cup to make room for the new volumes. The first was *Haverson's Library Sciences*, and the second, *The*

Fall of Imminia's Great Library. He cringed at the title but knew it was worth a read—it was wise to learn the mistakes of the past, even if they weren't always pleasant.

His stomach grumbled, and he glanced at the kitchen nook, where the empty pot of tea sat beside the bag of pastries. He couldn't keep summoning things in front of people, especially if this were to be a *public* library.

I wish I had a kettle of water over the fire, he thought. A black cast iron kettle on a long hook arm appeared over the cheerful flames in the hearth. As much as he enjoyed summoning endless cups of tea directly into his hands, he really needed to set up the cottage to entertain while other people were here. Plus, he had half a dozen stray cups already. So he waited for the water to boil, asked for a hearth-mitt to swing the kettle arm away from the heat, and carried the kettle over to the kitchen nook where he poured the water for a fresh pot of jasmine tea.

Kettle back on its hook, he used the hearth-mitt to lift the lid, peering inside. There was still some water left, but he wondered... "I wish the kettle was full of water."

In the blink of an eye, the line of water rose, filling the kettle to the brim. With a pleased smile, he replaced the lid and swung the arm so the kettle hung over the fire once more, ready for next time.

While he was waiting for the pot of tea to steep, he had a midday meal of two increasingly stale pastries, thinking it was about time he stopped for a reading break. He poured himself a cup of steaming tea and inhaled its floral fragrance with gusto.

As much as he wanted to dive back into *Turn of the*

Tides, he selected the library sciences book from the table.

The cat had stretched luxuriously on the chaise amid the soft blankets, snoozing, and Everson didn't have the heart to move the creature. He put his hands on his hips. He'd already given his landlord notice; it was about time he made this place more livable. He'd made a great start with the tea—a soothing beverage was one of life's requirements for relaxation. Next, he needed somewhere to sleep. Reading could wait...a bit. He frowned at the library sciences book, promising himself he would get to it later.

Everson climbed the ladder up to the loft and surveyed the area. The corner held a crate with some jars, the only remnant from the cottage's previous occupant.

"Hmm. If the main floor of the cottage is a library, I'm going to need my own space up here." He stared down at the ground floor, thinking. "I just wish there was a reading nook up here or something. That's really all I need for myself..."

He turned around to survey the loft again and jumped when he noticed something funny about the boards at the back wall of the loft. Dim afternoon light glowed through the cracks. It hadn't appeared like that a few seconds ago.

He hastily wished for a crowbar. It appeared in his hands, and he went over to the curiously-spaced planks, inserting one end of the crowbar into a crack. Levering it back and forth, it didn't take long to pop off a board, and what he saw behind it made his eyes water. He worked quickly to remove the rest of the boards and soon stood amid the discarded planks staring in wonder. He'd unearthed the most glorious bay window reading nook—something he'd only ever dreamed of.

Why in all the Omens would anyone board this up?

Or had the cottage only just granted his wish to find the reading nook? It was like the cottage had made him work to get a window up here.

"Thank you," he whispered to the cottage. He stood staring at it for several moments, hardly daring to believe it was real.

Soft red velvet covered the cushions that lined the nook, complete with matching plush pillows of red with gold stitching. It was deep enough Everson could probably sleep in the nook if he wanted to, and it certainly looked comfortable for any reading position. He wasted no time in running his hands over the cushions and testing it out by flopping down and putting his hands behind his head. He propped up a leg and sighed luxuriously. It was perfect. Through the mullioned windows, he could only see a blur of white snow, but that didn't matter. The afternoon sunlight filtering through was more than enough to read by.

The temptation to take a break and read then and there was overpowering, but he still had some work to do. He had to return to work at the courier's tomorrow and wouldn't have another day off like this for at least a week. He had to make the loft more functional. This place was his home now, and no one else could claim it from him.

So he tore himself from the nook with a groan. He

started by summoning a bed; the heavy oak bedframe that appeared rivaled the finery he'd had back in the palace and was a grand improvement from what he'd been sleeping on in his drafty flat. Luckily, he'd positioned himself when asking, so he didn't have to move the bed, as it appeared in the perfect place up against the slanted roof wall. Next, a nightstand for his nighttime reading, one with a cubby at the bottom to store the overflow of books that would inevitably stack up. A matching dresser next, complete with a few more sets of clothes. The ones at his apartment weren't much; he'd probably donate them to the poor once he moved all his things. He would need to retrieve his books from there too.

"Oh, then I'll need..." One more bookcase appeared at his wish, to fit his personal collection.

Next, he summoned a black velvet curtain on a rod, which would conceal his private loft from the public library. It was perfect. Except...

After all of his time spent wishing, the sunlight was quickly being stolen by the coming of night, and with the new curtains closed, the loft was growing blanketed in darkness. He asked the cottage for a small candelabra hanging from the ceiling, and two wall sconces in the reading nook.

"*Now* it's perfect," he said, flinging back the curtains to look down at the main floor. His proclamation startled the cat, who bounded from the chaise to lurk in a corner of the kitchen, perhaps smelling the pastry bag.

Everson grinned. The bookcases below looked spectacular, but he had a lot of work if he wanted to make this place a proper library.

But first, it was time to test out that reading nook.

"Another parcel for the palace," Filgaria informed him with a frown when he arrived at Hand to Hand the next morning.

Everson held in a groan. Franz and Sorcha were off today—it being Sylsday, which was normally slow—so naturally, Vastion chose this day to torture him.

He signed the gnome's clipboard and went back into the streets with the parcel and a few envelopes to deliver. This time, he headed straight to the palace without stopping at home.

Halmund was in the receiving chamber when Everson entered. The orc's large face burst into a smile. "Evers, my boy!" he boomed.

Everson eyed him warily. The way the orc's eyebrows perched halfway up his green forehead gave him a guilty look.

"I see you have another parcel to deliver?" Halmund prompted.

"I thought Vastion was done being a prick," Everson muttered, digging the small box out of his satchel.

"Actually, I'm the one being a prick," Druida called, striding into the chamber behind Halmund's wide frame.

Halmund's eyebrows rose even closer to his hairline, and he retreated from the room with excuses about checking on the new guardsmen. Everson shook his head as he watched the orc leave—he'd clearly known what Druida had done.

"Here you are, then," Everson said, striding toward Druida to hand over the package.

She took a half step back, her hands clasped together.

Everson rolled his eyes. "Did Vastion put you up to this? You know that's how he lured me here the other day, right?"

"Well, yes," she admitted. "Halmund told me. So I thought..."

"So you thought you'd force me to visit as well. I have a lot of work to do, so please take your parcel." He took another step, holding it out.

Still wringing her hands, she darted back to shut the chamber doors. Everson flung his hands up in frustration. The doors closed with a slam, and she whirled to face him, her back to the doors. "Omens, Everson, I wanted to talk to you."

He resisted the urge to tug on his hat to make sure it was covering his ears and hair properly. "About the wedding?"

"You know that's not it."

"Then I don't know what about," he lied.

Druida sighed. "What I saw when I was playing hide-and-hunt with Vastion on midwinter that year—"

At age eleven, Everson had been lounging in a nook in the palace library, reading a book on stagicorns when he'd fallen asleep. He'd been awoken by the sound of the library door being flung open, and twelve-year-old Druida calling triumphantly, "Found you!"

As he'd groggily sat up, Everson realized his hat had slipped off his head during his unplanned nap.

That was the last time he'd read anywhere but locked in his own rooms.

If anyone in Wrestia found out...he'd need a lot more than a magical cottage to solve his problems. In fact, he'd have to *leave* the cottage. If people knew the library was being run by a faerŭn, they'd run him out. He'd seen it before.

When Everson was nine, a traveling faerŭn had been run out of town after his hood had slipped at the tavern bar one night. The patrons assumed he was a witch of some kind, there to cast evil spells on them all. Vastion had recounted the tale with incredible detail to young Everson, who'd sat listening, pulling nervously on his wooly hat.

"Have you told Vastion?" Everson hissed to Druida, his hands shaking.

"No, I—"

"Consider this delivered by hand," he whispered, and set the package on the white marble floor before fleeing the palace.

Everson quickly delivered the other envelopes across Wrestia in a daze, slipping them directly into the recipients' hands, as usual. The image of that parcel lying on the marble floor haunted him as he trekked back to the courier's office. Filgaria normally didn't require them to return to the shop after making their deliveries, but obligation steered his feet through the cold streets.

Yesterday's snowfall had been shoveled out of the main pathways, only to be piled up against buildings. He kicked a snowbank before yanking the door open.

The bell rang, and Filgaria turned from where she'd been sorting letters into the rental mailboxes. "Something wrong?" she asked as she spotted Everson.

He frowned, nodding. "I—I have to resign," his voice cracked. "I delivered a package, and didn't...didn't... I left it on the floor." His gaze cut to the sign on the window, with the illustration of two hands holding a package from either side.

"Oh, Everson." Filgaria sighed, slapping her stack of mail down on the counter. "You needn't resign over that! I thought you'd lost it or something! Omens, boy, you gave me a fright."

"But my contract said..."

"Everson, I'm not a fool. That orc from the palace gave me that package to deliver...t*o the palace*. I'm glad you didn't play their game."

"Halmund arranged the delivery?" he demanded, irritation searing through him. "I *knew* he had something more to do with it."

"Franz and Sorcha will be back in tomorrow. I'll relegate any palace deliveries to them from now on."

Everson swallowed. "I... Thanks, Filgaria."

"Nothing to it. Oh, and your payout for the week is in your mailbox. I'll see you in the morning!" She winked and went back to sorting letters.

With more coins added to the box in his satchel and a lighter heart, Everson headed back into the snowy streets. He still had a lot of daylight left, so he headed to Stetler's Sleds to trade a silver coin for the use of a sled and a mule to pull it. The couriers occasionally rented from Stetler when they had large parcel deliveries, so Everson got a deal on the rental, and the man even threw in some empty crates.

He pushed Druida and his brother from his mind, not wanting his euphoria over the library to be ruined by old fears and new annoyances.

His apartment looked grimmer than usual when he let himself in, but compared to the cottage's warmth, it was no surprise. He set to work packing his books into the crates, covering them with blankets or spare clothes to cushion them and keep any precipitation out, should today's clouds prove snowy. The furniture was owned by the landlord, so he didn't need to pack any of that—not that he wanted any of the flimsy stuff. His landlord had slipped a note under his door, accepting his intention of departure, indicating Everson should leave the furniture, and stating that anything personal left in the apartment at the end of the month would be thrown away. Everson would be billed for the disposal fee.

Before long, all of his belongings were in the crates and being trundled on his sled down the city streets. Everson still had room in one of the crates, so he stopped at the Winter Market on his way toward the city gate.

He never thought he'd grow tired of pastries, but after eating them almost exclusively for more than a day, he'd decided he needed to stock the cottage with some essentials. And possibly learn how to cook.

Sylsdays were busy at the Winter Market, since most people had the day off from work. They called it the Winter Market, but it was here year-round, perhaps because it always felt like winter in Wrestia—with year-round snows, it was hard to argue. Shops lined Frostmar Street on both sides, each with a permanent display on the sidewalk and sturdy wooden roofs covering the stands. He passed the second-hand bookseller with a wistful smile and continued on to the food vendors. Everson bought bulging bags of oats, barley, and Imminian beans from the miller and sacks of potatoes, carrots, and apples from one of the farm stands. The produce came at a high price, since they had to import it from Vidgarde and Fehrgarde to the south, but Everson had a vague idea of recreating the stew he sometimes ordered from Beautemps.

He stood at the butcher's with his hand on his chin in thought. He wasn't much of a cook, and the cat would need some meat too. So he bought a wax-paper wrapped package of beef the butcher assured him would be perfect for the stew and was already chopped into pieces for him. Before he turned away, the butcher pointed to the herbalist across the way.

"Going to need some spices for that stew. Adrilla will set you right."

Everson nodded and set the package in his crate. The mule had stood by obediently while Everson did his shopping, so he fished a carrot out of one of the sacks and gave it to the old boy. The mule munched uninterestedly as Everson approached the herbalist, who loaded him down with small bags of thyme, rosemary, fennel, salt, and pepper. He handed over the required coins and carefully tucked the spices into his coat pocket so he didn't lose them among everything else on his sled.

When he finally arrived back at the cottage, the mule huffing white clouds in the cold air, three people were waiting on the porch.

LIZ DELTON

Library Card
A patron's key to unlocking books at a library.

-From Haverson's Library Sciences, by Acclaimed
Librarian Zachariah Haverson, who managed the
Melodïgha Library for forty-two years.

E verson tugged his hat tighter and led the mule up to the porch.

"I hope you don't mind," Nod said jovially, "but my nephew Hiron could use something to read, and their neighbor wanted to come too."

Delight tingled in Everson's chest, and he ushered them inside to warm up. Luckily, he'd asked the cottage to stock up on firewood before he'd left in the morning, so he tossed a few of those logs onto the fire while Nod's nephew and the elderly woman with them huddled close to the hearth.

Nod helped Everson unload the sled, stacking the

crates just inside the door. Everson gave the mule another carrot before he returned inside.

"I've already finished *Interpretation of Myth*," Nod confessed as they entered, Everson struggling to shut the door as usual. "You know, I could fix that door for you one of these days."

"Oh, it's fine," Everson lied, giving it another shove. Good enough.

"I don't suppose you have any more of that delicious tea?" Nod inquired.

"Of course," Everson said with a grin, glad he was prepared this time. He scooped a few spoons of leaves into the teapot, then retrieved the hot water from the hearth. After a few minutes, everyone had a steaming cup to warm them from the inside.

"So you need another story, eh?" Everson asked Nod. "I haven't quite put the books in order yet, but I'm sure we can find something."

"My nephew needs some books too. Hiron's teacher's been out with Fen flu these last few weeks." Nod shuddered. Everson turned to the nearest bookshelf, wondering if he had any books suitable for the boy. "Ms. Francesca, heard us talking and wanted to tag along."

"No, I *wanted* you to bring a book back for me," Francesca announced sourly. "I didn't want to make the trek all the way out to the woods, for Omens' sake."

Everson froze in his examination of the bookshelf, not sure what to say to that.

Nod winked at his nephew. "I can't very well decide on what *you* want to read, Ms. Francesca. Books are a very personal decision. Such a private experience, exploring a story in your head. And besides, it's good to get outside every once in a while, eh?"

Francesca grumbled something and went over to the shelf on the left of the hearth, her thin arms clutched about herself. Everson wasn't sure he'd be getting back any books he loaned to her, but that was all right. He could always ask for more.

Nod meandered away to browse the shelves—and inspect the woodworking, apparently, as he ran his hands over them—leaving Everson staring at little Hiron.

"Erm," Everson began. "What kind of books do you like to read?"

"We've been learning about the Trade War of 5220 in school," Hiron began, his hands finding their way into his pockets nervously.

"No, no," Everson clarified. "I mean, what do you like to read for fun?"

Francesca let out a derisive laugh from across the cottage. Everson narrowed his eyes at her, but she said nothing. He sank down to get on the boy's level. He looked maybe ten years old. "Look, you can read to learn things, or you can read to see things through someone else's eyes. Whether that someone else was a real person or not doesn't matter. The story is real in your head, isn't it?"

Hiron nodded, though he didn't look quite convinced. Everson frowned as he surveyed the cottage. He was sure he didn't have much reading material for someone Hiron's age, but now he was determined to find something. He just wished he could summon books without anyone noticing.

The crates by the door drew his eye, and he had an idea. He began digging about in one of the crates with his back turned to the others. *I wish I had some daring adventure books for a child and a history book that includes the Trade War of 5220.* He added the last request for good measure. He didn't want to be responsible for the boy falling behind in his studies.

To further cover up the magic, he took the new stack over to one of the shelves and pretended to sift through everything there. "Ah! Here's some you might like," Everson announced, pulling two of the adventure books from the shelf. Hiron took them and eyed them dubiously.

By this time, Nod had found not just one but five books to borrow, and Francesca had two. The old woman clutched the books to her chest, looking at Everson expectantly.

"Oh, um, I suppose I should write those down, so I know which books you've borrowed."

This seemed to mollify the woman, so Everson dug out a battered notebook from one of the crates. He would need to figure out a better system before he had more patrons.

He wrote today's date at the top of a fresh sheet of paper, then scribbled out, *Vincenzo and the Impossible Dragon,* and *Melinda the Magnificent* for Hiron. Nod's books were next, three more mythology books and two about glass-working. "Those are for my brother," he explained.

Francesca explained nothing when she handed over her two books, her expression hardened as if carved from ice. *Jams and Jellies* by Jeryd was on top, but beneath it was *The Dragon Lord's Queen*, a romance novel Everson had summoned on a crazy whim the other night. Everson said nothing, merely wrote out the titles, and handed them back to her with *The Dragon Lord's Queen* on top. Francesca hastily covered it with *Jams and Jellies* and turned toward the door.

"You know," Nod began, "we can return your sled to Wrestia for you, unless you have more business in town today?"

"That would be wonderful!" Everson said, nearly tripping on his way to open the door for them.

"What say you, Ms. Francesca?" Nod asked.

She sniffed. "I suppose I can freeze in the sled just as well."

"That's settled, then," Nod said. "We'll see you soon, I'm sure."

Everson's face was stretched in a grin all afternoon as he set about unpacking the crates and sacks and getting the stew started. As he stood staring at the large pot of water he'd summoned over the fire, he asked the cottage for a book on cooking.

After finding a suitable recipe that he could adapt to the ingredients he had, he attacked the stew with more confidence, finally producing an enticing aroma he knew he'd have to let simmer for a while.

With three new patrons to provide books for, he knew it was time to read the library sciences book.

Armed with a cup of tea and his notebook, he stood in the middle of the cottage, trying to decide where to read. The chaise by the fire looked inviting, but he was sure the soft blankets would lure him into sleep, just like the nook up in the loft. No, he needed to do this research, and for that, he should have...

He wished for a desk right in front of the window, which wouldn't take away any space from the bookshelves. It was narrow, with plenty of cubbyholes and little drawers. After populating it with pens and paper, he opened up *Haverson's Library Sciences* and flipped to the index. He had a lot to learn, but one pressing issue about running a library needed to be figured out first. Finally, he found a section that might help.

Borrowing Card

When a library patron checks out a book, it is best practice to insert a borrowing card inside the book to keep track of when the book is due back, and who is borrowing it. The library can also use these cards to track how often certain books are borrowed. Also included on the card is the patron's library card number.

Everson consulted the index again. He had a long night of reading ahead of him, but of course, reading was always the perfect way to spend a night.

LIZ DELTON

LIZ DELTON

E verson awoke early, having gone to bed at a reasonable time for once. It was probably because he'd gone straight to bed after his research and dinner of passable beef stew, instead of losing himself in an epic adventure until all hours of the morning. He had to report to work in a few hours, but that didn't stop him from sitting down at his new desk with a fresh cup of tea and an apple for breakfast, ready to work.

He didn't really expect any patrons today—Nod and Hiron both had a lot of books to work through, and Francesca seemed unlikely to ever return—but he was determined to streamline his process just in case. Now that he had real patrons, it all seemed so official, and the thought made him smile.

He'd made several notes on borrowing cards last night; it seemed straightforward enough. But for the library card... He wanted something different. He asked the cottage for a stack of blank paper cards and began sketching out what he wanted to put on them.

Though he had no intention of charging for

membership, he wanted his patrons to feel special; after all, not every pleasure in life required a great fortune, and they would always be welcome here in the library.

So he sketched a few ideas for a library card, crumpling his failures and tossing them toward the fire. He missed every time but kept trying.

The cat came over to rub his body against Everson's leg, and he gave him a scratch behind the ears. Everson had tried to feed him some meat last night, but it seemed the creature was fending for himself well enough. He didn't want mice in the library anyway, so it was an excellent arrangement.

The poor thing needed a name, but he was no writer, coming up with clever names for characters and creatures on a whim. Perhaps he'd peruse some books and find the right name that way.

The new timepiece that now sat on his desk indicated it was well past time to leave for work, so he tucked his best attempt at a library card in his pocket to look at later. He wasn't sure if he'd be able to ask the cottage for cards like this, but maybe he could get them made in town when he had some money to spare. They weren't terribly important for running the library, but ever since reading about them, it was all he could think about.

Before heading out the door, he picked up the crumpled-up papers and tossed them all in the fire. Adding a few more logs assured him it would still be warm when he got home.

Filgaria was busy sorting letters when he got there, and she greeted him by jabbing her thumb at his mailbox. He'd already gotten his pay, so he was surprised to see an envelope sitting there. That is, until he opened it and saw the heavy paper and swirly writing.

You are cordially invited to the wedding of Lord Vastion Wrestin and Duchess Druida Glace, to take place upon...

Everson's chest constricted. "At least they didn't try to trick me into going to the palace again," he muttered.

Filgaria made a snort of agreement and returned to sorting.

Another slip of paper fell out when he tried to put the invitation back in the envelope. He reached down to pick up the ice-white card.

Your presence is expected at the family rehearsal dinner on the eve of the wedding.

It was written in the same swirly script, likely done by a calligrapher. But underneath it, in an untidy scrawl, it said, *Everson, please come. We want you there for this. -V*

Longstanding Viridian tradition dictated the dates of noble wedding feasts by the moon cycle, and Druida's and Vastion's was no exception. Two weeks, the day before the full moon. Everson shoved the card back into the envelope with the invitation and stuffed the whole thing in his pocket. Then he accepted the stack of parcels and envelopes Filgaria handed him and set off to deliver them across the city.

A few times as he trekked through the snow-dusted streets, he pulled out his library card sketch to admire it. His fingers brushed the ornate wedding stationery, and he ignored it.

After his last delivery, when he passed Quill and Quandary, a small print shop, Everson couldn't help but pause. He pulled out the library card sketch again and strode inside.

A strange smell overwhelmed him, like that of a brand-new book but multiplied by a thousand. A woman with sharply cut short gray hair dressed in a formerly white apron bustled out from a back room, ink stains of black, blue, and even red covering the apron in splotches and smears.

"What can I do for you?" she demanded briskly.

"I was wondering what it would cost to get something like this printed?" He handed her the sketched card. "But I would need someone else to do the..." he gestured vaguely at the words and drawing.

"Oh," she said, eyeing it through her half-moon glasses. She only came up to Everson's shoulder, but she commanded more confidence than Everson had in his left pinky. She cocked a hand on her hip and set the card on the counter. "We have a library?"

"Um, yes," Everson said. "I've just started it. And I was hoping to get cards for members, and..."

"How much to join? You might want to add that on there."

"Oh, no, it's a free library."

She eyed him over her glasses. "Then you should definitely put *that* on there, son. People will be lining up to borrow books! Are you sure you don't want to charge? The cards'll cost money too, I'm afraid. This isn't a free printer!" she joked feebly.

Everson snorted in amusement. "No, of course. The books were...a gift to me, so I want to lend them to others as a gift too. I just wanted to see how much it would be to print a few; I don't expect too many patrons."

"I doubt that, son. I tell you, they're going to be lining up. Where're ya located?"

He explained, and she said, "Ahh, now I see why you're hesitant about getting patrons. Could be some folk won't want to trek all the way out of town, but for free books... Well, I can do you a deal if you want to get a hundred or more, but otherwise, it'll be six silver for twenty. And that includes typesetting and design."

"Six silver for twenty?" Everson echoed. "Well, maybe after I have some more patrons," he added forlornly.

"Actually," the printer said, "I have an idea. The setting of the type is what makes printing something like that cost what it does. Lining up all those tiny little letters, you know? And then a custom metal plate for the logo you have there. But what if it wasn't *printed*?"

"What do you mean?"

The printer turned to the back and called, "Geminigh! Come up front! And bring your latest one!"

Everson's brow furrowed as he waited. Another printer—judging by the state of his apron—but this one a gnome, emerged from the back. His turquoise and gray hair was mussed, and round spectacles perched on his long, light-turquoise nose. He had something wooden in one hand and a small carving knife in the other. "Yes, yes, what is it, Ada?"

"Show it to the boy."

"Oh, of course," Geminigh warbled, setting the thing down on the counter. It was a small block of wood, with a reddish substance glued to one side. The substance had been carved with what appeared to be words, as it looked half done. "We've been importing this stuff from Imminia—they call it 'rubber.' A few years ago, the traders discovered these trees whose sap—mixed with a few other ingredients—turns into this stuff. It's pliable and makes for excellent on-the-spot 'printing,' if you will. Here." Geminigh took the stamp and went over to a tray of black ink, gently settled the rubber portion into it, then brought it back over to the counter where he withdrew a sheaf of scrap paper from his pocket.

He gently placed the stamp on the paper, producing the words: *Til— Tinc—*

"Tilly's Tinctures," Geminigh clarified. "I'm not done carving." He held up the knife unnecessarily.

"That would be perfect!" Everson exclaimed. "I could make the library cards fresh on the spot."

"And however many you want, provided you have the paper and ink."

"Oh, I can get those easily," Everson blurted out, then his face warmed. "But how much would a custom stamp be?"

Ada muttered a few words to Geminigh, who was staring down at his incomplete stamp.

"Hmm, yes," he muttered.

"That'll be one silver," Ada said.

"That's it?" Everson demanded incredulously. "But—"

"Look, son, you're doing Wrestia a service," Ada explained. "And Gem's stamps are a new item we're selling, so you'll be one of our testers, all right? It's only fair we give you a discount."

A grin spread across Everson's face. "It's a deal then."

R omance Fiction. Everson tacked the placard to the top of the bookcase by the hearth, carefully balancing on a stepstool, and wondering if Ms. Francesca had enjoyed her *Dragon Lord* book yet. Not that the grumpy woman seemed likely to admit to enjoying anything.

Two days had gone by with no visitors, Everson spending his mornings delivering packages and his afternoons summoning books. The library was growing.

The library sciences book had given him some pointers about organization, and he made signs for each bookshelf to help with the process. The cottage had provided wooden placards to his specifications, and he'd painstakingly lettered them by hand with his new pot of ink and brush pen. His handwriting was all right, although nothing like the calligraphy on his brother's wedding invitation, which was hidden away in the top drawer of his new desk. He hadn't looked at it since receiving it.

Druida seemed nice enough for Vastion, but by the Omens, she knew he was faerŭn. She'd *said* she hadn't told Vastion, but Everson wasn't sure whether to believe her or not.

And yet…if Vastion knew, surely he wouldn't be insisting on Everson's presence at his wedding, right?

The uncertainty was too much. All he wanted now was to build the library and keep to himself.

He pinned up placards that read *Stories For Children of All Ages*, *Histories*, *Practical Crafts and Hobbies*, *Fantastical Adventures*, and *General Fiction* above the other bookcases.

"I think that's enough for now, don't you, Randalf?"

Randalf the Gray meowed and lazily reclined on the chaise, his favorite spot. Everson had named him after a mage in the *Whirl of the World* saga, when he'd made the connection with the cat's coloring. He'd been toying with book-related names, but Tome and Spine hadn't seemed fitting for the easy-going feline.

Footsteps thundered up the front porch, and someone pounded on the door. "Mister? Librarian, sir? Please tell me you have the next *Vincenzo* book!"

Everson wobbled on his stepladder and dropped the tin of tacks as little Hiron cracked open the crooked door and poked his head through. A gaggle of kids stood behind him, with Nod at the back of the group. Everson chuckled and waved them all in, climbing down from the ladder and stepping carefully around the half-dozen tacks that had spilled.

Ooohs of appreciation filled the library as the kids

filtered in. Some warmed their hands at the hearth, while others bounded straight for the *Stories For Children* section. Hiron was hastily scanning the titles, clutching his prior borrows to his chest with one arm.

Uh oh, Everson thought. He'd only seen the one Vincenzo book when he'd summoned the stack for Hiron the other day. He couldn't bear telling the boy he didn't have any more; Everson knew the look of a reader suffering from a cliffhanger when he saw one. He bent down to collect the tacks, and Nod came over to offer his assistance. The two of them got all the tacks back in the tin, and Everson returned it to his new desk.

"Er—let me check my desk, Hiron. I have some new books in here I haven't catalogued yet. I might have seen a few of those."

Everson wandered over to his new desk and quickly thought, *I wish I had more Vincenzo and His Impossible Adventures books inside my desk.* He stressed the last three words with all his might, crossed his fingers, and pulled open a drawer. Empty. But that was how it had looked before. He tried another and found five books in a neat stack.

He pulled them out. The spines indicated these were the continuation of the saga, books two through six, and Everson stood, grinning. "You're in luck, Hiron. These should last you more than a few days."

Hiron's eyes bulged, and he hastened over, holding out his hands to take the whole stack. The dwarf boy headed straight for the chaise and flipped to the first page as he sank into the cushions next to Randalf the Gray.

Nod chuckled, watching the boy. "That was a good

recommendation you gave him. You really are a fantastic librarian, Everson."

"Oh, thank you," he said, his face warming as he looked down at his shoes. "It's nothing." It was the cottage, really. Everson mentally passed the gratitude on to the cottage as he found his notebook and flipped to the page where he was keeping track of the book borrows, leaving it out on the desktop until everyone was ready.

Nod hadn't retrieved any new books, nor had he brought any back. He was busy stroking his thick braided beard and staring at the cottage door.

"I hope you don't mind," the dwarf said, "but I brought my tools. I'd like to help with your door."

"That would be—" Everson's voice hitched. "That would be—amazing. Thank you. But you don't have to do that."

Nod waved him away wordlessly and went to retrieve his toolbox from where he'd left it on the porch.

Everson didn't know what to do with himself while Nod began measuring the hinges and picking out new screws, so he pretended to study his book borrowing ledger while making covert wishes for books to appear in his drawers, just in case the kids asked for any others.

He carefully opened drawers and pulled the books out, pretending to check them off on a list—a blank page he scribbled abbreviations onto—then brought the stack of new books over to the children's section and began shelving them. A girl with dark braids was sitting on the wood floor, her nose buried in a book about insects native to southern Viridia, and two boys were looking at various covers and debating what the stories might be about. After Everson added the new titles, each of the boys seized one and began inspecting those too.

By the time Nod put his tools away, Everson was ready with a freshly made cup of jasmine tea, which the dwarf accepted gratefully. Everson stared at the door, then tested it. It opened and closed just fine with the new hinges, though it still stuck a little.

"If I could replace the frame and the door itself, then it'd be perfect," Nod mused.

"No, no, this is great," Everson said, a warm feeling in his chest that wasn't entirely due to the lack of the draft. "Thank you, Nod."

The dwarf waved him off. "Think nothing of it. You're bringing a great thing to Wrestia here, and when I found out Hiron and the kids wanted a trip today, I thought I would offer my services while I accompanied them."

"I'm truly grateful."

Nod turned to his nephew. "Hiron, did you check out your books already? We need to get back before your father misses you for dinner."

"Oh, right!" Hiron leapt up from the chaise, clutching all the Vincenzo books to his chest, his thumb stuffed in the book he'd been reading to mark his spot.

Everson readied his pen and ledger. "So you'll be returning the first one?"

Hiron shook his head. "No, I...might want to go back to it, you know?"

"I know," Everson said, nodding. "Then I'll just add these five to your account."

Each of the kids took out a handful of books, and Everson carefully marked them down in his ledger.

Nod gave him a hearty wave as he closed the door. Almost immediately, there were new voices outside, and a knock.

"Hello? This is the library, right?"

"Come in!" Everson called, hastily looking at the desk where he'd summoned a large stack of children's books as soon as the door had closed. But the new patrons entered with an awed expression, gazing up at the bookcases with a hungry look.

"Welcome to the Library at the Edge of the Wood." And so it began.

Everson still had his courier duties in the mornings, but he hastened back to the cottage as quickly as he could each day to open the library. He left a *Closed* placard on the door when he wasn't there, since he often found patrons waiting for him on the porch when he returned home, but it disappeared every time, perhaps blowing off in the wind, no matter how many tacks he used.

The door itself broke the very next day—just after Nod had fixed it. Everson inspected the hinges, which *had* seemed in perfect working order when the dwarf had installed them, but one of them had split in half, and all the screws Nod had installed had rusted so much they were immovable. He couldn't see how Nod could fix it this time and felt responsible for it breaking so quickly. But the new patrons didn't seem to mind once they'd come inside. They were enamored with the selection, and many of them asked Everson multiple times to clarify that borrowing books was indeed free.

Every day he added more books to the shelves, either summoning them into his desk when he had patrons or spending his nights adding to his inventory after he learned what was popular with his guests. He was still waiting on the solution to his library cards, but in the meantime, he continued using the ledger. He liked having all the borrowing information in one location, anyway.

He even had one regular patron who had started to come every afternoon just as Everson was having tea. When she showed up on the third day in a row, Everson offered her tea as well, and within a few days, had her cup ready and waiting at her favorite spot by the fire, where she read for a few hours before setting off back home. She reminded him of his mother, though she didn't actually look much like her. Perhaps it was the kindly expression she always wore. She offered him a big smile every afternoon and introduced herself as Lyla. Her black hair had white streaks coming from the temples, and shallow wrinkles around her mouth and eyes made him think she smiled a lot.

One afternoon, as he was topping up Lyla's cup of hora citrus tea—one she had recommended he try—another patron forced her way through the wonky door.

"You really should get that fixed," the gnome said,

unstrapping her snowshoes and leaning them against the wall. Everson's eyes bulged. It was Filgaria.

Her gaze slid off the door to take in the sight of the library. "Omens, Everson. You did all this?"

Everson couldn't help but grin. "Tea, Filgaria?"

She wrinkled her face. "Can't stand the stuff. Prefer a cup of strong brew from Arcavia, myself. Costs too much to import it at a reasonable rate, though, even with my connections." Everson had smelled the heady drink once, when a traveling tinker had brought some of the Arcavian beans through Wrestia.

Filgaria wandered past the histories section to stand before general fiction with her hands on her hips. "Anyway, I'd been wondering what you've been up to. Never see you coming from Munin Street anymore. But when I got this..." She held up a small parcel.

Everson's face fell. "It's not from the palace is it? Or *for* the palace?" He'd all but pushed Vastion's wedding from his mind.

She chuckled, the light airy sound filtering through the library like music. "No, dearie. It's for you! A package addressed to Everson Wrestin, at the Library at the Edge of the Wood. And I was mighty interested in what all *that* was about, so I had to deliver it myself. And the Omens sure rewarded me. You've been hiding a secret library from me! You scoundrel!"

He ducked his head, and she strode over to hand him the package. It was a small item no larger than his fist, wrapped in thick brown paper and secured with twine. He ripped open the paper and found a wooden block.

"Oh, I know what this is!" he exclaimed, then turned

it over. On the back was the strange red substance, with a reverse image that looked somewhat familiar—the stamp from Quill and Quandary. But he couldn't be sure how it looked until he tested it out. "Come here. Let me show you."

Amused, Filgaria followed him to his desk as she took it all in. "Didn't know you were making this much money working for me. Give up saving for the university, did you?"

Everson shrugged and set the stamp down on his desk. He'd barely spared a single thought for the university since opening the library. "The books were a gift," was all he said in explanation. *Let her draw her own conclusions from that,* he thought. Though, she might assume the gift came from the palace, and he wasn't sure what he thought of that.

Better than divulging the real secret about the cottage's magic.

He pulled out a scrap of paper and picked up the stamp. But he was missing one important ingredient— the ink. He had his desk for that, however, with its mostly empty drawers he used to summon things. The shallow top drawer held spare quills and odds and ends, and the cubbies on top of the desk were enough to store everything else he needed.

I wish I had a shallow tray of black ink inside my desk, he thought, thinking back to the tray Geminigh had used.

He began rummaging in the drawers—he'd noticed the magic liked to mess with him a little, putting things in different drawers each time. Finally, he found it in the top drawer, right next to the wedding invitation. He inhaled a painful breath, removed the ink tray, and shut the door without giving the thing another thought.

"Here," he said to Filgaria. "You might want to get one of these, come to think of it." He dipped the rubber side into the shallow tray as gently as he could, trying not to overload it with ink, then set it firmly down on the scrap of paper.

"I might want to get a library card?" Filgaria said, amused, looking at the final result.

"No—well, yes, you should—but the stamp! The rubber comes from some kind of tree in Imminia, and I can use this to create as many library cards as I like. Provided I have the ink and paper. You could use it for mail or parcels maybe."

"Ahh," Filgaria said, stroking her slightly pointy chin. "I can see where you're going with this. Instead of hand-writing *Hand to Hand* on packages, I could... Oh, Everson, you're a genius!"

"Not me," he said, holding his hands up. "Geminigh

at Quill and Quandary. He carved the logo for me and everything."

"That's *brilliant*. Gnomish ingenuity, right there."

"Then may I have the honor of presenting you with the very first library card, Filgaria?"

Her magenta-tinted face flushed a deeper shade, and she nodded. "The pleasure is all mine."

9

On Sylsday afternoon, Everson heard a groan outside on the porch. He and Lyla looked at each other, and Everson went to the door.

Nod stood there, hands on his hips. "What in the name of all the gods and Omens happened to the door?" he asked. He didn't sound mad, merely curious. The gaggle of kids standing in the snow peered out from behind him.

Everson's face burned. "I'm so sorry, Nod, I honestly have no idea. It happened when I was at work, and—"

"It's no trouble, son," Nod said with a shrug, motioning the kids inside the cottage after Everson opened the door farther. "I'll stop by on my way home tomorrow."

The kids dashed to the children's section and began hurriedly combing the shelves for new titles, amid whispers and gasps of excitement when their roving fingers were rewarded. Everson had been preparing for this all week, asking the cottage for books the kids would enjoy and stocking up the children's section until it was completely full. He'd been particularly amused the night he'd found *The Case of the Cantankerous Cockatrices* and *The Adventures of Nathaniel and his Faithful Steed* in the stack, stories he remembered fondly from his own childhood reading. The cottage had also provided a particularly memorable one entitled simply, *Larry!*, which Everson had flipped through out of deep curiosity the night he'd summoned it. Oddly enough, it was about a courier in the fantasy world of Garrion, where the courier was always getting into mischief. Hiron was now holding that one and laughing from deep in his belly, while the other kids pushed closer to get a look at it too.

"Shh!" The harsh sound came from right beside Everson as Ms. Francesca entered. He hadn't noticed her following behind the group, but it looked like Nod had rented a sled from Stetson for the trip, and she'd tagged along once more. "Don't you know it's supposed to be quiet in a library? People are trying to read."

She glared at Everson instead of the kids. He was grateful for that—he didn't want the kids to feel anything but joy for the books.

"Oh, it's quite all right," Lyla replied from her spot by the fire. Randalf the Gray was curled up on her lap as she read. "I can tune out anything when I read."

Ms. Francesca *harrumphed* and wandered over to the craft and hobby section, nodding approvingly at the new signs marking the sections.

Everson grinned at Nod, who was holding out his borrowed books. "So you're heading back home tomorrow?" Everson asked, taking the books and motioning for the old dwarf to follow him to the desk, as he tried to keep the disappointment out of his tone.

"Aye. Duty calls. My brother Raine's got the rest from here, setting up his glassware—not something I'm cut out for, anyway—already broke one vase! But I'm sure I'll be back through next spring."

Everson's heart fell. He enjoyed the dwarf's company and had been looking forward to discussing books with him over a cup of tea. "I'll miss you," he said. "You were the first to believe in my idea for the library."

"Oh, lad, if you hadn't believed in yourself, you never would have gotten this far."

Everson's face stretched into a welcome smile as tears pricked the corners of his eyes. "I have something for you."

"Is it a cup of hora citrus tea?" Nod asked, sniffing. He eyed the kitchen nook where the teapot sat on a warmer trivet with a small candle inside.

Everson chuckled. "In *addition to* a cup of tea. Let me present you with your library card. I already made it."

He sorted through the small stack of cards he'd made up in reference to all the patrons in his ledger.

Nod's eyes lit up when Everson handed it over. "Now, this is something, Everson. You're going to do really well here. And I can see you've been busy since last week!"

Everson ducked his head, eyeing the shelves. He'd already exhausted all the open space and had started stacking books on top. His personal bookcase upstairs was groaning with effort any time he tried to add any more too. Having access to unlimited books was quite dangerous for an avid reader such as himself.

"I'm not sure I can keep up with all the books needed to service Wrestia!" He chuckled. "I'm running out of room."

Nod stroked his pepper-flecked beard, done in three thick braids today. "You'd need more shelves." He pointed at the high cottage walls above the existing bookcases.

"But how would I..." Everson tried to picture himself carting out a tall ladder every time someone asked for a book on a high shelf.

A wild light entered Nod's eyes then. "I think a rolling ladder would do the trick. Or two."

Everson did indeed have time to discuss books with Nod while the kids picked out their new borrows, and he was grateful for the time spent. Everson insisted that Nod sit at his desk while they drank their tea, since the library didn't have many seating areas. That was another thing he'd have to change, but not with everyone here.

"Oh, I love that series," Lyla exclaimed from the chaise, as Ms. Francesca pulled a volume from a shelf in the romance section. It looked like the second book in *The Dragon Lord's Queen* series—Everson had summoned the rest of the series after she'd taken out the first one.

The old woman turned red, then shoved the book back in place. "Wrong book. I thought this was the *Ravenshold* section," she added curtly, storming back to the craft and hobby section.

Lyla shrugged and returned to her book. As Everson listened to Nod talk about all the improvements he'd made to his brother's new glassware shop, a timid knock came at the door, and two more people entered. Lyla waved them over excitedly to sit with her by the fire. They'd brought books from home, it seemed, since they weren't among the few patrons he'd seen this week. The trio got to chatting happily, books on their laps. Randalf the Gray vacated the chaise amid the chatter and bounded up the ladder to slink under the curtain and hide in the loft.

Everson briefly excused himself from his conversation with Nod, and the dwarf wandered over to see how the kids were getting on. Hiron had a tall stack of books under his arm and was reading the seventh Vincenzo book while he waited.

"Tea, friends?" Everson asked the group by the fire. Eager nods met his question, and he supplied them with fresh cups, pouring out the last of the batch of hora citrus. Just as he was scooping some fresh Queen Gray into the tea pot's strainer, Ms. Francesca came over with a small selection of books including a few histories and the well-known litany, *Omens Around Us*.

Everson settled in at his desk and frowned in thought at the stack. "Is this everything you wanted? Any other titles you might be looking for?"

Ms. Francesca's frown put Everson's to shame, and

she said, "That's it. I just wish I didn't have to come all the way out here to return them." Her gaze went, annoyed, to Nod, perhaps for the audacity of leaving town and not being available to escort her with the kids again after today.

Just then, Hiron and the kids shouted, *"Larry!"* in a singsong admonition just like in the book and burst into a fit of giggles. Before Ms. Francesca could chastise them for their loudness, Everson's mind skipped to the fictional courier, making his deliveries and spreading mischief.

A grin spread across his face. "I think I've got a solution for that, actually. I just need to work out the details."

"Good," Ms. Francesca sniffed. "These old bones really can't be out in the snowdrifts like they used to."

He nodded, then, in a moment of mischief himself, made a hasty wish for a book into his desk. He wasn't sure if it would buoy the old woman's spirits or cause even more discord, but a moment later he pulled a very discrete copy of *The Dragon Lord's Wife* from his drawer, the second in the series she'd been reading. The title wasn't visible on the cover, as he'd requested, but when he opened it, the title page confirmed his subterfuge had worked. While Ms. Francesca's back was turned—she was watching the kids again—he quickly scribbled a note on a scrap of paper.

Books are like magic for the soul. Read what makes yours happy.

He slipped the discrete book in the stack and handed them over with her brand-new library card.

"I'll find a way of contacting you when I have my

plan figured out, so you don't have to trek out here all the time," he said proudly, his heart thumping in his chest. Why had he slipped her that book? Ms. Francesca had been nothing but cantankerous since she'd first visited the library. But what he'd written in her note was true, even for people who sometimes weren't very nice.

That night, after all his patrons had left, Everson shut the door as best he could, and flopped onto the chaise, exhausted. A soft padding sound meant Randalf was slinking down the ladder, and soon enough, the cat was butting his head into Everson's limp hand, which hung over the side of the chaise. Everson grinned and scratched the cat's head.

"This is going really well, don't you think? I'm going to miss Nod, though."

The shelves were bulging, so he wouldn't be summoning more books tonight. Not until he looked into Nod's suggestion of high shelves with rolling ladders. As he thought back to his conversation with the dwarf, he remembered something he wanted to do tonight.

There was an open area on the other side of the cottage; he summoned two chairs with a low table between them. The chairs were plush red fabric like the chaise, and the table was sturdy oak to match the bookshelves. It was perfect for conversations or to read in. In fact...

A low freestanding bookshelf appeared next to the conversation chairs at his wish, which could be used as a surface to set teacups on or to stack even more books...

He grinned. So he *could* still add more books to the library tonight, after all.

10

"A book delivery service?" Filgaria repeated, skeptical.

"Yes!" Everson exclaimed. "I have at least one patron who doesn't want to make the trip out to the edge of the wood, and I bet there's a lot more people who would take advantage of it."

"It's a good idea," Filgaria said, tapping a pencil on her chin thoughtfully, "but I'd have to charge you. My best courier hasn't been taking on as many hours lately." She winked at him.

"I know. I'm sorry. I—"

"Nothing to be sorry about. I'm just worried you're investing more money and time into this library than you have. From one business owner to another."

"Ah," Everson said, the bottom dropping out of his stomach.

Her face lit up. "You should charge the patrons a fee for the service."

"Well, I didn't want to charge, so the place can be accessible for everyone..."

"Not for the library, for *delivery*. That's an extra perk."

He stroked his chin in thought. "You're right. That would make the most sense."

It didn't take long to work out a rate that Filgaria would charge the library for the service. She gave him a discount since he'd bring the books to the courier's office and the deliveries would all be made within city limits.

She whipped out a sheet of paper and began writing out the terms in her tiny, neat handwriting. He thought it over. "That won't be *too* much for people to pay."

"No, no, that's what you'll pay me. You have to charge them more than that, so you make a profit. You have your own savings to worry about, too. It's not like the library is paying you—is it?"

He gave a nervous chuckle. "Omens, no. It's just that the library is supposed to be a gift—"

"The gift is the books," she said firmly, drawing the contract toward her and signing on her line with a flourish. "But your generosity, organization, and execution of the gift should be rewarded. What happens when you get too busy for me and have to quit, eh?"

His face warmed. "Filgaria! That's not going to happen. I need to eat, you know."

"Exactly," she said triumphantly. "If you're not charging for library membership, tack a couple silver onto the delivery fees. You can make your money that way."

"That seems a bit much—"

"Fine, one silver."

His brief silent consideration was enough for her to

seize the moment. "It's settled then. Sign here, and Hand to Hand will start up a 'Book to Hand' service just for you." She smirked at her own cleverness.

He snorted at the phrase, then signed, wondering exactly what he was getting himself into.

"And I bet the librarian can even deliver some of the books himself," she said slyly.

With a chuckle, Everson said, "You're paying me a salary to make deliveries, but I'm paying you to make book deliveries. How does that even make sense?"

Filgaria shrugged. "Ask the Omens. Now, these packages aren't going to deliver themselves, you know."

On his way through town, Everson made sure to map part of his route so he would walk past Nod's brother's shop, which he'd looked up on Filgaria's city registry before departing. But first, he stopped at Beautemps to purchase some pastries. He missed having food around that he didn't have to prepare himself, and an occasional little treat was not just a luxury but a necessity.

He made his deliveries throughout the city, then wove his way toward Clear as Ice Glass Creations. The door was locked, but he could see people moving around inside, one of whom looked like Nod, so Everson knocked on the ice-frosted glass door.

The dwarf who came to the door wasn't Nod. He was a spitting image, except he had less gray in his beard and a few burn scars on his hands. His high-cheekboned face lit up, and he held out his arms, yanking Everson into the shop with a bone crushing hug.

"Oof," Everson said as the air was squeezed out of him.

"You must be Everson," Raine said, finally releasing him. "Hiron's told me all about your marvelous free library. Begs me to go every day, for Omens' sake! Why'd you choose a location so far out of town, eh?"

"Oh, um..."

"Is that Everson?" Nod's deep voice resounded from a back room.

Everson paused to look over the shop-in-progress. The whole place was painted in ice white, from the front counter to the shelves lining the walls; the lingering scent of fresh paint still hung in the air. The new shelves were mostly empty, but the counter held a few pieces: a large vase with blue swirls and a foot-high swan sculpture that could very well have been made of ice. The ice-white paint of the shop made every color and detail of each piece stand out.

Books were stacked at the end of the counter, and beside them sat a small glass horse figurine. A makeshift doll was mounted on the horse, holding what appeared to be...a satchel of parcels?

Hiron bounded into the room with his uncle, who carried a large knapsack. Everson pointed at the horse and messenger. "If I'm not mistaken, is that Larry the courier from the book?"

The little dwarf's face burst into a grin, and he began pulling the small "parcels" out of the little bag to show Everson. They were no more than pieces of parchment folded into cubes, but the messenger bag looked like the boy had sewn it himself. Everson shared a heartfelt look with Nod, and the dwarf came over to clap Everson on the back, almost shoving Everson forward half a pace in his enthusiasm.

"Best thing to happen to your little city," Nod said, indicating Everson to Raine. "A man with a generous spirit is a gift to his community and shouldn't be taken for granted."

Everson looked down at his shoes, his face warming. He hadn't come here for compliments, but Nod was a dwarf who knew his way around words.

"I just wish I could stay longer," Nod said mournfully. "And I wish Ravenshold had such a generous library as yours. I'm acquainted with the head librarian, but without a membership, I've never even been inside. Though, I don't know if they would have stocked such great books for the local kids," he added, ruffling little Hiron's hair as the boy stacked the packages back into doll-Larry's bag.

"Well, brother, you'll just have to come back next year and see how many more books we have than you," Raine said with a tug on his brother's beard. "But what can I do for you, Mr. Everson? Was there something you needed?"

"Yes, actually. I was looking for your neighbor, Ms. Francesca, and wanted to ask which house was hers. I figured out a way to do book delivery."

Hiron's eyes lit up, but Raine cut his son a look. "You're young enough to walk, my boy. The fresh air is good for you. And I doubt the delivery is as free as the library, am I right?"

"That's right," Everson said, feeling more confident

about his agreement with Filgaria now. "But I got a deal on delivery fees, so they're not too bad—I hope."

"Ms. Francesca lives in the house right across the way, bottom floor, you can't miss it," Raine offered.

Nod hefted up his satchel, and motioned Everson toward the door. "I'll walk with ye," he said. "I'm on my way out of town, late as it is. *Someone* broke the new lock on the door to the workshop." He gave Hiron a stern look, but his eyes twinkled.

Nod knelt down to meet the boy face to face and enveloped him in a bone-cracking hug. "I'll miss you, Hiron. And you'll simply have to write to me to tell me how the Vincenzo series ends. I can't wait to hear it from you."

Hiron nodded, pressing his lips together in a sad smile as his eyes welled up. "Goodbye, Uncle."

"I'll miss you," Nod said, then straightened and clapped his brother on the back. "Good luck with your opening, Brother. I wish I could stay a little longer."

"I know you have your own duties to get back to," Raine said. "Safe journey. And thank you."

Nod and Everson headed out the door, treading through the snowy street to knock on Ms. Francesca's door. After only a few seconds, the door creaked open sharply, almost as if she'd been waiting nearby.

"Yes?" she asked, arms crossed over her chest.

Everson couldn't help but smile. "I've got good news. I'm starting a book delivery service. All you need to do is return your books to Hand to Hand Couriers on Wreya Way and include a list of the books you'd like to borrow in return. The couriers will bring them right to you."

He suddenly wondered what she had thought of his adding the extra romance book to her stack, and whether that had been a terrible idea or not.

"Good," she said crisply. "And since you're here, I've already finished one from yesterday, and would like the next three in the series, please." She stuck out her chin as if daring Everson to mention the book title.

He smiled and nodded knowingly.

"Another voracious reader," Nod said. "If you ever want an escort to the library, Raine will be taking the kids every Myrsday from now on."

"Perhaps on the nicer days," she admitted with a frown that deepened her wrinkles. "These old bones...if you don't use it, you lose it, eh, Nod?"

Nod frowned down at his graying beard in concern, perhaps wondering if Francesca thought him as advanced in age as she. Everson chuckled while Ms. Francesca retrieved her book.

As she passed him the discrete copy of *The Dragon Lord's Wife*, she caught his eye and gave him a brief nod. "Thank you, young man."

"You're very welcome. I'm glad I was able to find that edition. I'll have Filgaria arrange to have your new books delivered as soon as I can get the rest."

He could summon them tonight, but he was starting to think he shouldn't provide book requests so quickly or people would begin to wonder where he was getting all these special books from so quickly. The tinkers only passed through every couple of weeks, though he could tell people he was getting them by special post...

Nod hitched his pack up higher and turned to go.

Everson started to turn too but then remembered something. "Oh, and there's a small fee for delivery," he told Francesca in what he hoped was a non-negotiable tone, since he'd forgotten to mention that from the beginning.

"I figured as much," Ms. Francesca replied, and shut the door in their faces with a grin.

The pair trekked to the cottage, discussing Ms. Francesca, though Everson kept her book preferences a secret—he felt that was his duty as a librarian—books they'd both read, and the shop duties Nod had to look forward to when he returned home.

"I'm the head of the Carpenter's Guild in Ravensh-old, and we've got a big meeting coming up. Then there's orders I scheduled for my return. I really didn't think I'd enjoy being up in this frigid city as much as I did. A lot of that is thanks to you, Everson."

Everson didn't know what to say. The cottage came into view, a thin cloud of smoke curling from the chimney.

Nod chuckled to himself. "I think if Hiron hadn't been so wrapped up in those new books, building out Raine's shop would have been a lot harder than it was. But the boy was occupied with those stories, so we both have you to thank for the entertainment. His teacher's still out sick, and Raine will have his hands full now, but at least the shop is built."

"I'm glad I could help," Everson said. "Books were always my favorite escape as a kid."

"I can imagine the palace had plenty of books for you to read," Nod said.

Everson looked the dwarf over. "How did you know I—"

"Now that word's spread about the library—between Francesca and her gossip circle and Ada at the print shop —everyone's talking about you. It didn't take long for us to hear who you really were."

Nod's last words hit Everson like a blow to the gut. *If only they knew who I really was, they'd never return to the library again.* He sighed.

"Yes, my stepfather's library was quite extensive. I had originally wanted to study at Ravenshold University, and I confess, it was mostly to have access to their library."

"And now you have your own and a much more welcoming one at that," Nod said. "Imagine that."

When they reached the cottage, Everson eased open the crooked door on its one hinge. He winced as it groaned.

"Only the Omens know how this happened," Nod said, then set down his knapsack and got to work.

Everson got to work too—on a pot of fresh tea. He also unpacked his bag from Beautemps, setting the pastries out on a dish in the kitchen nook.

Nod came over after twenty minutes, wiping his hands on a clean rag. "Don't know what got into those screws, but I've replaced them and the hinges. Should be as good as she gets now."

"Thank you, Nod. I'm sorry, I really don't know

what happened last time. Can I pay you for the repair? Especially since you had to do it twice?"

"It's all settled with a cup of tea and one of those pastries, I'd say."

"Oh, no, please, I—"

"I insist. But first, I have a surprise for you." Everson quirked his eyebrows while Nod began digging through his large pack, which had various tools and smaller satchels hanging off of it. "Here."

The dwarf pulled out a small box, about the size of a large book. It was dark polished wood, which matched the bookshelves, and it had a hinged flap to open at the top. On the front, someone had carved the word: *Donations*.

Everson gawked. "N-no, I couldn't possibly—"

"You can, and you should, son," Nod said, pulling out his hammer and a few nails. "Now, where would you like it?"

Everson stared around the cottage. He felt terrible asking people for money for his library, but he had a feeling Nod wouldn't take no for an answer.

They found a slip of wall beside the door that wasn't already occupied by a bookshelf, and Nod began hanging it by the two little hooks already installed on the box. Everson was wringing his hands when Nod said, "A donation is a gift, much like you're gifting your books to the people of Wrestia. People can give or not—it's merely a suggestion."

Everson frowned in thought. He did need to eat, and more than a few times in the past week he'd wondered how much longer he could keep working at the courier's.

It would be nice to have the library open in the mornings for people who couldn't make it later in the day, but that wasn't possible.

He loved sharing books with people, something he'd never imagined until Nod had given him the idea to turn the cottage into a library. Cranky Ms. Francesca, who secretly loved her romance novels; Lyla and her daily afternoon reading; Hiron and his friends, who were swiftly becoming obsessed with all the fantasy characters they read about; and all the other strangers he'd given book recommendations to. He nodded and looked on with a smile as Nod cleaned up his workspace.

"Now, where are those pastries?"

The dwarf selected a large pastry with almond slivers and cinnamon sugar sprinkled on top, and bit off half in one bite. Everson handed him a cup of Queen Gray tea, and the dwarf washed the pastry down with a satisfied pat of his stomach. Everson selected a biscuit and motioned toward the new chairs. They quickly made use of them, setting their pastries and tea on the low table.

Nod leaned forward, running a hand along the wood table. "Where'd you get this made? It's excellent crafts-manship."

"Oh, um, someone in Wrestia," Everson said evasively. Everson had wanted to experiment with the high shelves and rolling ladder last night too, but he knew Nod, in particular, would have been surprised by the speed with which Everson had acquired and installed those items. No, it was best to do the larger improve-ments slowly, so he didn't arouse any of the regular patrons' suspicions. Waiting was torture, though.

Nod continued to inspect the piece, but thankfully, asked no more questions about it. Surely, Everson could have bought it from a woodworker in town.

They fell to discussing the last book Nod had checked out, which Everson put back in the new section on the low bookshelf beside them. The placard on top read: New Arrivals. Then he pulled out a thin green and brown book from the shelf and handed it to the dwarf.

"I want you to have this—I just got it in last night. You might need something to read on the way home."

Nod grinned down at *Illusions, Folklore, and Artifacts: A Fantastical History of Villikry*, then knocked the breath from Everson's lungs with another clap on the back. "Thank you."

"You'll have to let me know how you like it when I see you next," Everson said. "I've got another copy I'll be reading after my current read."

"I look forward to it, my boy," Nod said, finishing off his pastry. "Now, I really must get on the road before your cozy cottage lures me in any longer! I could curl up by the fire for a nap any second! But I'm supposed to pick up a carriage in Fehrgarde for the rest of the journey home. They charge double in Wrestia territory, so I usually walk this stretch when I visit."

"A good plan," Everson agreed with a sad smile.

"Omens be with you, Everson," Nod said, and headed for the door.

"Are you sure you don't need any more books for the journey?" Everson blurted out, taking half a step toward the door.

Nod picked up his knapsack and gave him a grin. "No, but I'd take a hug from the librarian."

Everson's throat swelled and he went over to fling his arms around the burly dwarf, who did the courtesy of not cracking his ribs like his brother almost had.

"I'll send you a letter to the courier's office, aye?" Nod said. "And tell you my thoughts on the book."

"That would be great," Everson said.

ACT II

A week or so later, Lyla and her friends were sitting by the fire discussing their current read over cups of tea once more. Today was peppermint tea, and from what he'd overheard, the book was *Trivorin's Trials*, a biography of a traveling dwarf tinker.

As he half-listened to the conversation, Everson prepared another round of book deliveries for the next day; Ms. Francesca had apparently spread the word to many of her friends, and Filgaria had handed him five slips of parchment this morning featuring book requests, along with a pouch of money. Randalf the Gray had curled up in his lap and fallen asleep, his tail moving every so often as he dreamed. Everson had to summon several of the requested books into his desk drawers, as he didn't have them in stock, but he was happy to provide them to his new patrons. The coin they provided was also welcome. He had another stew on the fire with ingredients he'd purchased from the Winter Market after work, and the aroma was making his visitors peer at the pot with interest. He felt better about accepting money when he was putting it back into the pockets of other business owners.

The door burst open. A young woman about his age with large round glasses entered, a thick orange scarf wrapped around her neck, and dark straight hair pulled into a bun with a dozen flyaway strands framing her round face. Her eyes lit up at the sight of the cottage.

"The Library at the Edge of the Wood, right?" she asked in a light Imminian accent.

Randalf had awoken when the door opened. He darted off Everson's lap and up the ladder to the loft. Everson stood, finally free from his feline trap, to welcome the girl. She had trouble closing the door, and Everson strode over, apologizing.

"Sorry, I keep having it fixed, and it always manages to break again. I think the cottage is messing with me." He huffed, pulling the wonky door shut as best he could. The day after Nod fixed it, Everson had awoken to find it back in its previous state of disrepair. He wasn't going to bother having it fixed again—it was almost a good thing that Nod had gone back to Ravenshold, so he wouldn't start questioning the oddity of the door.

The girl let out a lyrical chuckle. "The cottage, eh? Perhaps it has a sense of humor?"

He looked down at his shoes, his face warming. "Perhaps it does," he said, wishing he hadn't spoken about the cottage like that. Clearly it wanted its door to remain broken—he had realized that by now—but he shouldn't be saying anything about its oddities to other people if he didn't want to arouse suspicion.

She reached up to push her glasses higher on her

nose, and Everson noticed her fingers were flecked with paint of all colors.

"Are there any particular books you're looking for?" he asked.

She scrunched her nose. "Erm, no, actually. I don't really read much. Do I need to borrow a book to be here?"

"Oh, no," Everson said. "That's fine. The free library is for everyone."

She gave him a wide grin and sauntered over to the conversation chairs, then began unpacking her satchel, which contained a large blank book of parchment with jagged edges and a set of charcoal pencils. The girl sat cross-legged in the chair and picked up a pencil before Everson realized he should stop staring.

"Would you like a cup of tea?" he asked. The cold tang of peppermint was evident in the air, competing with the scent of woodsmoke from the hearth.

"Oh, I don't have any money on me," she said.

"It's on the house," Everson explained.

"Not much of a tea drinker, but sure—it'll warm me up. Thank you."

Everson busied himself preparing the cup of tea, not sure what to do with a patron who didn't read. He had no recommendations to make, no books to covertly summon into his desk for her.

Finally, he brought the cup over and held it out to her. There was no space for it on the table, which was already covered with her things: loose sheafs of parchment with sketches and crossed-out drawings.

"Oh!" she said in surprise, taking the cup. "Thanks. I'm Miraluzana, but you can call me Mira if you like."

"That's a beautiful name," Everson blurted out, then turned completely red in the face. "Sorry, it—er—sounds like something from ancient Imminia, am I right? I read a lot of Imminian histories as a teenager." He added the explanation to cover up his awkwardness—though, he realized belatedly that the admission was perhaps even *more* revealing of his awkward nature.

Mira nodded. "Oh, yes, my mama was a fan of history as well. Imminia's first Queen of the Sword was Miraluzana de Varia, the Shadow Slayer, Bringer of Light, and a dozen more fantastic monikers I can never seem to recall. I wish I had just *one* fantastic moniker, you know? I don't need a dozen or anything."

A chuckle burst from Everson. "How *does* one get those, anyway?"

"Bringing light and slaying shadows, I suppose?" Mira said, then took a sip of the tea.

"Well, I'll let you get back to your..." He wasn't really sure *what* she was doing, and he glanced at her sketches trying to finish his sentence.

"Ah, ah, ah," Mira said, moving her papers out of view. "It's not finished. I don't share my art until it's done."

"Then I'll let you get back to your art," he said, giving her a slight bow and retreating to his desk, feeling the back of his neck warming. He reached up to make sure his hat still covered his ears, pulled a stack of blank library cards toward him, and began stamping them.

Stomping footsteps on the porch announced newcomers, and Everson looked up expectantly.

Lyla waved them over, beaming. "Oh, you made it!"

"Sorry, Lyla, couldn't find the place at first," one newcomer admitted. Everson recognized her as the herbalist from the Winter Market. "Oh, it's you!" she greeted Everson.

"Welcome," he said, nervously pulling his hat down. Six more people filtered in, crowding over by the chaise. They removed their coats, then warmed themselves by the fire. Each of them already had a book with them.

Everson got up and hovered nearby, unsure what was going on.

"Quite the book club you've got there," Mira said, looking up from her sketching.

"The what?"

"Book club. To discuss the book they all read, eh?"

"I've never...heard of such a thing," Everson admitted, folding his arms across his chest.

"And you, a librarian," Mira said teasingly.

His face warmed. Sure, he was a librarian *now*, but his only previous experience with books was reading them *alone*.

Lyla cleared her throat nervously and began asking the newcomers what they thought of *Trivorin's Trials*. Everson busied himself making more tea, but when he went over to the fire to get more hot water, Lyla stopped him.

"For those of you who don't know him, this is our generous librarian, Everson," she introduced him. "He runs the whole library by himself."

Everson flashed a smile at them, though he only recognized Lyla, her two friends, and the herbalist. A dwarf woman with two long braids sat cross-legged on the floor beside a girl who was glued to her book, a married couple leaned against the wall by the hearth, and another man with a short black beard on his pale face lingered near the door.

"Do you have any more chairs?" the man against the wall complained. Lyla shot him a quelling look.

"Or tea?" the dwarf asked.

"Tea I can do," Everson said. "But I don't have any more chairs than you see here."

He retrieved the kettle from the fire and hastily prepared the pot of tea. The book club-goers served themselves from the kitchen nook when Lyla announced a break in the discussion.

"Maybe next time I'll bring some biscuits for everybody," the herbalist said as she and the others poured their cups.

"I like the sound of that, Adrilla," the dwarf agreed. "And I could bring some cheese toasties, maybe."

Lyla waved Everson over, her gray-streaked black hair falling into her face. "I'm so sorry, Everson. I should have asked your permission! Mayline and Greta told a few friends about our little reading club, and they all wanted to come—"

"It's no problem," Everson said, a warm smile spreading. "I'm glad you're all making use of the library. I just wish—" He halted the words in their tracks and took a long time clearing his throat. "I'm sorry I don't have more chairs."

"Well, maybe next time?"

"Next time?" His eyes bulged.

"We were thinking of meeting every month. We haven't picked the next book we're going to read yet, but perhaps you can steer us in the right direction?" She held out a hand toward the little group gathered around the hearth. The dwarf had borrowed a pillow from the chaise and sat on the floor serenely drinking her cup of tea, *Trivorin's Trials* open on her lap. The couple was debating what really happened when Trivorin went to see the King of Imminia at the end of the book, and Greta and Mayline were comparing their favorite quotes, which they'd copied onto slips of paper.

Everson grinned. "Sure. I think I can make some recommendations for your book club."

LIZ DELTON

O n Myrsday, Everson stopped at the Winter Market to buy some more supplies for the library. He lingered at a woodworker's stall, inspecting the chairs she had for sale, but Everson's book delivery money wouldn't cover half of one of these exquisite chairs, and though beautiful, they were much too large for the library.

He'd considered asking the cottage for some chairs, but if he only needed them for the book club, where would he keep them the rest of the time? He'd have to figure out something else for the large gathering. The cottage *was* cozy, and he couldn't very well go filling it up with furniture.

He carried a sack of apples and baked meat pies, relishing the reprieve from the wintery winds that normally howled off Mount Wreya. By now, he and all his library patrons had beaten a path through the snow to the cottage, but the tracks were iced over and hard to walk on, so he walked on the fresh snow beside the path, which crunched satisfyingly as he broke the icy layer on top.

When he arrived at the cottage, a small group was waiting on the porch to greet him. Everson's face burst into a smile when he recognized Hiron and Raine, though it was tinged with sadness at Nod's absence. Only one of Hiron's friends accompanied him today, and she was bouncing on her heels clutching her books to her chest.

"Good afternoon," Everson said. "Let me get the door."

It was Raine's first time visiting the library, and the dwarf let out a pleased *hmm* as he wandered around the shelves. Everson nibbled on one of the meat pies as he put the rest of his food away and built the fire back up to make a fresh pot of tea.

Hiron and his friend were talking in hasty whispers over in the children's section, evidently deciding who was going to borrow which new book on Villikrian dragon myths he'd added to the collection. Everson noticed the *Larry!* book tucked securely under Hiron's arm, as well as the next Vincenzo book. It was the last in the series, so Everson would need to look for another series for the boy.

A pot of Queen Gray brewing in the kitchen nook, Everson went over to his desk to draw up a library card for Raine, who already had three books in his hands as he browsed. Everson pulled the neat stack of blank cards from their designated cubby in his desk and grinned. Stamping the cards was one of the most satisfying aspects of running the library—just after making someone's day by having the right book for them. He was already thinking of commissioning more stamps from Geminigh, the next being a *From the Shelves of the Library at the Edge of the Wood* stamp, which he was thinking of stamping inside all the books. Though he didn't really mind if one went missing, he didn't want to abuse the cottage's magic by needlessly summoning extra books.

While Raine and the kids browsed, Everson sipped his own cup of tea and went through the stack of notes Filgaria had handed him at the end of his workday. There were three book delivery requests, so he got to work summoning them into his drawers and packaging them up in brown paper to protect them from the elements. He secured the paper with string, and tucked each request note behind it so he would remember which was which. He needed to stop at the print shop soon. He also wanted to get a book delivery stamp. He'd been dreaming up something with lines where he could write the patron's name and address along with the titles of their books.

Just as he finished his task, he heard light steps on the porch. Mira came in, clutching a large bag. She waved at Everson with paint-speckled fingers and headed to the conversation chairs, staking a claim with all her art supplies. Today she had brought tubes of paint, brushes, and even a little jar of water. Everson raised his eyebrows and asked if she wanted a cup of tea.

Mira shook her head, flyaway hair framing her face. She chuckled. "Don't want to mix it up with the paint water."

Not far behind her, Lyla arrived, alone this time, but with a book clutched to her chest and a smile on her face.

She beamed at Everson and came right over to his desk. "Book club was a hit! Everyone's talking about it. I think... We might have more people next time, if that's all right with you?"

"I still need to solve the problem of chairs," he said thoughtfully. "I have nowhere to store them after the book club, you see. I'm happy to have more people utilizing the library, I just..."

Her face fell.

"But I'll figure something out," he said firmly. "Did you decide on a book yet?"

"We did," she said, her grin returning in full force. "*Whirl of the World*. You made it sound so wonderful— a far-off journey for someone from such a small community? Wizards, a quest, and a magic necklace? But only one of us already has a copy. Do you think we could buy the rest from you?"

He choked on his tea, and the bergamot of the Queen Gray clouded his senses for a moment. "Yes," he said slowly, thinking fast. "I think I can do that. I'll send for them right away. I'm delighted you chose that one, actually. Not everyone likes fantasy stories." He had just finished *Turn of the Tides*, so he was all caught up on that series, but it was a delight to share it with people who hadn't read it.

I'll have to wait a few days to hand them over, though, he thought with half a smile.

"Fantastic!" Lyla said, clapping her hands together. "I've collected everyone's address and written them all down for you. They've all agreed to purchase one, and everyone but me asked for delivery. You can do that, right?"

Everson gaped at the note. There were twenty names on it. Twenty book purchases, and twenty delivery fees... It would feed him for a year!

His face warmed, and he bobbed his head. "I—yes, I can."

"It's settled then," she said, delighted, and turned to head for her favorite spot on the chaise. Randalf the Gray was already there. The cat shifted closer to Lyla when she sat down to read her book, leaving Everson dumbstruck beside his desk. For a second he thought about explaining Randalf the Gray's name to Lyla but decided to wait to reveal it after she'd read the book when she'd appreciate it more.

I suppose the book club will work out rather well, he thought. *Only...how am I supposed to provide chairs for twenty people?*

He glanced around the library, thinking. He supposed twenty chairs could fit when everyone was seated, but where he would store them was the real problem. The cottage had no closets, only the loft above, which was just enough space for him and his bed, dresser, and private bookcase. The porch was too small, and he needed access to the kitchen nook...

Well, I've got a few weeks to figure that out, he thought, then got down to creating library cards for the new people on the book club list.

Then Raine and the kids came over with their stacks of books, and Everson grinned.

He loved being a librarian.

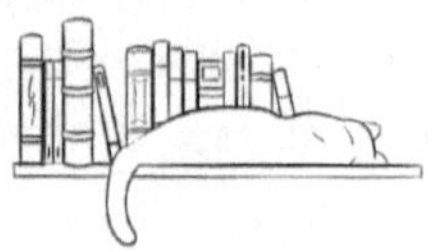

Mira stayed long after the others had left. Even Lyla, who'd yelped about having to get dinner ready an hour ago, had wrapped her scarf around her head and bustled from the cottage.

Everson didn't mind, as Mira was remarkably quiet, but he had wanted to experiment with the new bookcases Nod had suggested. He couldn't very well do that with Mira here.

So he tidied up the blankets on the chaise, making a silent wish to the cottage to make the cat hair go away. It did. Then he retrieved his current read from his desk: *Illusions, Folklore, and Artifacts,* the same book he'd sent off with Nod. Though Everson hadn't gotten any correspondence from the dwarf yet, he'd begun writing down some of his thoughts on the scrap of paper he was using as a bookmark.

He'd been reading for perhaps an hour before Mira started packing up her paints, and the sound jolted him from the chaise. "Omens, I forgot you were here!" he said.

Mira grinned. "I finished," she said, "Sorry for staying so late. Sometimes I just get so caught up, I forget what's going on around me."

"I was doing the same with my book," he assured her, tucking his paper in between the pages to mark his place. Randalf meowed sleepily as Everson scratched behind his ears. "Am I allowed to inquire about the artwork, since it's finished?"

Mira narrowed her eyes at him, and said with a grin, "I suppose, Master Librarian. Only because I haven't put it away yet. It's not *finished* finished, though. I forgot my gold paint at home. But it's still wet, so don't touch it," she added as he moved closer.

She flipped the canvas toward him, and his jaw dropped.

It was his chaise, his hearth—his library! A figure sat by the fire reading a book. At first, he thought it was him, and his face flamed hotter than embers. But upon closer inspection, the broad brushstrokes revealed long black and gray hair. "Is that...Lyla?"

"Do you think she would mind?" Mira asked. "I've been doing form studies of people, and it's so hard to find a place where anyone sits still long enough, where I don't have to pay to be there."

"Oh," Everson said, dumbfounded. "No, I don't think she'd mind at all. This is... It's beautiful. The yellows by the hearth are so warm, I just want to jump into the painting. Mira, this is beautiful!"

She laughed, the sound cascading over him. "Your library is just as cozy, I assure you. But thank you."

"You should show Lyla," he insisted.

"Perhaps after I add the gold," she allowed. "But it's late, I should head back to the city."

Everson glanced at the windows, which were nearly

black. "Let me walk you back, please. No one's ever stayed this late before."

"I'm really sorry, I—"

"No, no, please, I was simply stating a fact. And you should call me Everson, by the way."

"All right then, Everson. Everson, Bringer of Books. I like that moniker, don't you?"

His face warmed, and he didn't think it had anything to do with the coat and scarf he was pulling on. "Top notch." He wracked his brain but couldn't come up with anything suitable to nickname her that didn't sound ridiculous, so instead he offered to carry her bag, and opened the crooked door for her. It wasn't snowing, which was a blessing.

"The cottage still won't let you fix that door, will it?"

"Oh, I've given up," he admitted as she began to crunch her way through the snow. "Hold on, let me grab a lantern."

He had a few hanging from the porch, and retrieved one now, its oil reserve thankfully full. He'd gotten into the habit of summoning anything he could possibly think of in the mornings before work so he wouldn't have to ask the cottage to do magic when anyone was there. Tea leaves, water for the kettle, a stack of books next to his desk that he had nowhere to shelve. He really needed to stop summoning books until he'd figured out how to add new shelves.

Lanternlight spilling on snow ahead of them, they made for Wrestia in wintery silence. Mira carried her painting close to her body, holding it carefully so the light wind wouldn't take it.

"How come you chose a place so far from the city?" she griped good-naturedly after a few minutes.

He chuckled. "Everyone asks me that. I didn't really choose it...it kind of chose me." He immediately regretted saying anything. He really needed to stop talking about the cottage like it had a personality with her! But something about her continued to disarm him.

"Ah, I see," she said.

He really hoped she didn't.

"So what do you do when you're not running the library?" she asked.

"Oh, I work at the courier's in the mornings."

"No, I mean what do you do for fun?" she clarified.

"Read," he said simply.

She laughed again, the sound ringing through the night. "I think you need a new hobby, Bringer of Books."

"What, like painting?" he asked jovially, then his face warmed.

"Sure," she agreed. "Or cooking. Whittling. Bird-watching. Meditation. Everyone needs a hobby that sets their mind free, allows it to wander. That has nothing to do with money or your day-to-day. Art."

"What if I'm not an artist?"

"It's *all* art. Bird watchers master the art of identifying species and admiring their beauty from afar. Even playing a game of virnolz to allow your mind to explore all the avenues of winning is an art."

Everson didn't have anything to say to that. He loved reading, of course, and would never give it up—even if his library was a spectacular failure—but perhaps Mira, Master of Art, was right.

A light snow peppered him as he blearily trudged back to Wrestia the next morning. Unwisely, he'd stayed up late after walking Mira home, trying to work out the problem with the bookshelves, and he didn't have anything to show for it except bags under his eyes. He hadn't summoned anything—the precarious position of the proposed shelves didn't seem like something he could summon from so high, and he couldn't very well move heavy bookshelves up a ladder alone.

"You're late," Filgaria observed as he hustled into Hand to Hand.

Everson frowned. "I'm so sorry Fil, I—"

"Not to worry, it's a light mail day." She tossed a small stack of letters onto her desk, bound in twine. "Your pay's in your mailbox, minus book delivery fees."

A gasp ripped through Everson, and he smacked his forehead.

"What is it?" She leaned forward, concerned.

"I forgot today's books," he groaned. "I'll have to trek back to the cottage..."

Filgaria frowned at him again, but no admonishments came, not even teasing ones, for which he was thankful.

He flipped through the stack of envelopes—thankfully none for the palace—and mapped a mental route for the morning. He'd been planning on stopping by the print shop to order another stamp, but he'd also forgotten his sketches at the library. And since he'd forgotten the book deliveries...he was going to have to deliver those all himself. He groaned again.

"Thanks, Filgaria."

"Take care of yourself, Everson," was all she said, an uncharacteristically sad look in her eyes.

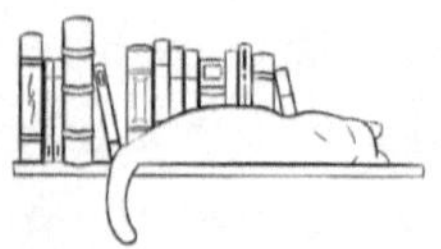

Despite the light mail day, he finished around midday as usual, so he decided to run by Stetson's and rent a sled. He needed to get to the library and back as quickly as possible before any patrons showed up.

Stomach grumbling the whole way back to the library, Everson was wondering if he should grab lunch at Beautemps when he returned to the city. Then he spotted the last thing he needed: patrons on his porch.

"Oh, no," he groaned under the sounds of the mule's clomping feet through the snow. He couldn't very well turn them away after they'd trekked all the way out here.

Lyla and Adrilla were among them, along with a

patron Everson had never met before. He pulled the sled up beside the porch and greeted them.

"The librarian arrives," Lyla announced, a delighted smile working wrinkles into her face. "We're a little early, but we wanted to show Ferrace the library. He works evenings, you see, so he hasn't got a lot of time."

"Oh," Everson said, "then I'm delighted I came when I did." And he *was* delighted about serving a new patron, although now he doubted he'd be able to make it back to the city unless everyone left early.

After he let everyone in past the crooked door, he scrounged up an apple in the kitchen for the mule, who seemed content to wait out in the snow under the boughs of the edge of the woods. He then got himself an apple and put on a pot of tea.

Two apples and a bowl of cold cooked oats later, he was staring at the stack of book deliveries on his desk with a frown. He hoped his paying patrons wouldn't be upset about the late deliveries.

Lyla was showing Ferrace around the library. "Oh, Everson, you got more new books?" she asked, browsing through the new arrivals stack on the bookcase by the conversation chairs.

Everson ducked his head. "Just a few. Your book club ones should be here any day now," he added. He didn't like lying, but an entire stack of *Whirl of the World* appearing a day after he ordered it would be strange indeed, as if summoned by the fictional Randalf the Gray.

Lyla convinced Ferrace to select the first *Of Dragons and Destiny* book by J. Andrew from new arrivals.

"Dragons and adventure. That's just what you need, Ferrace!" she urged.

Ferrace didn't look convinced. In fact, he hadn't shown much interest in the library at all. He hadn't pulled any books from the shelves or even touched their spines as most patrons did while they browsed, but he brought *Of Dragons and Destiny* over to Everson's desk all the same.

Everson bit his lip as he took the book. The cover displayed a dragon in shiny gold foil. "What sort of things do you like to read?" he asked as he pulled out a fresh library card and began filling it out.

Ferrace grimaced and wrung his hands. They were scarred and his joints knobbly, with black under his fingernails that looked like it would never wash out. Judging by his face, he appeared to be about five years older than Everson, though his worn hands made him look older. "Not much of a reader, though the story sounds interesting," he admitted. "It's—a bit hard for me to hold the books, you see. I work on repairing carriages all day, and my hands have taken a beating over the years."

"Hmm," Everson said thoughtfully. "I wish there was another way to read... Perhaps..." He paused anxiously, hoping his 'wish' wasn't something the cottage would interpret.

Lyla looked at him expectantly.

"Perhaps we need to arrange *another sort* of book club," he suggested, tugging on his chin in thought.

A wide grin spread on Lyla's face, and she put a hand on Ferrace's shoulder. "What do you mean?"

"Well, what if instead of discussing the book, we spent the time listening to someone read the book aloud?" Everson held up *Of Dragons and Destiny*.

Lyla clapped her hands together. "That would be so much fun!"

"Yeah," Ferrace agreed. "That sounds pretty neat."

"Like the storytellers of Ancient Rhapsodia," Lyla said, "gathering around a bard to hear a tale!"

"You know about the bards of Ancient Rhapsodia?" Everson barked. "I thought I was the only one who read about those."

Lyla shrugged. "I read all kinds. As long as it's good."

"We'll just need someone to read," Everson said. "I'm not really one for narrating aloud."

"Me either," Lyla admitted.

"We'll think of something," Everson assured them. "And in the *early* afternoon, then?"

Ferrace's delighted smile melted, and he nodded. "Aye, I should probably be getting to work soon actually. Last time I was late, I almost got a flogging."

Sick guilt swooped in Everson's chest. He wished he could offer Ferrace work here instead. Today had been difficult managing the needs of the library and his own job, and he could use some help. But perhaps he needed to consider taking on the library full-time before thinking about employing anyone else.

Of course, the money from the book club would support him for a long time—as long as he could figure out the chair problem—and that was just from one month of running it. Then there was the donation box he'd noticed a few coins clinking in after Nod installed it.

He hadn't dared look inside yet, not feeling as though he'd earned the coin.

Could he take on the library full-time?

"Ferrace," Everson began, pushing those thoughts aside, "would you like a ride back to Wrestia? I've got to drop something off at the courier's, and it'll be faster for you."

The man's eyes lit up. "That would be great, Mister Librarian, sir—"

"Please, just call me Everson. Though, I'll have to leave the library unattended..." He glanced at Lyla, uncertain.

The older woman nodded. "It would be an honor to watch over it for you, Everson." *Thank you*, she mouthed silently, nodding at Ferrace.

Everson returned her nod and tossed back the rest of his tea before grabbing the stack of book deliveries. It was the first time he'd left someone else alone in the cottage. He hoped nothing strange occurred while he was out...

He quickly showed Lyla the blank library cards and his ledger. Though he didn't think they'd get any new patrons while he was out, it was better safe than sorry. He didn't know if the wish magic worked for other people, but his theory so far was that only he could use it, considering *someone* must have made a wish of some kind these past few weeks, and nothing strange had been reported.

Was it because he was faerŭn?

For once the idea filled him with warmth instead of dread, knowing the cottage magic might be faerŭn. The thought of others knowing his true self was like a blade hanging above his head most of the time.

With the book deliveries secured in a crate at the back of the sled, Everson and Ferrace set off for Wrestia, and he finally felt like his day was turning around.

That is, until he dropped Ferrace off at his shop and snow began to fall. The carriage mechanic had opted to leave *Of Dragons and Destiny* behind at the library, not wanting to get any grease on it, he'd explained.

"Looking forward to the 'bard' reading!" Ferrace called with a grin as he stepped off the sled. "Thanks for the ride, Everson!"

Everson waved, a smile warming his face at his new patron, then he consulted his mental route for the book deliveries as the flakes began to fall faster.

Yet again, he had been hoping to stop at the print shop, now that he was out of the library with some time on his hands, but the falling flakes prevented any detours. Knowing Wrestia, it could turn into a full-scale blizzard at any moment. Hopefully, it was just a passing snow cloud.

He didn't even stop at Beautemps for soup and bread like he wanted, just dropped all the books off with his five delivery patrons and headed straight back to the cottage with the sled. The mule didn't seem to mind it when he left him out under the tree boughs again, which offered a respite from the snow since there wasn't any wind for once.

Everson stomped the snow off his boots on the porch and pulled on his crooked door. It was odd coming home knowing there were people already inside, but it was also kind of nice.

The herbalist had gone home, but Lyla waved at him

from her spot on the chaise. Mira had arrived and set up shop in her usual spot, her painting spread across her lap. Gold paint glinted from the end of her paintbrush.

"Everson, have you seen this?" Lyla asked, standing and pointing at Mira's painting.

"I have," he said, unwinding his scarf and hanging it on the rack behind the door. "I take it Mira showed you?"

"It's wonderful," Lyla said, beaming. "Did Ferrace get to work all right?"

"Perfectly on time."

Her face visibly relaxed. "Good. I really wish I could help find him a new job, but they've got a baby on the way and he doesn't want to take any chances."

Everson frowned, his thoughts going back to his earlier quandary.

As much as he wanted to offer to help Ferrace, Everson had to help himself first. He didn't want to risk someone else's livelihood until he knew the library would be sustainable.

And that meant he had work to do.

LIZ DELTON

14

Mira and Lyla prepared to head home together, and Everson offered them the sled, as long as one of them returned it to Stetson's. Lyla agreed to take it since it was closer to her home on the west side of the city. Mira held firmly onto her canvas, which she'd promised to give Lyla when it was finished and framed.

He watched them go on the sled, lantern bobbing in the dusky tundra as they headed for Wrestia. *I wish I had one of those all the time*, he thought idly as he closed the door halfway and kept watch. Then he blanched, hoping he hadn't just accidentally wished a sled and mule into the library. Whirling around, he didn't see anything, but his heart was racing.

"Gotta be careful what I wish for," he said to Randalf, who'd perked his head up at Everson's quick movement. Luckily, his wish had been vague—or the cottage simply wasn't capable of summoning something so large. He suspected live animals were also one of the cottage's restrictions, but he wasn't willing to test it.

He had tomorrow off from the courier's, a day he

desperately needed to catch up on all the tasks and planning he'd been putting aside. But tonight, he had some reading to do, and his nook in the loft was calling to him.

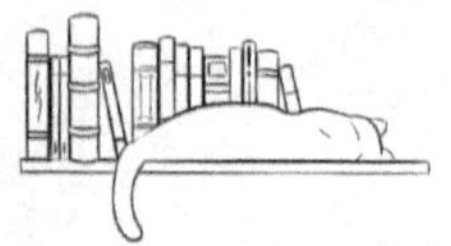

The next morning, Everson had a few more notes to include in his letter to Nod, which he planned to send as soon as he finished *Illusions, Folklore, and Artifacts* unless Nod wrote to him first. The book was a fascinating take on Villikrian history—a much different approach than *Exploration of Villikry*, which he had practically memorized. It made him want to run away to Villikry and bask in the history of the faerŭn—but with the magic of the cottage, he couldn't imagine ever leaving.

He stretched lazily in bed, disturbing Randalf for only a moment before the cat went back to sleep—or went back to pretending to be asleep, he couldn't be sure.

For once, he didn't have book delivery orders to fill, so he took his time making breakfast—porridge with apples and raisins—and sipping his tea on the chaise.

His work called to him, notes left out on his desk, but he put them off for two whole hours, recalling Mira's words about finding another hobby that wasn't books. He'd been living and breathing books for the last few weeks, and though he wasn't complaining, he suspected she was right. He didn't think he'd be interested in bird-watching, though.

Finally, after pouring himself another cup of tea, he sat at his desk and pulled a fresh sheet of paper toward him. He kept paper stocked in all the cubbies of his desk. He had a variety of sizes and thicknesses: small heavy cardstock for library cards, slightly larger for bookmarks or notes, and large sheets like the one he'd just selected.

The Library at the Edge of the Wood
Full Time Hours
Weekdays: Noon to Sunset (Open early on
Myrsdays at Eighth Chime)
Weekends: Eighth Chime to Sunset

"There," he said, admiring it. After several crossings-out, he thought he'd come up with a passable schedule. Most days he'd have the morning to get things done or bring deliveries to town. But that didn't leave much time for non-book activities...

Closed Sylsday

"That's better." Noon to sunset was already pretty close to the current library hours, though sometimes he got home from deliveries a little later. Patrons might like more predictable hours. *And* I'll *like having a whole day off from work of any kind. I just have to figure out a way to break it to Filgaria...*

As much as he didn't want to go out into the cold, he donned his scarf, hat, mittens, and boots and readied for another trip to Wrestia. He vowed on his first real day off he wouldn't leave the cottage for anything. No errands, no deliveries, just books, tea, and whatever new hobby he might find. He'd consult Mira the next time he saw her to see if she had any non-avian suggestions.

The print shop was his first stop. Ada beamed when he entered. "The librarian!" she called. "I've been hearing about you all over town! How's business?" She put an elbow on the counter as she peered at him expectantly.

Everson chuckled and ducked his head. Based on what Nod had said, he wondered if Ada had been the one spreading the word in the first place.

"The library is great. More than great." His stomach did a little flip as he thought of his plans to take it on full-time. "In fact, I'd like to order two more stamps. At the regular price, please."

"Library must be doing great then," Ada said with a wink. "What do you need?"

He pulled out two sketches from his pocket: *From the Shelves of the Library at the Edge of the Wood*, and his book delivery card sketch. Ada looked them over.

"Geminigh!" she called loudly. "Stamp order for the library."

The old gnome ambled out, holding a newspaper under his arm and a small porcelain cup in his other hand. "*What?*"

"Stamp order for the library," Ada repeated with a roll of her eyes.

Geminigh's eyes lit up, and he set down his newspaper. An overwhelming and vaguely familiar scent cascaded Everson, rich and bitter all at once.

"What is that?" he asked, nodding to Geminigh's cup.

A wide grin came over the printer's face, and he said, "Arcavian mountain blend coffee. My grandniece sent me some all the way from Arcavia for my hundred and fiftieth."

Everson grinned, congratulating Geminigh and wondering if that was just what he needed to gift Filgaria as a peace offering when he gave his notice.

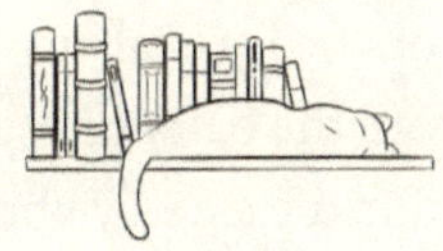

For the second day in a row, Everson headed to Stetson's to rent a sled. A young hostler gave him the same mule as yesterday, and Everson patted the creature's neck.

Before he left, Everson leaned over to the hostler and asked, "Does Stetson *sell* sleds and mules?"

"Oh, o'course," the young hostler agreed, rubbing his eye with a corner of his threadbare mitten. "Looking to buy?"

"Not today," Everson assured him. "What's this one's name, anyway?"

"Princess," the boy replied. "She's very easygoing, ain't she?"

Everson agreed, patting Princess on the neck and taking his leave. He led Princess toward the Winter Market to purchase food for the week. *If this keeps up*, he thought, *I'll have paid more renting one than owning one. I just wish I had somewhere to board her...*

He smirked at how easily wishing came to him, but he suspected *that* wish was something the cottage couldn't grant. He'd attempted to add extra rooms or make the cottage larger, but those requests were clearly too much for the cottage's magic. Perhaps if he had a small barn built in the woods, that would work. If only Nod were still in town, Everson would have asked him.

Shaking his head, he turned his thoughts to things he *could* afford, like sacks of apples, potatoes, carrots, and a basket with a couple loaves of bread from the bakeshop that had recently opened a stall in the market. A few rounds of cheese from the dairy farmer, some spices from Adrilla—who exclaimed excitedly about her anticipation to start *Whirl of the World* for the book club—and his sled was nearly full.

He hadn't even dipped into the book club money. The book delivery fees were enough to pay for his rations, and even the extra pastries he'd grabbed from the bakeshop at the last minute. The lemon and hora citrus scones must have been fresh out of the oven, because even as Princess trudged him and his load back to the library, their deliciously sweet and tart steam wafted over him.

The mule was content to munch on a carrot and an apple under the branches of the wood while Everson went inside. He figured he'd send the sled home with Lyla or whoever else came to the library today.

He had maybe an hour until any patrons showed up, so as soon as he came in the door and dropped the sacks in the kitchen nook, he took care of the most urgent task requiring secrecy.

I wish I had twenty copies of Whirl of the World, he thought.

A grin formed on his face when the stack appeared on the floor in front of him.

"You know, I was wondering how you got all these books," a voice said.

Everson nearly jumped out of his skull as he turned to see Mira paused in the act of browsing books on the other side of the cottage. He hadn't noticed her bag sitting on the conversation chair.

He made to bolt for the door for some reason, then froze.

"No, I'm sorry, Everson," she blurted, taking a step toward him.

He reached up for his hat, thanking the Omens he hadn't dispensed with it.

"I thought I could come in—yesterday you left Lyla in charge, and I kind of assumed she was already here," she explained, trying to take another step toward him. "I didn't mean to intrude on—"

Everson opened and closed his mouth several times, finding no words to fill the space. The stack of books sat on the floor like a dark Omen between them.

"I..." he finally croaked. "I need a cup of tea."

He kept his gaze off the stack of books and walked to the kettle, making a silent wish to fill it with water. Mira couldn't see that, at least. Swinging the kettle over the fire, he strode over to the kitchen, tears pricking in his eyes. Was this the end of the library? She'd seen him do magic—would she make the connection that he was faerŭn?

Vision slightly blurry, he dug in the tea cabinet and pulled out his favorite Queen Gray, scooping a few teaspoons of black leaves into the strainer of the teapot. It vaguely reminded him of his plans to ask the cottage for Arcavian coffee, but now that seemed as far off and distant a dream as the conversation that lay before him.

"Everson, I—"

He cleared his throat and strode over to the fire when the kettle whistled. Part of him wanted to ignore Mira and pretend like nothing had happened, but he knew that was childish and wouldn't work anyway.

Finally, when he had a steaming cup ready on the counter, he crossed his arms over his chest and leaned against the counter in the kitchen nook, facing her.

Before he could say anything, she blurted, "You can do magic." It was hard not to see the wonder in her eyes. Perhaps this wasn't the end of the library after all.

He shook his head, a reluctant smile turning up the corners of his mouth slightly. "No, the cottage can do magic, actually."

"Ahh. Does that have anything to do with why the door kept breaking?"

Everson picked up his teacup for something to do with his hands, though it was still too hot to drink. The warmth spread to his fingers, much like the heat rushing through the rest of his body. She wasn't afraid or running to Wrestia to declare him a witch... That was a good sign, right?

"It does, I think," he admitted. "I think the cottage really does want the door to remain broken."

"And the books? How does it work?"

A chuckle ripped from him. She was taking this rather well. "Y-You're not—"

"Not what? This is amazing, Everson!" She seemed to think it safe to continue her approach, and she came over to inspect the stack, a finger to her lips, which he noticed were a lush shade of red. "How does it work?"

"I just...wish," he said, finally testing out his tea. It had cooled to the perfect temperature, and he took another sip. "I wish I had another copy of *Whirl of the World*."

The stack grew by one book as the new volume appeared.

Mira's eyes grew even wider.

"And it's not just books," Everson said, excitement building as he put down his cup. "I wish I had...a set of paintbrushes," he supplied on a whim.

Half a dozen paintbrushes appeared on his desk, with varying brush sizes and shapes. The handles were smooth polished wood. One brush head was shaped in a flat arch like a fan, another as skinny as a quill nib. Mira reached out to touch them but then pulled back.

"H-How? Is it real?"

"As real as anything," he said with a shrug. "I even checked one of the books against an original copy. It was word for word. Go ahead."

She leaned over and picked up the fanned brush, running her finger lightly along the tip. "This is incredible, Everson! It's magic!" She jumped up and down on the tips of her toes and lurched toward him, arms spread wide.

The scent of vanilin and terrazzo—one of the spices

he'd bought from the herbalist—engulfed him as she hugged him, and his chest tingled. His fingers moved seemingly of their own accord, running down her soft black hair, which was half up and half down today. The long black strands were like silk, and his face warmed when she pulled away.

He buried his flushed face in his teacup as he took a sip, watching Mira whirl around, as if admiring the cottage in a new light.

"How do you even...get anything done, with all this magic at your fingertips?"

A real laugh burst from his lips and he set his tea down once more. "It was hard, in the beginning. That's—er—how the library idea came about, actually. I'd wished for hundreds of books, there were stacks of them lying all around the place, and someone came in looking for directions and assumed I was opening a bookshop. But I couldn't sell these, not really. Not when the cottage just *gives* them to me."

She nodded sagely, tucking a flyaway strand of hair behind her ear, but it fell away just as quickly. An odd urge to reach out and move her silky hair came over him, but instead, he blurted, "Do you want to try an experiment?"

Her dark brown eyes seemed to twinkle. "You don't mean..."

Everson held up his hands. "I don't know if it will work for you," he said in a rush. He didn't want to get her hopes up. "But I haven't been able to see if it worked for anyone else yet. You're the only one who knows about it besides me."

"What do I do?"

"Just make a wish."

She put a finger to her lips in thought, the expression both surprisingly alluring and serenely thoughtful. "I... Is it crazy that I can't think of a single thing? The possibilities are almost too much!"

"It doesn't work on food or money. Those are the only limitations I've found. Well, it also won't make the cottage any bigger," he added. "Or fix that Omens-cursed door."

She laughed, saying, "Then I wish I had a lovely doormat for people to wipe their feet on."

Nothing happened.

"It doesn't work for me, does it?" Her smile hadn't faded; in fact, it only brightened. She reached out and poked him in the chest. "So you are magical in a way, then, yes?"

His face flamed again, hoping this conversation didn't turn to faerŭn and witches. "Or maybe it's because I found the cottage first," he improvised. "And claimed it somehow?"

She stroked her chin, nodding. "Could be. I don't know much about magical cottages, dear Everson, Keeper of the Cottage. That's two monikers you're up to now." The shadow of a wink drove a flutter through his stomach.

"While I've yet to come up with any for you," he said, shaking his head in mock shame. "What a terrible friend I am." Of course, he'd thought of some, but didn't dare say them out loud.

"That's all right, I wasn't born for a dozen monikers, you know. I'm just Mira."

"Well, 'just Mira'"—the sound of footsteps on the porch made Everson's stomach flip, and he lowered his voice—"I trust you can keep the cottage's secret for me? I'm not ready—I mean, I don't know if—"

"Of course, Everson," she said, all hint of frivolity wiped from her face. "I'll take it to my grave if I must. A little magic is what makes life worth living—whether you know the magic is there or not."

"Thank you," he said, just as Lyla knocked and shoved open the door, followed by Adrilla and Greta.

Mira floated off to her chair and began unpacking her charcoals as if she hadn't just uncovered one of Everson's most closely kept secrets. She had a new blank canvas today, and she called over to Lyla that her frame would take a few days. Then she began sketching, turning her canvas so that Everson couldn't see it. He gave her a knowing smirk and headed for his desk, where he had twenty new books to process. Twenty-one now.

But when he heard Mira curse under her breath and saw her stare down at a broken charcoal stick, he got an idea. Lyla and her friends sat by the fire, sipping tea and chatting about a recipe Adrilla had found in one of the library books.

He got up and wandered over near Mira and thought, *I wish I had a new set of charcoal pencils on the conversation table.*

His heart thudded against his ribcage as he watched four charcoal sticks wrapped in paper and twine appear right next to Mira's sketchbook. He'd gotten quite good at making his requests specific.

She looked up at him with a conspiratorially delighted look etched on her pretty face. He ducked his head and grinned. He felt so light having shared the secret with someone, he practically floated back to his desk to finish wrapping up the books for delivery.

Perhaps it wasn't so bad—sharing secrets with a friend.

When Lyla and her friends made to leave around suppertime, Everson presented them with their own copies of *Whirl of the World*, which they happily paid for. They clutched the neat little packages to their chests and headed out the crooked door, declining Everson's offer of the sled. Evenings were growing lighter these days, and the wind and snow had let up for once. Summer wasn't far off—a brief reprieve from Wrestia's snowy mantle, lasting a month or two, though the occasional snowburst still broke through the chilly landscape.

Lyla gave a knowing look toward Mira, who was entranced in her sketching, and waved goodbye before shutting the door.

The sound seemed to jolt Mira out of her trance, and she looked up to find the cottage empty. Her expression changed from surprise to something else, something mischievous. Everson couldn't help it, he grinned at her, then ducked his head.

"Did you want a ride back on the sled?" he offered. He inhaled the delicious scent of the cottage—he'd put on a virleek and onion soup while everyone had been busy reading or drawing, and the smell had taken over, competing only with the scent of the fresh bread and scones he'd bought at the market. His stomach growled.

"Not just yet," she said with a sigh, setting down her charcoal and revealing blackened fingertips, which she brushed off on a corner of her black tunic. "But you probably want to get to your dinner, eh? I can pack up if you want me to go."

"No," he blurted. "I mean, you're welcome to stay for dinner if you'd like. I actually have some, uh, magic to ask the cottage this evening. I thought you might be interested."

Her mischievous look returned, and she carefully rolled up her canvas, tucking it away in a tube she pulled from her bag. "Now *that* I want to see."

He noticed she'd left the new charcoals on the table, and he nodded toward them. "You can keep those, you know. A gift from the cottage."

"Thank you," she said, but she kept her eyes on him. "Now what is this magic you're doing?" She came over and leaned against the back of the chaise, watching him unabashedly.

"*I'm* not doing the magic, the cottage is," he clarified.

With a shrug, she said, "Whatever you say, Keeper of the Cottage."

He gave a light snort. "Tomorrow, I'm planning on..." He hesitated, turning to his desk and shuffling his papers there. The plans he'd made. The new hours, the tallies of fees from the book club, and projections for income from deliveries and book club orders for the near future. "I'm planning on quitting my job at the courier's to take on the library full-time."

"Oh, that's fantastic, Everson! But what sort of magic do you need for that?"

"Coffee. From Arcavia."

Her forehead wrinkled. "Huh?"

He chuckled. "A parting gift for my boss, Filgaria, to soften the news."

"Ahh, I see. Well, go on then."

"I wish I had a bag of Arcavian coffee beans."

A small sack appeared in his open hands, and it didn't take long for the scent to reach his nose. They both inhaled deeply at the same time and burst into a fit of chuckles at the synchronicity.

"Omens, that smells good," she said. "What do you do with it?"

"Drink it, but I'm not sure how." He gave the bag an experimental squeeze, feeling the beans inside. "I was hoping Filgaria would know. But maybe... I wish I had a book about Arcavian coffee?" he asked hesitantly.

A thin paperback appeared precariously balanced on his knee and promptly fell off. Mira lunged for it at the same time he did, and their heads collided.

"Oof!" Mira exclaimed, pulling away and sinking back to sit on her heels, book in hands. "Sorry."

Everson rubbed his head, apparently having been hit the hardest; Mira was already thumbing through the book.

"Growing conditions...taste profiles... Ah, preparation!"

He set the sack on his desk and got down on the floor

beside her so he could look. "What is that?" he asked, pointing to an illustration.

"A grinder. I guess the beans need to be ground first. And this one here's an *espresseaux* machine, for brewing it."

Everson pursed his lips. "That looks...complicated. I don't know if the cottage can handle that kind of thing."

Mira frowned in thought. "If it can produce books with thousands of words correctly, I don't see why this wouldn't work too."

"Maybe you're right."

"Does Filgaria already have one?"

"I wish I had a cup of coffee to try first," he said idly. "I'm not sure I want to lug such a big machine all the way out there."

A porcelain cup appeared beside him on the floor filled with brown liquid, a fine tan foam lining the top. The scent of coffee duplicated tenfold as the steam wove around them.

Mira let out a delighted laugh and leaned around him to get a better look, leaning on his crossed knee. Everson had to stifle the urge to reach out and stroke her hair again. Instead, he scooted back to give her room.

"I wish I had one," she said teasingly.

"I'm sorry," he said. "How rude of me. I wish I had another cup of coffee for Mira."

A second one appeared next to the first, and he handed it to her. She sank back onto her heels, holding it with both hands and inhaling the steam. "Omens," she moaned. "This smells *delightful*."

"I couldn't agree more," he said, lifting his own cup

to get a better scent. The rich aroma pervaded his senses, and his eyes closed in bliss. The two of them looked at each other and took a sip. Everson's eyes rolled up briefly in pure joy as the warm, almost-nutty flavor hit his tongue.

"You definitely need an *espresseaux* machine in the library," Mira said in a tantalizingly low voice after taking a sip.

"I quite agree. But this…I think I want to do this the right way." His gaze strayed toward the donation box, where he'd heard a fair number of coins clinking ever since Nod installed it. "Maybe I'll send to Arcavia to see about ordering one. I know a gnome who brews his own coffee—I bet he'll know where I can get one. If the Arcavians go to this much trouble to harvest and brew the stuff, I want to make sure we get the best."

Mira nodded, taking small sips of her coffee, a peaceful expression coming over her that had become familiar to him. After a minute, he realized it was the face she made when she paused in her sketching or painting to stare off into the distance, looking at nothing and everything all at once. And he had been the one to put it there. Suddenly his gaze was drawn to her lips, and he had an overwhelming urge to kiss her.

But that wasn't something a faerŭn librarian should do.

Instead, he got up, taking his cup with him and setting it on the desk beside the beans. He distracted his racing heart by saying, "I think the beans will make a good preliminary gift for Filgaria. I can tell her I'm ordering a machine if she doesn't have her own."

Mira's eyes fluttered as she drained the last of her cup. "I think it's nice of you to get her a gift at all. I apprentice for a master artist here in Wrestia, and he doesn't let me touch his supplies even when I run out in the studio. Though, I think it's more because he's *particular* about his own things."

"Filgaria gave me a chance, when she hired me. I...had a hard time keeping a job when I first left the palace. Not many jobs in Wrestia for someone who likes to keep to himself and would rather read books all day if he could." He shrugged.

"The palace, eh?" Mira asked, hugging a knee to her chest and taking another sip of her coffee.

"Oh, well, yes. You didn't know? I'm Vastion Wrestin's stepbrother."

"I'd heard something of the like. He's getting married soon, isn't he?" she asked. "I met Lady Glace at the solstice celebration at the ice gardens—she always wears the most beautiful dresses. I'd love to paint her someday."

Everson nodded mechanically. "That's them."

"You're not happy about it?"

"No. I mean, yes! Of course I'm happy for them. It's just... My life at the palace was always a little difficult, and then our parents died from the Fen flu, and I didn't want to be there anymore. Things are a little...complicated."

"I see. But now you've carved out your own haven here. I'm sure they would be so proud of you."

Everson just nodded, his throat swelling. "Perhaps I should respond to Vastion's wedding invitation."

Mira gave an incredulous laugh. "You haven't responded yet? The full moon is in three weeks, isn't it?"

He ducked his head. "Yeah."

"I wish I could see it," Mira added wistfully.

"Can't you?" he asked, thoughts whirring. The ceremony was open to the public, but if he invited her to come with him personally...would she want to?

"I can't," she explained. "I have to travel to Melodïgha next week. Master Raymyn—the artist I apprentice under—his work is being featured in Duchess Floratiño's new gallery."

"Oh." Everson's heart dropped. "How long will you be gone? I mean, what will we do without our resident artist?" he added, finding he sounded more forlorn than he meant to.

"I'm not sure," she said, hugging her knee tighter. "I hope to get some sketching done on the carriage ride, but I'm sure it'll be too bumpy for that. At least, I'll get out of the snows for a few weeks."

Everson forced a smile. "That's a bonus. I wish you could come with me to the wedding," he admitted.

"I do too," she said. "It would give you something to do that wasn't just *books*. Have you decided on a new hobby yet?"

He snorted. "I'm learning about brewing coffee, aren't I?"

"A noble pursuit," she said. "Coffee is a beverage of the gods, to be sure. I'll need another cup next time we're alone."

Everson shivered at the last four words, but he nodded heartily. "Of course. Maybe you can come in the morning sometime, before the library opens, since I'll be quitting the courier's," he said, swirling the last of his cup before finishing it.

Then he straightened as the realization of what he'd said hit him.

"How did it feel to say it out loud?" she said, poking him in the shin.

"Good. *Good*. I think this is the right decision. I mean—" His gaze went to his papers on the desk as if seeking reassurance.

She poked him again. "You'll do great. Everyone loves the library—loves you. I think this is what you were meant to do."

His throat felt swollen again, and he nodded. "Do you want a ride home?" His stomach had started to do flips at the thought of quitting tomorrow. Or perhaps it was the coffee. Or Mira.

"Actually... Can I take you up on that offer of dinner? It smells divine—maybe not as divine as the beverage of the gods," she added, gesturing to her empty coffee cup. "But still."

"I would love that," he said, his heart racing faster. "Do you want any more coffee?"

She grinned, shaking her head.

As he busied himself in the kitchen nook, scrambling for bowls and a serving ladle, finding his cloth napkins, and generally darting about like mad at the idea of having dinner with Mira, the artist took the coffee book and wandered over to the shelves at ease.

"Where do you want this book?" she asked as he set two bowls of virleek and onion soup on the table by the conversation chairs. He normally had dinner at his desk, which was, perhaps, not the healthiest habit. He really needed another hobby.

"Right there is fine," he said, pointing at the low bookshelf beside the chairs. "It's a new arrival, after all."

Mira grinned and slipped it in. The book ends—large carved chunks of a blue and white stone he'd wished for —were dangerously close to the edge, the section bulging with as many new books as would fit.

"I really need more shelves," he grumbled to himself.

Mira chuckled, the airy sound filling the small space.

He retreated to the kitchen to grab the basket of bread and set it in the middle of the table.

"I can take you back on the sled after," he offered.

"I know," Mira replied, pulling her bowl toward her.

Somehow he'd run out of things to say now that they were sharing a meal together. He couldn't remember the last time he'd had such an intimate meal with someone. Back when it was just him and his mother? After they'd moved to the palace, he'd taken many of his meals alone or been forced to attend large dinners. At the large dinners, Everson had often been tormented by Vastion's great-uncle Overforth, who was a worse tease than Vastion had ever been. He'd always found something to criticize about Everson, whether it was his appearance, his silence, or his well-known adherence to wearing hats indoors. It was no wonder Everson had eaten in his rooms more often than not.

But the silence with Mira was comfortable, and his mind wandered freely instead of wondering what he should say to fill the space, which was good, because his mind was filled to bursting. It felt like he stood on the precipice of change, between Mira finding out about the cottage and quitting his job tomorrow. But he already had a steady income from the library deliveries, which hadn't tapered off since he'd begun. Every day, he had at least one new person requesting some book or another. Often, the new patrons didn't ask for a specific title, just a vague request, which Everson usually repeated word for word to the cottage, unless he knew of the perfect recommendation himself. All the new books were starting to become a problem. He gasped.

"What is it?" Mira asked.

"I was thinking about my book storage problem. I can't add any more new shelves, but I had another idea. I've never asked the cottage to make something *go away* before, but"—he glanced over at the chaise, where he often asked the cottage to clean the cat hair off the blankets—"I think it's possible."

Mira tore off another piece of her bread to dip in her soup, watching with interest. "Well?"

Everson frowned. He'd finished his soup and bread already; he had always been a fast eater, perhaps due to all those years of eating alone and having no one to share the time with. "I wish this napkin would disappear."

The blue cloth winked out of existence, crumbs and all.

That mischievous look was back in Mira's eyes, watching his expression. "You're not going to make me disappear, are you?" she teased.

Everson laughed. "Of course not! And I highly doubt it would work on people, anyway. No, this will be great! I can return the books that people haven't checked out in a while. I'll have to go through my ledger and rate the popularity..."

"That sounds like a truly riveting *bookish* task, though you might need some coffee for it."

He gave her a look. "I *like* books, you know."

"And they suit you. How about next time I stay for dinner, you can try painting!"

Everson swallowed. "I-I'd like that. Though I won't be any good at it."

"Not with that attitude," she said with a wink.

The bell above the door at Hand to Hand jingled as Everson walked in, sack of coffee beans in hand.

Filgaria was sitting at her low desk, the surface clear of its usual letters, clipboards, and papers. She seemed to be waiting for him, though he was right on time today.

"H-Hey Filgaria," Everson said, his voice cracking uncharacteristically.

"Morning, Everson," she said, leaning her sharp chin on her propped arm.

"Listen, we need to talk."

"Sure."

"I-I..." His throat seized. He'd never quit a job before. It had always been the other way around. "I got you this."

He handed her the sack of beans, and her smooth expression morphed into delight as the scent wafted over her. "Arcavian coffee? Everson! Where did you get these? This is...wonderful!"

"Oh, um, I've been ordering a lot of books and just happened to..." He trailed off vaguely. But then he glanced back at the sled outside, stacked with books to deliver, and he straightened up. "I wanted to get you a little something, for all that you've given me while working here. I just...I need to quit."

"Finally." She pulled on the sack's tie so she could peek inside. Everson's heart dropped, but she continued. "You've been working yourself to the bone doing both things. I was waiting for you to realize what you needed to do."

He gaped at her. "Really? You knew I was going to?"

Filgaria cocked an eyebrow at him. "You've been rushing around, getting book orders from all across town. I can tell the library's going well. Everson—I'm happy for you."

He swallowed the lump in his throat. "I—Thank you, Filgaria. For everything. And the coffee beans... I don't suppose you have a machine to brew them?"

She shook her head wistfully.

"I'm going to order one for the cottage," Everson declared. "I...um...smelled the stuff at the print shop, and I'd love to brew my own. You're welcome to come anytime for a cup."

"That's right, Geminigh has an *espresseaux* machine. Maybe when I buy another stamp, I'll ask him if I can use his in the meantime." She took a deep whiff of the open bag. "I suppose you have book deliveries for me?"

Everson bit his lip and nodded. This was the other part of quitting he'd been worried about. He couldn't possibly handle all the book deliveries himself.

"Hand them over, then."

"Really? I'll pay more, now that I'm..."

"I won't hear about it," she said. "I don't want that Ms. Francesca complaining to me about the delivery price going up—she's in here all the time with her lists, you must know. You're giving me more business than ever. People dropping off book requests are using the mail more too since they're already here, and then the book deliveries themselves—it's been a tidy profit, Everson, and I'll have no trouble hiring another courier. I gave Franz your deliveries today anyway, so you can take off after this."

"R-Really? Thank you, Filgaria," he gushed. "Thank you. I have—erm, eighteen books today, and, um, a letter for Arcavia." To put off quitting, he'd gone to the print shop first to ask Geminigh if he could help him order an espresseaux machine from Arcavia. The old gnome had handed over a slip of paper with an address from the box of his own *espresseaux* machine.

Everson's head was spinning. He was done! He didn't even have to make deliveries today. His gratitude welled up, and he was doubly glad he'd gotten Filgaria the coffee beans.

"See?" she said. "I knew the library was doing well! You should think about having a grand opening or something, spread the word more."

He stroked his chin. In the haste of the morning, he'd forgotten to shave, and he would need to do so before he opened the library today. The hair looked blond when stubbled, but noticeably faerun-silver when it got any longer. "Maybe," he hedged, thinking about the people he'd like to see there, and wondering when exactly Mira was leaving for Melodïgha.

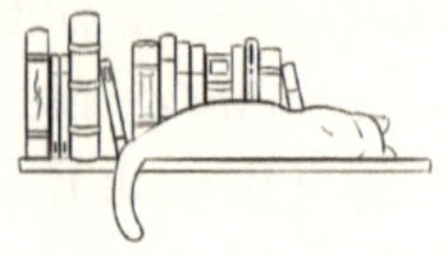

The Library at the Edge of the Wood
New Hours

Weekdays: Noon to Sunset (Myrsdays:
Ninth Chime to Sunset)
Weekends: Ninth Chime to Sunset
Closed Sylsdays

Everson tacked the sign to the crooked door that afternoon, hoping the mischievous thing would allow the sign to stay there, but he doubted it. He'd made a second copy just in case and left it on his desk. He'd decided eighth chime was too early and pushed it to nine so he'd have a little more time to sleep in, now that he was his own boss, and was quite looking forward to taking the day after tomorrow off.

After stopping at the courier's, he'd taken Princess back over to Stetson's—the mule had already spent one night out in the cold. Everson tracked down Stetson and explained he was interested in buying her, but he wasn't yet ready to accommodate her long-term. Stetson wasn't worried. Princess was used to the cold, and the trees offered enough shelter. But Everson wouldn't consider it until he had a barn or lean-to of some kind. If only Nod were still around.

Tomorrow would be his first full day, from ninth chime to sunset, so before anyone arrived today, he had some cottage magic to do. Half-hoping Mira would show up early again, he went over to the general fiction section and began browsing the shelves. He pulled a handful of books he didn't recall anyone taking out and asked the cottage to make them disappear. It wasn't as pleasing as watching a new book pop into existence, but more room on the shelves meant he could rotate the stock, and that meant more room for new books.

By the time he'd gone through that section, he'd gotten it down to a science. He'd put the tip of his finger on the book and say, *I wish this book were gone.*

He was able to shelve the excess books from new arrivals onto the main bookcases and even make a dent in the random stacks he'd kept by his desk before any patrons arrived.

When the knock came on the door, though, the person didn't come in when he called. *Must be a new patron*, he thought, striding over to the door to open the crooked thing.

He was greeted by a tall gentleman dressed in black, a black bowler cap shading his face. A well-to-do carriage sled with a team of horses sat just outside the forest, awaiting the man.

"H-Hello," Everson said. "Welcome to the library."

"Library, is it?" the man asked gruffly. "I didn't know we had a library."

"Yes, it's—"

The man pushed his way in and took off his cap, revealing a bald head with a scar running down the back, shaped like a jagged crescent. Everson's eyes bulged. He'd know that scar anywhere.

"Mr. Overforth?"

Havilon Overforth, uncle of Vastion the First, and great-uncle to Everson and Vastion, turned sharply from where he'd been surveying the room with his cold gray eyes, and adjusted his cravat. "How do you—ah, the youngest Wrestin. Your brother put you up out here, did he?"

Everson bristled. "No, I—"

"Any books on law? Ravenshold Library has an extensive collection, I'm sure you know."

"No, I don't," Everson said coldly, his voice shrinking. Uncle Overforth surely knew Everson hadn't attended Ravenshold University and wouldn't know a tick about their collection.

"Ah," Overforth said, waving a hand at Everson's carefully curated shelves as if dismissing them for frivolity. "I'll proceed on to the palace then. Vastion will be expecting me. Perhaps I'll find more suitable reading materials there."

"I'm sure."

Bile rose in his throat as he watched Overforth head back outside. The man didn't even bother to close the door behind him, perhaps thinking the task beneath him. Like everything and everyone else. Everson had no doubt Overforth was in town for Vastion's wedding, which made him even less inclined to attend.

Curse Overforth and his looking down on him. So he didn't have any books on law. What he was most angry about was Overforth's assumption that Vastion had set him up with the library. As if Everson couldn't have carved out this place for himself?

His anger died out as he gazed around at all his books. Of course, anyone might assume the Wrestin money had purchased this. This many books *would* cost a fortune. He rolled his eyes and strode over to shut the door.

Everson managed to get it closed and then, inadvertently, wished for a cup of tea.

The sight of the fresh steaming cup on the floor in front of him made his eyes prick.

"Thank you," he muttered to the cottage, picking it up.

His collection of teacups had grown to an unreasonable number, though, so before anyone else showed up, he decided to start cleaning out his kitchen cabinets.

In the beginning of his cottage days, before he'd started brewing his own tea, he'd amassed a large collection of various teacups and mugs, all of different shapes and sizes. He made most of them disappear, keeping only his favorites...and plenty for his patrons.

The magic lifted his spirits a little, or perhaps it was the fresh start the decluttering bestowed.

Lyla's face lit up when she entered half an hour later, accompanied by Ferrace and someone new. "New hours, Everson?"

Her excitement buoying his spirits, he nodded. "I'm working at the library full-time now." His chest swelled at the admission.

"That's fantastic! And I found you a reader for the Bard Hour," she said, pulling the newcomer forward.

"Already?" Everson asked.

"This is Wren Malone. She's actually a singer, but when she heard about the storytelling, she said she'd love to," Lyla gushed.

Wren, with short tawny hair and a serious expression, didn't look like she'd said any such thing, but she nodded at Everson shyly, so he introduced himself.

"I was hoping for an hour of reading aloud," he explained. "Is that something you'd want to do? Maybe next Myrsday—early afternoon?"

"Oh, yes," Wren said. Her voice was clear and melodical. "I sing down at the Snowed-In Inn every weekend, so a Myrsday is fine."

"She's got such a beautiful voice," Lyla chimed in. "A natural performer."

"Oh," Everson said, surprised. Wren's demeanor was reserved and quiet—not someone he'd have pegged as the type to read to strangers for an hour. *Guess I shouldn't judge a book by its cover*, he thought with a grimace. "It's settled then. And I'll pay you, say, three silver?"

Wren's eyes widened. "I normally only sing for tips, but sure."

He thought it only fair to pay a performer for their time, considering it was a service he was providing for the patrons. *And there I go, already employing someone on day one. Let's hope this works out.*

"Fantastic. Let me make you a library card while you're here."

Wren browsed while Lyla perched in her favorite spot on the chaise, *Whirl of the World* in her lap.

Ferrace bustled out soon after. Everson thought it

was sweet that he'd escorted Lyla to the library, when the mechanic had no interest in reading physical books. Everson kept an ear out for Mira while he worked through his ledger, crossing off the books he'd gotten rid of, and making little *X*'s next to the other books that had never been checked out for future cottage cleaning.

Eventually, Wren selected a couple of books: one about Viridian flowers, and the *Dragon Lord's Queen*. Everson smiled but said nothing, not after Francesca's secrecy. Wren clutched it to her chest and tucked her new library card in to use as a bookmark.

Lyla availed herself of another cup of tea, and a couple of gnomes came in to check out books from the histories section, but there was still no sign of Mira. Everson began to wonder if she'd been put off by their late-night coffee and dinner. He'd walked her home to the edge of Wrestia in the cold, and the silence on the walk had been comfortable—or had it?

He shook off his doubts. Mira was his friend, and they'd shared a warm and delightful evening together. Even if he'd wanted to run his fingers through her hair or the back of his neck warmed at the memory of her lips.

He cleared his throat loudly to derail those thoughts, and the two gnomes looked up from the books that they were reading at the conversation table. They stood up to leave, and Everson gave them a cheerful smile, hoping they hadn't thought he was giving them a signal to depart.

Sighing, Everson pulled out the wedding invitation from his top desk drawer and stared at it. The guilt for not responding as the days drew nearer had him biting the inside of his lip, but now that he knew Overforth was attending... Well, he didn't know if he could go through with it.

It was almost sunset when Mira blew in through the door; she'd wrenched it open with the help of a blustery gust of wind. She seemed to have more things with her than usual, a bulging bag and a bulky-looking cloak fluttering about her.

"How'd it go?" she asked, a knowing look in her eye. She shut the door with a practiced shove and headed over to her usual spot to deposit her things.

"Great," he said. "Did you see the new hours?"

"What new hours?"

"On the door?" he asked, standing up and coming closer.

Mira shook her head, and Everson groaned.

"They probably blew away in all this wind."

"Yes... Probably."

"So you'll have plenty of time to learn how to brew coffee, eh?"

His insides warmed as he thought of last night, when they'd sat on the floor together looking at the book, coffee steam coiling in the air around them like a pocket of warmth. Was it too much to hope he'd have a moment like that with her again?

"The wind almost blew my painting away," Mira said with a grin, pulling the awkward thing from under her cloak. It was framed now, which would explain the danger of the wind. Her cheeks were red with the cold, and she shivered as she removed her cloak to hang on one of the pegs behind the door. "The frame took a little longer to dry than I expected. Here you go, Lyla!"

Lyla gasped in delight as Mira handed her the canvas. As they admired it, the two women were outlined in a golden glow from the hearth, not unlike the gilded hues of the portrait.

"It's beautiful," Everson said.

"Would you keep it here for me until a less windy day, Everson?" Lyla asked as she stood to go, carefully handing it to him.

"Of course," he agreed, his heart thudding an extra beat at the thought of being alone with Mira again. "And I'm sorry I don't have the sled today. I thought the mule could use a night in the stables."

"Oh, it's fine, dear. I'm a Wrestian, I can handle the cold. Have a good evening, you two." She wrapped her thick scarf up over her nose; her thick wool hat and mittens also looked warm enough to combat the wind.

Everson swallowed as he watched Lyla go, giving her a little wave, then running over to close the door behind her. "I really wish people didn't have to walk through all that just to get here," he said, though he knew it was one of those wishes that the cottage couldn't grant for him.

"I think it just makes it more of a reward when you finally get here," Mira said. "It's going home that's the worst part."

Everson's face warmed, and he cleared his throat. "The painting is beautiful."

"So you said," she remarked with a grin. "Any more magic this evening?"

"Is that the only reason you trekked out here?" he said, unable to keep the teasing from his voice.

"No, I brought you a surprise, actually. But I wouldn't say no to magic."

"Oh?"

She began digging in her bulging bag and removed a casserole dish wrapped in towels. "Hopefully, it's still warm. If not, we can put it by the hearth."

Everson's eyes bulged. "You cooked...for me?"

She gave an airy chuckle and brought the casserole over to the hearth, peeking inside. "Stone cold. Shouldn't take too long to warm up over here though. The cat won't touch that, will he?"

Randalf was in the loft, napping. Everson shook his head, still aghast at Mira's kind gesture. "W-Why?"

"You gave me dinner last night, eh? And that *delicious* coffee. It's only fair I return the favor."

"Well," he said. "I can't deny I would love the company."

He blanched at the words that had tumbled from his mouth. He turned toward his desk to pick up a piece of paper he didn't need, pretended to check something on it, then put the paper back.

"And," Mira said, "I brought these."

He turned to see her holding up a small collection of paints—little white tubes marked with a dab of paint on the outside to indicate the color. Though, many of them were marked with more than just one dab of paint—clearly accidental swipes from paint-stained hands. He smiled.

"I—really? I don't want to use up your supplies. I can ask the cottage—"

Mira held up a hand, one that was indeed paint-stained, this time with gold. "Much like your desire to do the *espresseaux* machine the right way, I *insist* you do paints my way. At least to get started. Who knows what kind of magic the cottage will put in them, anyway?" she added with a wink.

"Can I offer you a coffee?" he asked, seizing on the subject.

"No, though I hate to turn it down. I was up all night. I think that is a morning kind of beverage. But I *did* clean out my studio, which I've been putting off for ages. That's when I found these paints. You can keep them."

"Are you sure?"

She studied him for a moment, then moved closer. "You give so much, Everson. Allow other people to give things to you for once, eh?"

Somehow, he'd gotten closer to her too. "Very well, then, I accept, Mira the Master Artist." He could see in clear detail her dark lashes and her lush red lips.

A giggle spilled from her, and she shook her head, her charming flyaways wreathing her face. "It'll be a long time before I'm a master. My apprenticeship is for another five years, then journeyman—"

"Not in my book," he said quietly.

"You and your books," she said, now tantalizingly close. He could smell vanilin and terrazzo again.

A spark popped in the hearth, and they jumped apart. Everson cleared his throat, and Mira went to check on her dish, but the stray spark landed on the stones of the hearth.

He went to the kitchen nook and opened the cupboards to look for dishes.

"What do we need?" he asked.

"Bowls would be best."

He got a whiff of unfamiliar spices that made his mouth water as he took down two bowls and retrieved the breadbasket.

After Mira filled the bowls and set them on the table, Everson summoned a pair of blue cloth napkins and handed her one. The bowls were filled with spiced Imminian rice with a mixture of black beans and topped with grilled virleeks, the green vegetable adding a splash of color.

"It's not much, but it's one of my favorites," she said.

His mouth was watering. "It looks—and smells—delicious."

I wish I had a bottle of Melodïghan wine and two glasses, he thought suddenly. It was impulsive, but when the items appeared—the glasses on the table and the wine bottle on the floor for some reason—she grinned, sending a jolt of energy through his stomach.

He had to ask for a corkscrew as well, but was soon pouring the pinkish liquid for both of them. Before he could come up with a suitable toast, however, he noticed Mira's expression go distant.

"I have to tell you, I have another motive for making you dinner," she confessed.

"Oh?"

"I'm leaving for Melodïgha tomorrow. Master

Raymyn got a letter from the duchess—the gallery opening got moved up and..." She sighed, gazing up at him through her thick brown eyelashes. "I'm sorry, I-I've really enjoyed coming to see you."

"I...really enjoy seeing you too," he said quietly, then cleared his throat. "But we'll have plenty of time for coffee and painting and dinners after you get back, right?"

"Well, I just hope Master Raymyn doesn't follow through on his musings about moving to Melodïgha..."

"Would-Would you have to go with him?"

"To finish my apprenticeship with him, yes. But I'm not sure he's entirely serious, and it'll depend on how the gallery opening goes."

"Could you find another artist to apprentice under?" he blurted. If Mira left Wrestia, he'd probably never see her again. The cottage was more than a home for him, it was the library, the warm haven serving not just him but everyone in Wrestia. A place where everyone was welcome, no matter what they read, or even if they just needed a place to go. How quickly it had carved out a place in his heart.

Mira frowned, looking away. "It was hard to get this position. Not many masters accept new artists these days. A master is not only responsible for teaching an apprentice, but they provide us with a small stipend. Not that I'm paid much, but I do a lot of work around the studio."

Everson couldn't help but frown too. Deciding his original idea of toasting art was too sore of a subject—for both of them, now, it seemed—he picked up his glass and said, "Then, to the library, may it always be here to welcome you."

With a gentle clink of glasses, their eyes met over the wine, and he couldn't drop his gaze even as they sipped. It was delightfully fruity but somehow not too sweet. He saw her expression morph from somewhat dejected to impressed. "You can wish for this stuff anytime?" she blurted, holding her glass up.

A laugh roared out of him. "Yet this is the first time I've done so," he admitted. "Here, I'll send a bottle home with you." With a silent wish, another bottle appeared on the floor.

The two of them tucked into the meal, which, as Everson had predicted, was just as amazing as it smelled. Spices burst across his tongue, and the virleeks and beans added contrasting textures to the rice.

Again, a comfortable silence settled over them as they sipped and ate, the flavor of the wine perhaps not the most suited to the spiced meal but eliciting a welcome heat in his belly regardless.

Maybe I'll add a wine pairing book to the collection, he mused to himself after all the bowls and glasses were empty. "That was amazing," he told Mira. "Maybe instead of painting, you can teach me how to cook!"

She giggled and tossed her napkin onto the table. "You're just trying to get out of learning to paint, aren't you, librarian? But I can give you the recipe."

"Not trying to get out of it at all, I'm just getting sick of soups and stews," he said, holding up his palms. "Here, let me clean up, and we can start."

With a wish, the dirty napkins disappeared, and he

brought the bowls to the kitchen nook to soak in his wash basin. A thrill ran through him when he turned around and saw Mira was refilling the wine glasses. A blank sheaf of parchment was laid out on the table, along with the set of charcoals he'd gifted to her.

"I thought we were painting?" he said, his steps hesitant as he approached.

She whirled around mischievously. "First, you need to plan out what you want to paint, my dear librarian."

He wasn't sure, but his heart seemed to skip a couple beats. She was incredibly close, that mischief dancing in her eyes.

"I'm not sure what I want to paint," he whispered.

"It can be anything," she said softly, taking a step even closer to him. A charcoal found its way into his hand, and she guided his fingers toward the paper. She continued speaking in his ear. "Once you put your mark on the paper, it becomes your unique creation—it becomes art. And even if every artist in the world drew the same thing, yours would still be unique. Because no one will mark the paper just the same as you, and no one will see the vision in their head as you do."

Her words seemed to trail down his spine, and he shivered. He wasn't sure he could draw *anything* right now with her so close to him.

He turned to suggest they move toward the fireplace as a distraction, saying, "Mira, I—"

She'd moved her face in front of his, and suddenly, those bright red lips were much too close. Before he could even think of whether he *should* or not—she kissed him.

Everything around him seemed to disappear. Something fell from his hand, and he reached up to stroke his thumb along her jaw. Her presence surrounded him, from the scent of vanilin and terrazzo, to the silky hair tumbling through his fingers.

She pulled away, that mischief like fire dancing in her eyes as he reluctantly dropped his hands. He'd wanted to live in that moment forever.

"You're not what I expected of a librarian," she whispered, her sweet breath caressing his cheek.

He blinked. Nothing clever or coherent bubbled to the surface to say, except, "I'm sorry, I-I got charcoal on your cheek."

His own face warmed at the thought of his hand running down her jaw, his fingers slipping through her hair.

"Oh, that's nothing new," she said with a sly smile.

With a wish, Everson summoned a cloth napkin. "May I?"

Mira nodded, and he stepped forward, stroking it down her cheek. It took a couple attempts, but he finally got the black streak off. He couldn't help looking at her lips again.

"You're just trying to avoid painting, aren't you?"

His face burned, and he shook his head, "What, no, I—"

"I'm only kidding," Mira said with a light laugh, then leaned forward and planted a soft kiss on his cheek. "Come on, my librarian. Let's sketch together."

LIZ DELTON

LIZ DELTON

"I like that," Mira said, leaning over his shoulder. They'd moved to the fire where the light was brighter, Mira's supplies scattered across the low table amid teacups, wine glasses, and scone crumbs. They'd asked the cottage for toasting forks and warmed up the orange and hora scones for dessert.

Everson looked down at his sketch. It was his third one, and he finally felt happy with it. At first, he'd tried sketching the hearth—something he could look at for reference had seemed an easy way to approach it. But he hadn't been happy with his proportions and angles, and after the second attempt, began to suspect that realism might not be his thing.

So he'd ended up just moving the charcoal around the paper in pleasing shapes and patterns, overlapping arcs and swirls. It wasn't a picture of anything in particular, but the shapes made by the overlapping lines created something pleasing to look at.

He heard a stifled yawn and turned to look at Mira. His insides simultaneously burst into flames and tried to wriggle towards his stomach. "What time are you leaving tomorrow?"

She sighed. "Midday. Master Raymyn's final painting is still drying—he's hoping it'll be ready by then. Maybe I can convince him to stop on our way out of town and say goodbye?"

Anguish rippled through his gut. He set down his drawing and turned to face her fully. "I wish you didn't have to go."

"I don't want to leave, either, Everson. But I'll be back."

Her last words didn't sound as sure. Were Master Raymyn's plans of moving to Melodïgha more concrete than Mira had let on? They *would* come back, wouldn't they?

"Hopefully, I'll see you tomorrow," he said, his hand seeking hers where it sat on the back of the chaise.

"I hope so too."

He squeezed her fingers, enjoying the feeling of them encased in his.

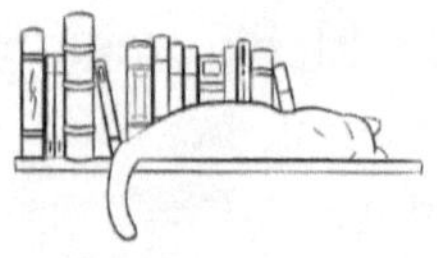

He awoke to his first real day off with far less enthusiasm than he should have felt; the idea of Mira leaving Wrestia had put a damper on everything. Even the weather was grayer, from what he could see through his reading nook windows.

But he had the cottage all to himself, plenty of books

to read, and tea and scones for breakfast. Randalf *meowed* when Everson flung back the covers.

A pot of tea steeping in the kitchen, he ignored his work desk and went straight to the chaise where he and Mira had left their sketches from last night. He'd been surprised when she'd insisted on leaving hers, which had made him all the more melancholy. Between that and the dinner, he was starting to feel like she was giving him parting gifts, like when he'd given the coffee to Filgaria.

He took his time toasting a scone over the fire, then reclined on the chaise to start rereading *Whirl of the World* for the book club. He knew some people thought rereading was a waste of time; for him, it was like visiting an old friend. An old story. An old memory.

A timid knock came on the cottage door.

He frowned. It was much too early to be Mira, so perhaps a library patron. He had only posted his new hours yesterday, so not everyone would know he was supposed to be closed—a hazard to his first day off that he'd reluctantly expected. Whoever it was, he was sure he could read and relax just as easily with them there. Though, he didn't normally open the library this early.

"Come in!" he called, getting up and jamming on the hat he kept by the door before assisting with the crooked door.

He lifted it by the sturdy doorknob and swung it open. Druida Glace stood on the porch, shivering in her white fur wrap. She'd come by sled, the mule unbothered by the light morning breeze.

"Why'd you pick somewhere so far out of town?" she demanded, storming inside.

Everson took a hasty step back. "What are *you* doing here?"

She strode in and parked herself in front of the fire, still clutching the wrap around her shoulders. "What do you think? Your brother is getting married in a week's time, and we haven't received your response."

"I—well, I—"

"My, you've been busy," she remarked, turning on the spot.

"I have," he said, crossing his arms over his chest. This was *not* how he wanted to spend his day off.

Druida's expression wrinkled into a frown. "You know, you don't have to shut yourself away from everyone—especially all the way out here."

"I like it here," he said through gritted teeth, forcing himself to uncross his arms. "And I'm not shutting myself away. I have *plenty* of patrons who come every day."

"Oh, it's a gorgeous place. Warm fire, books, and is that Queen Gray I smell? It's downright delightful. Except the part where you make people trek all the way out of town."

"I started doing book deliveries," he said defensively.

"So I heard," she drawled.

"Did Filgaria tell you where I was? What, were you trying to trick me into coming to the palace again?"

"No, and I'm sorry I did that to you. We crossed a line, interfering at your employer's. Ada at the print shop told me. They're doing our cards and programs for the wedding feast." She let the ends of her wrap drop. "You're the only one who hasn't responded to the invitation. Are you coming to your brother's wedding or not?"

His arms crept back into their crossed position of their own accord. Mira would be out of town, and he'd have to deal with Uncle Overforth. But somehow...after spending last night with Mira, he didn't care as much about his prior worries and the massive black stain of anxiety had receded. "Yes, fine, I'm coming."

"And the family rehearsal dinner?"

He held his breath for a second. That sounded more intimate. Vastion, Druida, and Overforth. "I..."

She stared at him pointedly.

"Yes, fine," he repeated.

"Good, because as Vastion's only close family, you're part of the ceremony at the wedding feast, and we need to go over a couple of things."

"I'm *what?*"

Druida threw her arms up in the air. "Everson, with all the books you read, don't tell me you know nothing about the Wrestia noble wedding customs. Your own mother..." she paused, pursing her lips.

"Of course I remember," Everson said, his gaze becoming unfocused. "I just didn't think Vastion wanted me to be part of the ceremony."

"Whyever not?"

He shrugged, shaking his head.

Druida sighed and wandered over to the romantic fiction section, putting her attention on the books instead of him. "I promise you, I've never told him what I—"

Everson's eyes bulged. He fought the urge to check

that his ears were covered. Why were Druida and Vastion fighting so hard to have him at the wedding, anyway? What if Vastion, in his infinite needling, deemed his covered head disrespectful and forced him to remove his hat in front of everyone? His own mother's wedding feast—when she'd married into the Wrestin family—had gathered half the city.

"On second thought, maybe I shouldn't be there," he blurted out.

"Why in the name of the Omens not?" she demanded, whipping around to glare at him. "No, no. This is exactly why I've been trying to chase you down, for your brother's sake. This is why you hide yourself away, isn't it? You're faerŭn. Just admit it."

The word lay like a dark ink stain on a brand-new sheet of parchment.

He turned toward his desk, focusing his attention on the library cards there, hoping that someone would knock, Mira would come early, or Randalf would smell something delicious and leap down from the loft, pouncing on Druida by accident.

"Everson," she said, "there's nothing wrong with you. It's just hair and—"

"It's not *just* hair, thank you very much. It's getting shunned for the rest of my life if anyone finds out. It's getting run out of town, out of my *library*." Pain bloomed in his chest. His library. He'd only had the cottage for a few weeks but losing it now would break him. He never wanted to leave this place.

A quiet sigh rolled from her, and she walked around the chaise so she was again in his line of vision. "Your brother loves you, no matter who you are. And I can't think of a single person in Wrestia who would run you out of town, particularly with all the good work you're doing here."

"And what of the next faerŭn stranger who gets run out of town? Am I supposed to just expect a free pass because I'm me? Look by when my patrons shun another with my heritage?"

"Of course not," Druida said. "Good people don't look by when ill befalls their neighbors. And we should extend that charity to strangers. We're all under the watch of the Omens, aren't we?"

"You really should write poetry," Everson muttered, dropping into his chair, his argument spent.

She laughed. "No, I want to make a difference in Wrestia."

"Then I wouldn't laugh at poetry," he said seriously. "Words are our most important weapons, our best tools, our only way of expressing the inner turmoil of our hearts...or seeing into the heart of another. You should arm yourself with them."

She stared at him. "Perhaps *you* should write poetry, Ev."

He looked down at his desk with a private smile. He couldn't pretend he hadn't thought about it. "I'm not much of a writer. I prefer the words of others."

"Look, maybe you should talk to Vastion yourself, about...you know, being faerŭn."

"I really don't think that's a good idea."

"But if you told him—"

"Look, Druida, I didn't tell him in the ten years I

lived in the palace, being taunted by him any time I ventured out of my rooms. Why do you think I barely played with him? Not to mention he constantly"—he huffed, reaching for his hat and yanking it off— "*constantly* harassed me about my hats. Well? You can see why I kept to myself." Warm relief stole over his scalp as air hit it. He ran a hand through his hair to loosen it.

Druida, to her credit, didn't stare. In fact, she didn't change her stance one bit. "Fine. You know, for not sharing any blood, you're both remarkably the same kind of stubborn. I'll let him know you're coming, though, and I'll see you at the rehearsal."

She stalked out of the cottage, getting the door shut with a hearty slam. Everson strode over and smacked the door with a wordless groan. Of course *she'd* gotten the door closed all the way.

He shook his head and paced the library. His hat was still on the floor; he kicked it in annoyance as he passed. Curse Druida for ruining his day off.

Just as he was shakily pouring himself a fresh cup of tea, someone pounded on his door. Everson huffed. Was it Druida come to harry him some more? He stalked over to the door as the pounding continued.

"Everson?" a familiar voice called. "Open this gods-cursed door!"

"N-Nod?" Everson choked incredulously, picking up the pace, and nearly tripping on Randalf who'd just decided to dart in his path.

The door was stuck fast for once—after Druida had slammed it. His heart lifted as he wrenched it open, elated by the dwarf's return.

"Nod!" he shouted, throwing his arms up, ready to hug the dwarf.

But Nod just stared at him, blinking.

"What's wrong? You came b—" Everson choked. The porch was completely devoid of snow and ice, much like the landscape around them. Green leaves fluttered in a light breeze from the verdant forest. Everson blinked. "But...where did the snow go?" he whispered.

He'd never seen Wrestia shed her icy shroud so quickly. He'd *just* seen Druida stomp out into the snow...

"Not *where did the snow go*," Nod said haltingly. "How did your cottage get to Ravenshold?"

18

"W-What?" Everson demanded. "What are you talking about?"

Nod yanked Everson's arm and pulled him outside. Everson protested at first, wanting to get a coat, but he quickly realized that it was hardly needed. His dressing robe was enough to ward off the slight dawn chill in the woods.

"Ravenshold," Nod insisted, pointing at something Everson couldn't see through the trees. "You're in the Ingwood, just outside Ravenshold. How in all the Omens..."

Everson's knees buckled, and he wobbled.

Nod was stroking his beard, staring at the cottage. "That place is magic. I knew there was something funny about it!"

"I...no...I couldn't possibly..."

But the birds were singing, and sprigs of dew weed and clumps of delicate violets bloomed on the ground. The air was cool yet lacked the bite of the winter winds that continuously barreled down from the mountains around Wrestia. There wasn't a hint of ice, the fallen leaves were dry, and the air smelled foreign without the scent of snow.

It was impossible. It was magic.

It was the cottage.

Everson realized his mouth was hanging open in shock. He promptly closed it.

"I'm right, aren't I?" Nod asked, an odd sort of urgency in his eyes.

"Perhaps," Everson ceded quietly, his mind racing at the newly revealed power. If there was anyone he'd trust with the cottage's secrets, it was Nod. "But how did you find me?" He still wasn't even sure how he got here.

Nod grunted, then began pacing. "I was debating hailing a carriage back to Wrestia. I got word from Raine in the post last night—he and Hiron came down with Fen flu, and it's just the two of them there, all alone, no one to care for them. But I didn't want to leave my assistant Helenia here with all the orders and was out here pacing back and forth between the hosteller's and town when I happened to...happened to think of you and the cottage...and then it just...appeared."

Everson's mouth was still hanging open, and he slowly closed it. "I can't believe it," he whispered.

"Can't you?" Nod asked with a hint of his former joviality. "I noticed how you always just happened to have the *exact* book at the right moment, my boy. And master-quality bookshelves that appeared overnight?"

Guilt turned Everson's awe into a frown, but Nod was all grins at the confirmation of his apparent theory.

"Well, yes, but I can't very well tell everyone the

cottage is magic. And I didn't even know it could do *this!* Which means—I can help you get to Wrestia! I think, anyway. *I hope so.* Here. Come inside."

Nod glanced around the lush woods, shrugged, nodded, and followed Everson inside. He muttered some good-natured curses at the broken door and managed to get it shut all the way just as Druida had. He looked at Everson expectantly.

Then Everson realized he had never put his hat back on.

It felt like the bottom dropped out of his stomach and fell onto the floor. His hand went to his hair and covered a pointy ear, and he blanched. "I—"

He clamped his mouth shut, wishing he hadn't drawn more attention to himself, though his eyes had gone blurry. He forced his gaze away from Nod because he didn't want to see the dwarf's reaction. First Druida's judgment, now this?

He spun, turning his back to Nod and striding over behind the chaise where he'd kicked his hat. He made to jam it on his head, when Nod cleared his throat.

"Will that help get us to Wrestia?" the dwarf asked. "If not, I really don't see the need, my boy."

"You...don't?" Everson choked, his back still turned. His face was turning red, and it felt like his pointy ears were warming too.

"I've been staring at you for five whole minutes, now, Everson. Couldn't care less. I *would* care to go see my brother, though. Very much so."

"Of-Of course," Everson squeaked, turning back, face flaming. "I just...um... I don't actually know how I got to Ravenshold in the first place, and..." He gasped. "And Mira's leaving today! *Oh no, I wish I knew how to get back to Wrestia.*"

He strode over to the door, intent on going outside to take a look at the cottage. Maybe there was some clue in the Ingwood about why it had magically appeared out there. But when he wrenched the door open, a cold wind bit at his face, and he was nearly blinded by the blanket of white snow.

"Wrestia," he breathed. "How is this possible?" Of course! He'd made a wish! He wracked his brain to wonder why he'd never accidentally moved the cottage to any other part of Viridia, but he must not have made any explicit wishes. Or...the door had never been shut firmly until now.

"I'd like to know that myself," Nod said, clapping him on the back. "But a mystery for another time, maybe. I want to get into the city. Raine sent that letter *days* ago."

Dread filled Everson's stomach at the thought of his friends lying at home with Fen flu and no one to care for them. Little Hiron, who loved his adventure stories. Raine, a father all on his own. Everson's own mother and stepfather had had a whole palaceful of attendants, and they'd still succumbed to the illness.

"If you give me a minute," Everson said, "I'll come with you."

Nod gave him a grin. "Omens know I want to hear all about the cottage on the way into the city."

"And you don't know where the wood comes from, do you?" Nod asked as they reached Wrestia's gates.

Everson could tell the dwarf was worried for his brother and nephew and was using Everson's tale of the cottage as a distraction, but he happily obliged. After spilling the wish magic secrets to Mira, it hadn't been as difficult to tell Nod.

"Of course you're interested in the wood, and not how the magic works," Everson muttered loud enough for Nod to hear.

Or about my faerŭn heritage. Neither of them had mentioned it since the cottage, and Everson had crammed on his hat before heading out the door, decked out in his boots, coat, and cold weather gear. Contrary to Everson's every belief, it seemed Nod truly didn't care. Unless the dwarf was withholding his judgment until after he'd seen his brother. A cold feeling that had nothing to do with the wintery wind settled over Everson's shoulders. And he knew the feeling wouldn't go away until Nod said something about Everson being faerŭn. For better or for worse.

The dwarf let out a guffaw, stroking some frost from his beard and lowering his voice now that they were inside the city walls. "What kind of carpenter would I be if I wasn't curious about the wood? It looked like oak, but from what tree? I wonder where it all comes from?"

he said, though not in a way that indicated an answer was needed.

Everson shook his head. He'd already explained how he'd checked the books, making sure the content was correct—he still wasn't sure whether the cottage created things from nothing or took them from somewhere else. Though, he supposed he would have heard of a large number of books going missing from Ravenshold Library by now, considering that library held the largest collection in all of Viridia.

Nod was quiet for a few minutes as they passed the outskirts of the Winter Market, not wanting to get caught in the heavy foot traffic first thing in the morning. Bright-eyed farmers and shop owners, bundled against the cold, happily bagged up goods and accepted coin as customers hurried on to the next shop. The morning wind was brisk and carried the strong smell of oncoming snow in the air.

"You should head back," Nod said finally, when they got to Raine's street. "I don't want you coming in and getting sick."

Everson frowned. "But—"

"I know you care about them too. But if I was going to risk you, I'd have sent you instead and stayed in Ravenshold. No—go back to the library, and I'll send word later. I might need some books delivered," he added with the ghost of a smile.

Everson hesitated, but the dwarf's expression was resolute. "Of course. Please, let me know how they are, when you can."

"I will. And Everson? I'm glad I found out who you

are. It's an honor to know the true soul of such a good friend."

Everson's throat swelled, and he nodded, tears pricking the corners of his eyes. Nod clapped him on the back and turned to leave.

And with that, they parted ways, leaving Everson standing forlornly on a snowy street corner, his hands stuffed in his pockets. He was far too anxious to return to the library, but Mira was supposed to meet him there. And since he didn't know where Master Raymyn's studio was, he headed to Stetler's and rented a sled and Princess to hasten his journey home.

He was soon pacing the library, his hat still on in case he had any more surprise visitors. A cup of tea cooled on the conversation table, untouched.

He couldn't stop thinking about Nod, Raine, and Hiron. *I wish there was something I could do*, he thought, but as usual, there were some wishes even the cottage couldn't grant.

A gasp ripped through him. "Maybe there *is* something I can do! I wish I had a book on treating or curing Fen flu!"

He shut his eyes, half-worried nothing would appear. But when he opened them, he spotted a book sitting on the floor in front of him with *Fighting the Fen* written in simple black letters on a gray cover. He swiped it off the floor and practically threw himself into one of the conversation chairs to flip through its pages.

It seemed to be a healer's guide to all the remedies the author had tried, in fighting the flu over what looked like decades. Every time Everson started another chapter with another anecdote, his heart leapt, but the chapter inevitably ended with the healer indicating the treatment didn't work. Foxfire seeds. Leeches. Blackfork leaves. Nothing touched the sickness. Some of the methods were familiar to Everson, having seen them used when his mother and stepfather had fallen ill.

He huffed and flipped to the back. Surely, if the healer had found anything...

He reached the very last page and then thumbed back a few pages. The words were scrawled in a shakier hand than previous chapters.

> At last, I have succumbed to the Fen myself. It was only a matter of time, and I'm entirely surprised I made it this long without feeling its touch. I will only work all the harder for a cure now that it curses mine own body. Benson tells me I should try bloodletting again, but I'm no fool...

Everson skipped ahead again, where the writing was less shaky.

> I write to you with clear eyes, in awe of the Omens and their mercy. Unless my body has developed a resistance to the Fen, I believe I have found a treatment after all these years. I don't know if I am more overcome by gladness at my own survival or finally finding the

*answer. Benson sent to Villikry for lynchber-
ries, whose leaves carry some component of
healing. The berries themselves were useless.
We had to wait for a month. All the while my
body grew weaker, the coughs more ragged. I
steeped the leaves with a tincture of silverleaf
and garlic for two hours. The lynchberries were
dear, but I believe the key to this cure. I'll write
to Ravenshold Library post-haste so my find-
ings may be spread across Viridia.*

Brows wrinkled, Everson was torn between elation and confusion. If the author had written to Raven-shold Library to publicize the cure, what had happened to that information? The dates in the jour-nal's entries were *decades* ago. He shook his head. He needn't bother with that now. Right now, he needed...

Dried lynchberry leaves, silverleaf, and garlic appeared on the table before him, as he realized belatedly he'd made a silent wish.

He stood, looking about the cottage, then glanced back down at the journal, his mind racing. He was no healer—no herbalist—but the instructions in the journal were straightforward. He had to steep them for two hours. Steeping he could do; it was basically brewing a really strong tea.

After dumping the rest of the Queen Gray into his teacup, he decided perhaps he shouldn't put garlic and the other ingredients in the same pot he brewed tea in, so he asked the cottage for another one.

He stuffed the dried leaves and garlic in the pot and hastened over to the fire for the kettle, which was luckily already filled with hot water. He poured it over the ingredients, his heart leaping.

But he wasn't familiar with lynchberry at all, so he asked the cottage for a book on herbs and looked it up to ensure he wasn't about to poison anyone. The entry only told him it was native to Villikry and included no known uses, explaining the leaves had a bitter taste and the berries were edible.

"That's it, I guess," he said. And soon, he was back to pacing. He had no idea if this would work, but he had to try.

When someone knocked on the door, he thanked the Omens for the distraction. The clock on his desk said the brew was only halfway done, and he'd been unable to stop wondering if this cure worked and had been available to his mother and stepfather, how things could have been different.

Relief struck him like it had been fired from a cannon when he opened the door to find Mira standing there, an orange scarf wrapped around her head and neck.

"Everson, what's—"

He flung his arms around her, and she squeezed him back. "What's wrong?" she murmured into his ear.

Everson swallowed and waved her inside. "Do you have a moment or—"

"Yes," she said, coming in and helping with the

crooked door. "Master Raymyn has been uncharacteristically nice this morning, so much that I'm worried he's buttering me up for bad news once we get to Melodïgha. He even loaded half the carriage before I got there."

Everson didn't want to think about what that bad news might be. That Raymyn *would* be moving to Melodïgha?

"But enough about me," Mira said. "What's happened?"

"How can you tell?" he blurted out.

She frowned, taking off her mittens, and reaching a cold hand to take one of his. "I've never seen your eyes look so sad."

He closed them, and traitorous moisture slipped out. He wiped it away. "My friends are sick. Raine and Hiron came down with the Fen flu, and—" His chest constricted as he drew in a breath. He couldn't say anymore.

Mira nodded and squeezed his hand even harder. "I'll pray to the Omens for them the whole way to Melodïgha."

Everson nodded, his chest still tight. He cleared his throat. "I might have found... I might have found a treatment in a book." He gestured vaguely to the kitchen nook. "I'm going to bring it to them as soon as it's ready."

Outside, the mule pulling Master Raymyn's covered sled brayed.

"Good," Mira said. "I hate that I have to leave you here like this."

"No, no. You have a good trip, and good luck with

the gallery opening. Be careful on the roads, and...and take care of yourself."

"I will," she said. She leaned forward and had to rise onto her toes to kiss him. Her lips still held a chill from the outside, but her hand, which he was still holding, had grown warm. "I hope not all of your days off are this frightening."

He snorted. She didn't know the half of it. Druida. The cottage going to Ravenshold. Nod. "I can't wait to tell you about some thoroughly boring days off when you return."

He brushed a flyaway hair from her face and tucked it back under her hat, then leaned close to brush his lips against hers as he took her in his arms, perhaps for the last time.

"Thank you, Everson, for everything."

Before she turned to go, she ducked her head and gave him one of those smiles that turned his insides into honey. "You know, something that takes my mind off the bad things? Losing myself in a painting. Maybe you should try it."

"I will," he whispered, then watched her expertly maneuver the crooked door open and head out into the blindingly white landscape. Would he see her again? Would she return from Melodïgha? He had no way of knowing. He watched as Mira got into the carriage-sled and closed the door with a wave. The driver flicked the reins, and the mule began a slow trot to get the heavy sled to move, with its bulky compartment for the paintings behind the passenger area. Everson watched them head south and slip out of sight.

With the door safely closed as best as he could, he glanced at the clock once more. He still had a long wait ahead of him.

He found his sketch from last night, but he didn't feel like adding any more to it. She had left so quickly. Was it only last night they had holed up in the library drinking wine and sketching together? And that kiss...

Mira hadn't shown him the paints yet or how to use them. Though, he thought he could use a brush pen with ink well enough. How hard could it be?

But no matter where he tried to position himself downstairs, he couldn't help but look at the time ticking by and remember with longing the moments he'd spent sitting in that same spot with Mira last night. So he slipped the set of paints into his pocket and climbed the ladder to the loft. Randalf trotted up the ladder after him and curled up on his bed. Everson shut the black velvet curtain behind him with a sigh, enclosing him inside his own personal haven.

He asked the cottage for a lit taper to light the candles in the chandelier. He even wished for a cup of Arcavian coffee, a set of paintbrushes, and a stack of parchment.

Surrounded by all of his favorite books, wisps of coffee steam unfurling around him, it was becoming easier to set his anxieties over the dwarves and the ravages of Fen flu aside. Mira was right. And he hadn't even started painting yet.

He uncapped the first tube of paint—a deep wine color—and perched on his reading nook, staring at the sheaf of parchment. Paintbrush in hand, he froze, not sure what to do. Last night his swirls and shapes had been enough. Why not try that again?

He picked a sturdy brush and dabbed some paint on the end, not sure if he was doing it right. He wished Mira was here for this. He set the brush to paper and made a little swirl, the corners of his mouth turning up in an unexpected smile. The color was beautiful, a rich purple with undertones of red. He continued swiping and swirling his brush until the parchment was covered in shapes and swirls. It wasn't a masterpiece by any stretch of the imagination, but it was quite fun to look at.

He'd only used a couple dabs of paint from the small tube. Everson frowned, not wanting to use up all the paint Mira had given him all in one go. So he made a sneaky little wish. *I wish I had a large tube of wine-colored paint in my hand.*

One appeared, similar to the tubes he'd seen Mira wielding when she was working on her portrait of Lyla, although Mira's had been nearly used up, the metal tubes rolled so she could get every last drop out of them. This one was plump and, when he opened the cap, revealed a color not unlike the one Mira had given him.

With a sly look at Randalf, he dabbed some on his paintbrush and pulled over a new sheaf of paper. She wasn't here to question his use of the cottage for paint. And besides, he was just experimenting.

This paint flowed from the bristles onto the paper just as smoothly, the color only marginally different, but the weak afternoon sunlight filtering through the snow-speckled windows glinted off the swirls in a glittering kind of way. He squinted at the new lines he'd painted. They all held a kind of glimmer to them.

He went through dozens of parchments and asked for more colors: a light mint green, an auburn reddish-brown, a gray like Randalf. Eventually when he'd used up all the paper, he stood, admiring the work. He still had some paint on his brush though—the mint green—and a mischievous smile overtook him as he looked up at the ceiling.

Why not?

Not wanting the paint to go to waste, he swooped and swirled his brush on the angled ceiling until he ran out of the minty color. Then, because he'd already committed to decorating his ceiling, he dabbed more of the wine paint onto his brush, the two colors an unlikely provoking pairing. The swirls overlapped, weaving in and out of each other, a fine glimmer flickering in the chandelier light.

At last, standing on his bed with paint-flecked hands, he deemed it finished. The weight on his chest was noticeably gone. He hopped down, careful not to get paint on his bed or blankets. Randalf had slipped under the curtain and retreated back downstairs, probably finding a spot where he wasn't in danger of being flecked with paint like his master.

Everson left his parchments to dry where he'd scattered them about the reading nook and over the floor. He moved the velvet curtain aside with his foot, still holding his paintbrush. He'd need to rinse it off and clean his hands before he checked the teapot...

The teapot! Carefully, he headed down the ladder

using one hand since he held the brush with the other. A blanket of relief slid over him when he saw the time on his desk. The concoction should be ready, if a little over-steeped. Hopefully, the more potent, the better.

Wishing for a jar of fresh water, he stuck the paint-brush in it as he'd seen Mira do and found a cloth napkin with which to clean his hands as best he could.

Finally, he wished for a second jar, this one empty. He peered into the teapot, and the pungent mix of garlic and strange herbs assaulted his nose. It wasn't pleasant by any means, but that didn't matter. He poured the concoction into the empty jar, and watched it swirl around until he wished for a lid.

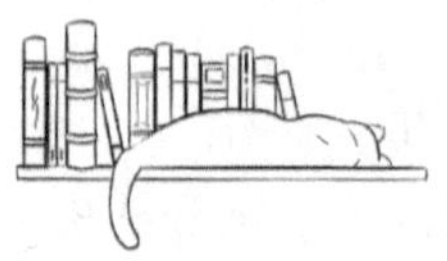

Princess trotted through the gates of Wrestia while Everson clutched the cooled-off concoction securely. It was in an inner coat pocket, but with all the jostling, he hadn't let go of it since he'd left the cottage. A light snow had picked up, and he hoped it would remain light, although the dark gray clouds to the north threatened otherwise.

He led the mule to Clear as Ice Glass Creations, dismounted, and knocked decisively on the door.

Nod, looking harried, came to the door, but didn't open it.

"You shouldn't be here," Nod called through the glass window.

Everson reached inside his coat pocket and pulled out the jar. "I have something that might help. A gift from the cottage."

Nod's bushy eyebrows rose, and he unlocked the door, only opening it enough to reach his hand out.

Everson handed it over. "I found it in a book. A healer discovered it decades ago..." He trailed off as he realized he was babbling.

"We'll try it. The healer's already been and gone with her remedies, but they haven't improved much." Nod gave a helpless shrug, then pulled the door closed again, the concoction in his hand. "Thank you," he added, the glass between them once more.

Everson nodded and watched Nod hasten toward the back of the shop, no doubt heading to the apartments upstairs. Everson only hoped that the author of the journal had been correct, and his recovery hadn't just been a coincidence.

His breath clouded before him as he noticed the snowflakes getting bigger. He should return to the library and make another batch of the concoction, should the dwarves need more of it, but something kept him tethered there for a few more minutes. It wasn't as if he thought Nod would return with news that they had recovered instantly; simply he didn't want to leave them, didn't want to be so far away when they were suffering.

Though he'd only known Nod for a few weeks, the dwarf had carved out a careful place in Everson's heart, almost like family—no, he *was* family. You couldn't choose who shared your blood, but you *could* choose who you respected and who respected you back.

For the first time in weeks, Everson wished he could stay in the city for the night.

He patted Princess on the neck, looking up at the dark clouds that now covered the city. They were in for a storm and a big one. All his swirling thoughts about Nod, Raine, Hiron, his mother dying of Fen flu, and even the warm memories of Mira condensed into one thought. He knew what he had to do.

He would go to the palace.

LIZ DELTON

19

"Where's my brother?"

Halmund stirred from his post outside the receiving hall, its doors now closed. Garlands of elegant paper snowflakes were looped over the archway, the delicate papers swaying lightly.

"Oh, Everson," the big orc rumbled in surprise. "He's in his study."

Everson's gaze slid to the doors of the hall, realizing it was probably after receiving hours.

"Thanks," he said, and stalked back the way he'd come, running into a few servants dashing about. Most of them kept their heads down, though one pair was overseeing a carpenter as he repaired a tiny dent in the chair rail that ran the length of the round hallway encircling the palace. Others polished furniture, dusted corners, or in one case, touched up the paint on a doorframe. All preparations for the wedding, no doubt.

Finally, his steps slowed as he reached the section that housed Vastion's rooms, but he didn't remember Vastion having his own study. He'd never been one for books or writing.

Realization dawned on him. Vastion would have taken over his father's study—Vastion the First's—now that he was the ruling noble. He kept walking, wondering how many times his mother had trod these halls and thinking of how much he missed her. Everson had always tried to slink about when no one was around, a ghost in his own home. Mother visited his chambers, but it was nothing like their life had been before. It wasn't her fault. She was her own person, in love with Vastion the First, and busy with the duties that had quickly piled upon her in taking care of the city.

What would their life have been like if she hadn't married? Would the Fen have still taken her? It might have been just the two of them for a long time.

But he probably never would have found the library—or met Nod or Mira.

The study doors were closed. Everson rapped sharply on one side of the snow-white double doors.

"Come in," a voice called.

Something fluttered in his chest as he pulled open one of the doors and entered. He'd only been in his stepfather's office once before, in his early days at the palace, when the cook had hauled him in, complaining about Everson lurking around the kitchen when no one else was there.

To his stepfather's credit, he had only suggested that Everson clean up after himself if he was going to make midnight trips to the kitchen.

His brother looked up from where he was writing at

the desk, looking like a slimmer, less-lined version of Vastion the First. His eyes lit up, and Everson held up a hand.

"I'd like you to listen, Vastion," Everson said, every emotion from the unexpected day swirling through him and making his voice hoarse. It also suddenly struck him that Overforth was somewhere in the palace.

He strode toward his brother. "Look, Vastion, you're the only brother I've got, but I can't pretend you weren't a total jerk from the moment I moved into the palace. You want to know why I kept to my rooms? Why I always wear hats indoors? I'm *faerŭn*, Vastion, that's why." He ripped off his hat and flung it onto Vastion's desk.

The words he'd flung at him felt surprisingly good.

To his utter shock, Vastion's expression curved into a smile. "Of course you are. I've known since the day I met you, you dolt. Snuck into the nursery when you and your mother were talking. I never knew what the big deal was."

"Then what—*what*," he spluttered, running out of words. He ran a hand through his hair. "Why were you always teasing me? And Druida—she really didn't tell you?"

"Why would she? Wait! *She* knows? Is that why you've been standoffish with her?"

The surprise in his brother's eyes was genuine. A chuckle burst from Everson as he shook his head. "You really knew this whole time?"

"Yes, and I was waiting for you to tell me yourself. I

just didn't think it was going to take this long or be this... dramatic." He flourished a hand. "Why don't you sit down, brother."

Everson collapsed into one of the large wood and leather armchairs, and Vastion seemed to summon a drink of amber liquor almost as fast as the cottage could. The desire to return home was strong, but his need to finally tell Vastion had been stronger, particularly with the situation of Hiron and Raine stirring up all the old memories of his mother.

"Vastion." Everson's voice was filled with urgency, his friends' plight resurfacing in his thoughts. "Did you know there might be a cure for the Fen flu? I found it in a book and was able to get the ingredients. A few of my friends came down with it recently, and..."

Vastion set down his glass thoughtfully. "There *has* been a recent spate of the flu in the city. That's actually what I've been going over." He tipped his drink toward the papers on his desk in acknowledgement. "I'd hoped the weather would turn warmer soon—to lessen the spread—but winter seems to have dug in its heels."

"Like it always does," Everson supplied. "I'll let you know if the treatment works. We could—We could brew enough to supply the healers and distribute it to anyone in the city! I remember hearing Hiron's school teacher came down with it...it might have gone through the children in Hiron's class..."

"I didn't think you were much of a healer, let alone potion-brewer. I guess there's a lot I don't know about you."

Everson ducked his head. "I'm not either of those. I merely learned it from a book."

"I can't say I'm surprised," Vastion drawled. Then he tipped back in his chair to look out the mullioned window behind him. "You're not going back out to the woods in this, are you? Druida told me how far your library is. You should stay here. I'll have Halmund alert the staff." His fingers trailed toward the bell pull on the wall behind him.

To Everson's own surprise, he found himself nodding. Between having divulged his decades-long secret at last and his concern for his friends, he felt the unfamiliar urge to surround himself with family.

A grin bloomed on Vastion's face. "Druida will be *beside* herself to have you stay for dinner."

"Dinner?" *That* drew cold into Everson's core, and he considered changing his mind. "Will Uncle Overforth be there?"

Vastion snorted, tossing back the rest of his own drink and standing. "That old curmudgeon? How'd you even know he was here?"

"He stopped in at the library." Everson didn't feel like explaining more than that about Overforth's distasteful visit.

"He's almost as reclusive as you, dear brother. He takes most of his meals in his rooms, as it were. So there's no need to worry."

Everson returned his hat to his head regardless. Though he'd confided in Vastion, he wasn't ready for the whole palace or city to know just yet. And apparently, it hadn't been news to Vastion, anyway.

Halmund arrived a minute later, fangs protruding in an endearing grin, perhaps at seeing the two brothers together, with no evidence of a fight between them.

"My brother will be staying the night," Vastion announced. "Have his rooms prepared, and place an extra setting at the table."

The idea of an exquisite dinner from the palace cooks and the plush blankets of his old rooms filled his insides with warmth. Though he loved the library, it *was* beginning to feel like he was surrounded by work all the time.

"Halmund?" Everson inquired as the orc made to leave. "Would you send a message to Clear as Ice Glass Creations that I'm staying at the palace, in case they need to contact me?"

"Of course, m'lord," the orc rumbled.

Halmund's departure left the two of them alone once more, and Everson blurted, "Who else knows? Halmund?"

Vastion shook his head and stood before heading around his desk to a wall of books. "No one that I know—"

The study doors burst open and Druida strolled in. "Little brother," she announced.

Everson wrinkled his nose, "Not yet, I don't think."

Vastion and Druida were silent for a moment, then Vastion choked out, "You're *joking*, Everson! I didn't think you had it in you!"

The smile that came to his face felt right, and he stood as well. After checking that the study doors were indeed closed, he said to Druida. "I told him, but he already knew."

A wide grin burst onto her face and she looked between the two brothers, "I *knew* it! I knew you knew somehow!"

Vastion stepped toward her and kissed the back of her hand. "You're ever perceptive, my dear Druida. Now, let's feast my brother like he's never been feasted before."

Though the palace kitchens laid out the most delicious meal Everson had ever eaten—roast turkey stuffed with wilberries and apples, sourdough rolls so fresh from the oven that their steam preceded them into the room when the servants brought them in, peas and carrots swimming in butter, and enough small round potatoes to feed a dozen more people—he still couldn't shake his worry about the dwarves.

Druida nudged Vastion's shoulder as they concluded their meal—a delicacy their cook had learned from the far-off island country of Honzu, small gooey sweets made from rice—and Vastion cleared his throat.

"Is it your friends?" he asked from across the table.

Everson nodded, his mouth stuck tight with the gooey sweet. He reached for his goblet of wine to wash it down. He'd never been more content—a full belly, new flavors alongside old favorites, and mending things with Vastion—yet he couldn't help but worry.

"I only met Nod a few weeks ago," Everson explained

as the servants began clearing the meal and the three of them took their wine goblets to the drawing room.

Everson had never been in here before, but at the few formal dinners he'd attended, he'd watched the adults withdraw through these doors after dinner to have drinks and talk. He found a fabulously plush burgundy chair, upholstered in smooth velvet and paired with a matching footstool. He set his goblet on the round side table made of dark wood, just large enough to hold a drink or a book. Everson reached out and touched the wood gently.

"Nod's a carpenter from Ravenshold, and he came across my cottage—" He halted, rethinking where he was going with the story as he remembered who he was talking to. *Too many secrets,* he thought.

"He came just as I was setting up the library, then he came back with his nephew, even though he was helping his brother open his glass shop. They're really quite nice." He skirted around how Nod made it back to Wrestia when Hiron and Raine had come down with the Fen, but Vastion and Druida didn't seem to find any holes in his story. Knowing the two of them, they'd speak their mind if they had.

"And this cure..." Vastion began.

"I don't know if it will work," Everson said. "But I have a book—more of a journal, really. The healer tried dozens of cures over the years and ended with this one. The ingredients were hard to come by, so perhaps, that's why it's not well known."

They lapsed into silence. Everson still wondered if this cure had been publicized, whether their parents would still be alive right now. Perhaps that was also the reason for Vastion's stillness.

A merry fire had been lit in the drawing room hearth, and Everson was content to sit there in silence. Druida took to wandering the room, inspecting paintings of the Wrestins of old. There was even a landscape painting of somewhere outside the city; from his chair, Everson stared at the edge of the woods where he knew the cottage sat and wondered if he spied a slip of woodsmoke above the forest.

They waited. Whether Vastion and Druida stayed out of politeness, Everson wasn't sure, but he couldn't go to sleep until he got word from Nod.

Druida offered to engage Everson in a game of virnolz, but he declined. He wished he'd brought a book, but by the Omens, he wasn't sure if he could even lose himself in a book right now.

It felt too much like the night when the Fen took their parents—when their fevers had spiked past the point of no return. Except that night, he'd waited in his chambers, alone.

Vastion took up Druida on the offer of virnolz, and Everson shot him a smile. Vastion lifted a steep pyramid playing piece and captured one of Druida's.

Everson's eyelids began to droop as he watched them play, and he found himself wishing for a cup of Arcavian coffee to jolt his senses.

"You'll have to come visit the library soon," Everson said to his brother. "I've got a lot to show you."

"I'd like that," Vastion said, "but it might have to

wait until after the wedding. We've got quite a lot of work ahead of us, in fact."

Everson watched as Druida lifted her empress piece and smashed down Vastion's emperor. Guilt wiggled into his chest as he wondered if his unplanned visit had derailed some of their preparations.

"Is there anything I can help with?" he offered.

"Not unless you can get us a hundred satchels of white rose petals," Druida said with a groan. "These ridiculous wedding traditions! I wish we could do away with some of them."

"Maybe when we're married," Vastion said, frowning as he reset his pieces in defeat. "Though I quite like the wedding feast rule—if you didn't show up on time, I'd be devastated. And timing it by the moon makes it so mysterious, don't you think?" He waggled his eyebrows at his intended.

"Fine, we can keep that one," she conceded. "I think the other Viridian nobles do the same, anyway. But what's with the white rose petals? If we don't provide satchels to all the guests, how does that void the ceremony? That Omens-cursed merchant is two weeks late now."

Everson bit his lip. "I...actually think I can help you with that."

"Really?" Druida turned, her white lacy gown fluttering as she stood. "How? Where? We've scoured all the herbalists, florists, and even the tea shops—"

"I have some great contacts with the traveling tinkers," Everson improvised. "It's how I get my books, you know."

"You think you could have them by the wedding feast? *Pure white* rose petals?"

He remembered the little satchels from his own mother's wedding. White for the snows of Wrestia. He nodded. "Absolutely."

"Oh, Everson!" Druida cried, hopping up and down on her blue satin-slippered feet and clapping her hands together. "That would be fantastic!"

He ducked his head. "It's nothing. Consider it a wedding present."

As Everson debated over how—and whether—he should divulge the secret of the cottage to his brother, the couple took up another game of virnolz amid the occasional yawn hidden politely behind a hand.

Hours later—the clock had struck the midnight chime almost an hour ago—a knock came at the drawing room door, and Halmund poked in his head, holding a note.

Everson stumbled as he went to retrieve the note. Druida and Vastion got up from the virnolz board and followed close behind him. His brother's hand on his shoulder, Everson opened the folded note.

Hiron and Raine's fevers broke, by all the gods and Omens. Whatever you gave us worked, Everson. It's a miracle. I've never seen the Fen flu turn around after it got that bad. I owe you a new bookcase or ten.

Everson gave a watery chuckle, tears streaming down

the corners of his eyes. He turned to Vastion, and his brother hugged him for the first time in his life.

"It worked," he muttered as Vastion patted him on the back and then pulled away. *It worked!*"

"Those books of yours really are magic," Vastion said. "Come now, I think it's time we all got some sleep."

LIZ DELTON

ACT III

"Leaving so soon?"

In the middle of quietly closing the door to his old quarters, Everson turned to see Vastion striding toward him, dressed in a freshly pressed coat of light gray with a blue neckcloth nestled in the sharp coat collar.

"Yes," Everson hedged.

"Weren't even going to join us for breakfast?" Vastion asked, a hand to his heart as if stricken.

Everson gave him a lopsided smile. "I wanted to get back to the cottage and start working on brewing more of that cure for the Fen. I have some ingredients left." He didn't, but they would be easy enough to acquire.

Vastion drew level with him and clapped a hand on his shoulder. "That's actually what I was coming to talk to you about. If you've got a cure that works, we need to distribute it to the whole city. I'll fund whatever ingredients we need. We can get the healers brewing it all across Wrestia. No one else needs to succumb."

Everson nodded. "Would-Would you like to come see

the library? I'm actually supposed to open it at the ninth chime today. I started running it full-time recently."

His brother's face fell. "Druida and I have to meet with the cleric, I'm afraid. How about I come later this afternoon?"

"That would be great. Maybe you can take the Fen cure back into the city when you go! It has to brew for two hours anyway. I'll write up the instructions, and we can share it across the city."

"Perfect," Vastion said, reaching out and lightly rustling Everson's cap. "I'm so glad you came last night, brother. And not just because of your cure."

Everson ducked his head. "Me too."

Princess had been pampered in the palace stables— her coat was brushed, her sled had been cleaned, and its paint retouched. Stetson would be amused.

Everson felt like a new person too, but it wasn't from the soft sheets or fine feast from the night before. He felt lighter than he had in years.

As soon as he arrived at the cottage, he took the time for a quick shave to keep his faerŭn silver hairs hidden. Then he bustled about, asking the cottage for everything he might need for the day: fresh water in the kettle, kindling for the fire, and a few more fresh sheets of paper at his desk.

With the fire built back up, he gave Randalf a scratch behind his ears—the feline had settled on the chaise— and returned to his desk. Yesterday's day off hadn't been the restful day of peace he'd imagined, but today, every-thing was looking up. He'd discovered the cure for Fen flu, Raine and Hiron were doing well, and he'd finally mended things with Vastion. He only wished Mira were here. Every so often he caught a whiff of the spices from the dinner she'd made for him just the other night, and he smiled sadly.

But he had work to do. He was behind on delivery orders, but he'd get to those after he got the concoction brewing.

He asked the cottage for more of the ingredients he needed, summoning large tins, which he could hand over to the healers in town. And now, he'd get the first batch brewing before Vastion came. The teapot was a little small for making a large batch, though, so he summoned a dozen jars and a length of cheesecloth. Just as he was cutting pieces of cheesecloth to serve as steeping bags of sorts, he heard a knock on the door.

"Is the library open?" came a voice at the other side of the door.

He smiled, made sure his hat was on securely, and went to open it. Two new patrons came in, dwarves with tall leather boots, their ruddy noses looking frosted after coming in from the snow. They warmed up by the fire before browsing the books with delighted murmurs between them.

Word must have traveled about his new hours, because his sign had again disappeared from the door. He wasn't surprised. It had either blown away in the wind, or the cottage still wouldn't tolerate even a small modification to the door. So while the two new patrons browsed, Everson tacked his backup sheet of hours on the wall next to the door, just above the donation box.

Midmorning, after Everson had gotten all the Fen

cure ingredients steeping—a cheesecloth bag of herbs hanging in each jar—Lyla came through the door, *Whirl of the World* clutched to her chest. She grinned at Everson.

"I'm so excited for the Bard Hour!" she said, and the bottom dropped out of his stomach. With all the chaos of yesterday, he had forgotten. Was that *today?*

"I know some of the book club is going to attend, and I told them to spread the word. Wren even posted a flyer at the Snowed-In Inn."

Everson swallowed nervously. Where would everyone sit? He couldn't summon chairs now...

He nodded and smiled vaguely, then offered her some tea.

She gave a long inhale, nose wrinkling, and said, "That's not the tea I'm smelling, is it?"

"Oh, no," he said, hastening to the kitchen. "That's something else. I put on some orange vanilin tea, though, which promises to taste much better than what you're smelling."

Lyla meandered over to look at the concoctions steeping in their jars. "Er—what are you making?"

Everson paused, not sure if he wanted rumors of the cure spreading before they had a chance to test it on anyone else. He also wanted to deliver more to the dwarves to make sure they were truly on the mend and that the Fen wouldn't come back.

"Oh, it's something I found in a book. An experiment."

She nodded sagely. Perhaps she knew that he was keeping secrets—likely even, from that glint in her steel-gray eyes—but she smiled and accepted the cup of orange and vanilin tea he poured for her, then headed for her usual spot, where Randalf was snoozing.

Everson sat down at his desk with his own cup of tea, being careful not to make an accidental wish for Arcavian coffee, though he desperately wanted one. He couldn't wait for his *espresseaux* machine to come in.

Bard Hour was in a few hours, and he still needed to find a way to accommodate the patrons. It wasn't as if he could summon chairs into his desk drawers...

He glanced around the cottage, and his gaze strayed toward the loft. He could summon something up there, but he still didn't think chairs were going to work. He thought back to the book club; some people had stood leaning against the wall, while one dwarf had taken a pillow from the chaise to sit on the floor. His eyes lit up. *I can summon floor cushions into the loft! I can bring those down the ladder and make them disappear when we no longer need them.*

Everson took a sip of his tea and thought, *I wish I had two dozen floor cushions* on my bed. He carefully stressed the last three words.

Nothing odd appeared on the main floor—thankfully—so he got up to go check the loft. Before he did, something from upstairs fell and toppled through the curtain.

A floor cushion. A wild chuckle escaped him, and he said, "Whoops!"

Lyla looked up from her book.

Everson held up the maroon and gold cushion. "Ah,

yes, I solved our seating problem," he said. "The stack upstairs must have fallen over."

"That's wonderful! Do you want help bringing them down? I bet Ferrace and Wren will be here soon."

Everson bit the inside of his lip. He didn't think he had anything magically odd upstairs, but he wasn't sure about the state of his bed with the stack of cushions on it, so he said, "How about I toss them down and you catch."

As he climbed the ladder, he heard Lyla telling his new patrons about the upcoming Bard Hour, and they settled into the conversation chairs in anticipation.

Two dozen floor cushions, minus the fallen one, sat piled neatly on his bed, if the pile was precariously high. A few leaned a little too close to his nightstand, where his already towering pile of books was in danger of being toppled. He rescued the books and took those cushions first, tossing them down into Lyla's waiting hands. She began setting them out as he went back for more. In no time, his bed was clear, and the floor of the cottage was dotted with all the cushions.

"I'm not sure how many people we're going to get," he said as he hopped down from the ladder. "But the cushions seemed like the best solution."

"They're perfect, Everson," Lyla gushed, picking up her book from the chaise and claiming a floor cushion for herself. "And just in time."

Footsteps on the porch announced newcomers, and Everson wove through the cushions to open the door, his excitement rising, despite everything that had occurred yesterday. This was just the thing he needed.

But instead of Wren and Ferrace, Vastion and Druida stood shivering in the light breeze. Everson's grin was cut short when he spied Uncle Overforth behind them.

Vastion gave him a forced smile. "Brother! So glad to finally see your marvelous library. I still can't believe you created this place all by yourself!"

The specific words made Everson wonder about his own conversation with Overforth. Perhaps their uncle had been repeating his doubtful thoughts on the way over. Everson gave his brother a cautious smile.

"You're just in time," Everson said. "We're about to have our first reading. A singer from town is going to read a book aloud every Myrsday, so patrons can *listen* to stories instead of reading them."

Overforth sidled in, and Everson thought he heard the word "Preposterous," but he staunchly ignored it— and his uncle.

"Can I offer you some tea?" Everson said, ushering them farther inside and closing the door.

"You really ought to fix that door," Overforth grumbled, stepping around the cushions with an annoyed look on his face, as if he were walking through a field dodging cow pies.

Everson gave a forced laugh. "Oh, we've tried. With the help of a master carpenter and everything."

"And what is that awful smell?" Overforth asked, his nose wrinkling.

Vastion and Everson exchanged a look, and Everson nodded.

Overforth's distasteful look shifted to reluctant appreciation as Vastion leaned over to whisper in Overforth's ear. It seemed their uncle had been informed about the cure. The older man wandered over to the kitchen nook and examined the jars. Everson was glad they all seemed to think keeping the cure quiet for now was a good idea, since he didn't want to get anyone's hopes up.

While Everson joined him in the kitchen nook to get tea for his brother and soon-to-be sister-in-law, Overforth lifted the ingredient jars one by one, holding them up for inspection. He studied the lynchberry leaves longer than Everson would have liked. They came from Villikry and were hard to get. He wasn't looking forward to any questions about them. Instead, however, Overforth simply muttered, "If this really works, you should get a patent on the cure."

Everson's face warmed, and he pulled down his hat, stuttering, "Oh...um...I'd rather it was available to everyone—anyone. And I didn't invent it anyway. I found it in a book."

Overforth nodded thoughtfully, and wandered away, hands clasped behind his back. Everson couldn't picture the uptight man deigning to sit on a floor cushion and wasn't surprised when Overforth stood stoically in the back with his arms crossed.

"This place is very *you*," Vastion said, as he and Druida sidled up next to him in the kitchen nook.

Pleased, Everson handed them their tea just as the door opened to reveal Wren. She was followed by Ferrace and a whole trail of people. Evidently, everyone had set out for the cottage at once. Library patrons bustled about, removing their coats and hanging them on hooks behind the door, stomping snow off of their boots and claiming floor cushions while Wren got settled by the hearth. Randalf slinked through the busy feet and disappeared up the ladder into the loft.

"Mister librarian, sir," Ferrace said, bobbing his head as he came over, his eyes bright.

"Please, just Everson," he replied with a smile.

"Everson, sir, would you mind if we turned the chaise around for Wren? She thought that might be better to read from."

"Oh! Of course! I didn't even think of that. Please."

Ferrace recruited one of his friends to lift the chaise and spin it around, being careful not to get too close to the table or any of the patrons seated nearby. A murmur of excitement ran through the crowd when Wren sat down to face them all, gently silhouetted in the glow from the hearth.

Everson guided an older dwarf to his desk chair while his gaze roved over the crowd. There weren't enough floor cushions, but those standing on the edges of the library seemed content. He spotted Ada leaning against the shelf in the children's section, and then Filgaria over by the New Arrivals shelf, to whom he gave a hearty wave. The gnome waved back, an approving look on her face.

Then the gazes started turning toward him, led by Wren's expectant look.

"Oh, yes," Everson said. "The book! You'll be needing..." His face warming again, he stepped through the crowd to pick up *Of Dragons and Destiny* from the new arrivals shelf. The gnome beside him held out his hand,

and the book was passed from person to person until it reached Wren, who gave Everson yet another expectant look.

Everson cleared his throat, tucking his thumbs in his pockets to keep himself from fidgeting with his hat, which was exactly what he wanted to do once everyone's gaze landed on him.

"Yes, thank you. Thank you all for joining us for our first ever reading, which we're calling Bard Hour. Wren Malone has graciously agreed to read aloud for us, on the first of what I hope are many occasions. Wren?" he ended, relieved to turn the crowd's attention to someone else.

Like a wave, heads turned to Wren, the singer outlined in golden hues from the hearth. *That would make a lovely painting*, Everson thought, wondering just how Mira was doing on her trek to Melodïgha.

"*Once upon a twilight glen,*" Wren began, "*two brothers met, though who knows when. Their purpose? A broken heart to mend. Listen, then, and hear their tale, of woe and unbeknownst foes, of victory and villainy, of dragons and destiny...*"

Wren's voice was clear and melodic, which was no surprise with her being a singer. The lyrical prose was fitting coming from her, and Everson was pleased with the choice of books for this first reading. The patrons sat in rapt attention, some with their eyes closed as they took in the story.

It had been a long time since anyone had read aloud to Everson—perhaps not since his mother had read him bedtime stories, before they'd moved to the palace.

The entire hour went by in an incredible blur. Everson forgot about Overforth; he even forgot about the dwarves' brush with the Fen. He lost himself in the tale of the brothers, Julius and Leonis. And before he knew it, Wren was closing the book and saying, "I think I'll leave it there. It seems I've gone over time too." She glanced at the clock on Everson's desk.

Everson jerked, realizing his concoctions had finished steeping as well. Before he could spare a thought for the jars, a burst of noise echoed around the cottage, mostly applause, with some voicing, "Another chapter!" and "Please, let's keep going!" and "More!"

Everson joined in the clapping, Vastion and Druida beside him just as enthusiastic as anyone else. He'd almost forgotten they were there; they too had been enraptured by the story.

A swarm of patrons rose, making the library seem even more crowded than a minute ago when they'd been quietly seated, listening to Wren.

New patrons swarmed his desk to get library cards, current patrons selected a book or two to borrow amid the chaos of the cushions being stacked on the chaise. Filgaria came over with the book on Arcavian coffee to borrow, and Everson grinned as he logged it.

"We miss you at the courier's," she said. "I have some book delivery requests for you, actually, and your stamp order from the print shop."

His old boss dug in her small satchel and drew out a handful of papers. Everson almost groaned upon seeing them, but his heart soared at the sight of the two small, wrapped stamps. He couldn't wait to try them out.

How incredible that only a few days earlier, he'd worried that he wouldn't stay afloat running the cottage full-time, but he was already so busy he could hardly handle it without assistance. He *would* need to hire help soon. He tucked the slips in his pocket and assured Filgaria he'd drop off the deliveries tomorrow—the new ones *and* the ones stacking up on his desk.

Everson had to seek out Wren amid the crowd to thank her for her time. She was surrounded by a small group of admirers, still clutching *Of Dragons and Destiny* to her chest. Everson sidled into the circle surrounding her and lifted a hand to get her attention.

Her wide eyes lit up. "Oh, Everson, that was so much fun!"

"You were amazing!" he said. "Are you still interested in coming back to do more?"

He held out his hand for the book and slipped her not just the three silver coins he'd promised, but five.

Wren cocked her head and gave him a grateful smile. "This is too much," she declared.

"Then consider the extra a tip from me for the truly magical performance. And we'll see you next Myrsday?"

"Wouldn't miss it for the world," she said, tucking the coins away and running a hand through her short tawny hair. "I should get going back to town, though, I booked an extra set tonight at the inn. There's more people staying in town for the noble wedding."

Everson bit his lip and nodded. The nobles in question were having an animated discussion in the kitchen nook, Druida's tea in danger of spilling as she gestured.

Wren wasn't lacking for company on the trek back,

among them Ferrace and his friend Josephus. Many of the library patrons expressed interest in not only accompanying her but heading to the Snowed-In Inn to listen to her sing as well.

Everson tapped Ferrace on the shoulder. "Ferrace, would you mind taking my sled back into town? Along with anyone who needs a ride?"

He wanted to make sure Ferrace was on time for work, and Princess would probably prefer to be back in her home stable for the night. He'd need to bring book deliveries back into town tomorrow, though, so Filgaria could distribute them...

He gasped as an idea struck him—one that could solve many of his increasing problems.

"O' course." The carriage-mechanic bobbed his head, saying, "I can't thank ye enough for arranging the Bard Hour, Everson, sir. It was—"

"Like magic," his friend Josephus finished for him in a soft baritone. "Can't read, meself. Never knew what the fuss was about with all them books." He gave a nod to the wall-to-wall bookshelves.

Everson's heart lifted. "I'm so pleased you both came. And Ferrace?"

"Aye?"

"Would you be interested in some part-time work for the library?"

"That's not part-time work," Ferrace whispered, face paling after Everson explained the job and the pay. "That's...that's as much as I make at the carriage shop."

"For half the time," Josephus hissed, elbowing him. "Go on, Ferrace. Do it!"

Everson crossed his arms. "The trouble is, I have all these book orders, and nowhere to keep a sled. And I could really use someone familiar with Princess to bring her here and into town perhaps a few times a day."

"I-I," Ferrace stammered. "I'll do it."

Josephus clapped him on the back. "Glenda will be thrilled," he murmured.

"Oh?" Everson asked.

"Me wife," Ferrace supplied, a punch-drunk look on his face. "She's expecting, you see, and if I'm not at the carriage shop all hours of the night, it'll be a huge help for her, Everson, sir."

"*Please*, no more 'sir,'" Everson urged. "And I'm so glad to be able to offer this job to you. I'll talk to Stetson about purchasing Princess and boarding her there. You can be the library's official sled driver."

Ferrace straightened and held out his hand, which Everson shook happily. Then Ferrace and Josephus rounded up Wren and some of her admirers who could use the extra assistance of the sled and led the way out into the afternoon light.

Feeling a little punch-drunk himself, Everson turned to speak with his brother about the cure when Lyla stepped in front of him.

"That was a very nice thing you did, Everson," she said, a soft smile on her motherly face.

"Oh, it's nothing," he said. "I really *do* need a driver..."

She put a hand on his shoulder and nodded. "I think I'll walk back early. Unless you want help putting the cushions back?"

"No, no. I can take care of them. Thank you, Lyla. Bard Hour was incredible."

"No need to thank me," she said, retrieving her coat from the hooks, and wrapping her scarf around her neck. "I think it was destined to happen. And book club will be a hit too!"

Everson nodded. "I think so, too."

"You should really do a grand opening," Lyla insisted.

"People keep saying that," Everson said slowly. "What if...what if we have a little grand opening party right before the book club? That way people aren't trekking out here just for one thing. I'm sure it will be a lot of the same people."

"That would be wonderful!"

"I'll print up a couple flyers for you," Ada said, over-hearing. "On the house."

"Oh, you don't have to…"

But it was too late. Lyla and Ada were already chatting excitedly about the prospect, and Everson shrugged helplessly.

"I suppose I'll have the *espresseaux* machine by then," he said to no one in particular, excited and nervous all at once.

Lyla gave him a wink and headed through the crooked door, the last of his patrons. The sudden quiet of the cottage descended on him as he turned to his less bookish guests.

Everson tried to ignore Overforth, who was scrutinizing titles in the histories section, but Vastion and Druida were still in the kitchen, inspecting the bottles.

"Oh, I just sent away my sled," Everson said, his smile falling.

Vastion chuckled. "We brought one, dear brother. Can't have Druida catching a chill this close to the wedding!"

"Or you," Druida interjected, elbowing Vastion with a sly grin. "Ten minutes into the ice gardens and you're always, 'I can't feel my toes. Let's walk faster.'"

The two leaned a shoulder into each other with knowing smiles, chuckling, and then Vastion continued. "No, no, we can easily bring these cures back to the city for you. I'll have Halmund contact the healers at once. Let's bring these out to the sled, then, and we'll all ride back together. There's plenty of room."

Everson's gaze slid to Overforth, and he shrugged. "You know what? I think I'll get another batch brewing. It takes two hours, you know. I don't want to waste any time—all of Hiron's schoolmates might have caught it."

Vastion cocked an eyebrow, then said, "If that suits you. I don't suppose you have a crate for these?"

"Um, sure, in the loft," Everson supplied.

Up in the loft, Randalf had made himself comfortable on Everson's bed, away from the chaos of Bard Hour. Everson asked the cottage for a crate and carried it down the ladder, feeling Overforth's scrutinizing gaze on him.

"Brought some books up there the other day," Everson lied, setting the crate in the kitchen. His brother and Druida helped pack the jars into the crate, and Everson found some sacks to pad them so the glass wouldn't crack from the sled's jostling.

"That's settled then," Everson said, hands on his hips. "Do you want to take the ingredient jars with you to distribute to the healers?"

"Don't you need those to make more?" Druida asked.

"Oh, right." Everson's ears flamed under his hat. "Sorry. It's been a long day. I'll have to write to my contacts right away to get more immediately. Along with your rose petals," he added with a nod at Druida.

Her face lit up. "Thank you *so much*, Everson. All of Wrestia is in your debt—and not for the rose petals, but for this." She gestured to the crate.

He shrugged. "I found it in a book is all."

"What book was that, anyway?" Overforth inquired, turning toward them. "I'd love to inspect it."

"Oh, I think I left it in the loft." Everson vaguely waved his hand up. "A journal from a healer."

He didn't want to explain any more than that, not with the way Overforth was studying him. What if that book had been lost to the ages and wasn't supposed to be here? What had happened to the cure being publicized by Ravenshold Library, anyway? Was the only copy locked up there? Everson wondered if a trip to Ravenshold was in order. But not before checking in on the dwarves.

The trio headed out the door, Vastion carrying the crate and the recipe Everson had written down for him.

As soon as he was certain they were gone, Everson set to work, requesting more jars and cheesecloth from the cottage and getting another batch steeping. He wanted to summon more ingredients, but he didn't think he could get away with lying about how they arrived so quickly, not with Vastion's natural curiosity or Overforth's unsettling scrutiny. But what if it meant the difference between life and death in the city? Would he risk being discovered as some kind of faerŭn magician? He shook his head. He wasn't sure.

No. By the Omens, he'd find a way. He wouldn't let his own fear rule him anymore. The fear of being discovered had guided his life since he could remember. Hiding in his rooms and keeping to himself, even as an adult. Holding anyone he knew at arm's length, not letting anyone get close.

But ever since stepping into the cottage, something

had begun to chip away at his fear—from his first visitor, Nod, to Mira. A flash of heat surged through his chest at the memory of her closeness—not just physically, but the closeness of letting her in on the secret of the cottage.

For once, he had the power to do something, to really help his people with the cottage's magic. There had to be a way. He could drop off the ingredients at the courier's anonymously if the Fen got out of hand before he could "rightfully" acquire the ingredients.

Or he could toss his ever-present caution to the wind and hand them to the healers himself.

The Fen wouldn't take any more from him.

Nod appeared in the window of the darkened glass shop and opened the door a crack.

"Everson, my boy!" the dwarf called. "I'd let you in, but I still don't want to spread the sickness and—"

"Everson!" Little Hiron ambled out of the back room with a lit candlestick, looking pale, but up and walking all the same. The cure really had worked; there was no doubt in Everson's mind. But it made his confusion and anger at the journal being lost for so long even stronger. If only this knowledge had been shared as it should have.

"I'm so glad to see you're all doing all right." Everson choked, his breath clouding before him and forming a fog on the glass of the door. "Here, I brought some more of the medicine—it's still steeping, just give it another hour before you take it. Oh, and I brought you some books!"

He pulled the satchel off his back, a new one the cottage had provided, full of Vincenzo books for Hiron and a few others he'd picked out for Raine and Nod based on the previous borrows noted in his ledger. "For recovery."

"You're a blessing from the Omens," Nod rumbled, accepting the satchel through the cracked door and handing it to Hiron. "Where did you ever find the cure? I couldn't believe my eyes—their fevers subsided minutes after taking it!"

"With a little help from the cottage," Everson managed with a wink. "And I'm going to make sure this cure is shared across not only Wrestia but all of Viridia."

Wearing a brand new fine gray suit, tailored almost to perfection by the cottage, and a dark blue neckcloth tucked between the high collars, Everson thought he must look a little like Vastion as he strode down the unfamiliar streets of Ravenshold.

It would be helpful to present the demeanor of a confident noble as he demanded to see the head librarian of the private institution he had no right to be in.

The town was just waking up; the air had a slight chill, but nothing close to what he'd left behind in Wrestia. Everson could hardly believe his eyes as he studied the cobblestoned streets, free from snow. Some of the tightly packed houses even had early spring flowers bursting from the pots hanging beneath the windows. Everywhere he looked, the black and white flag of the Ravensons soared above the town, a raven in a white circle, surrounded by a sea of interwoven black designs.

The dark buildings with slate roofs provided a dark contrast to the gray sky. And the tallest and darkest building of all: the library.

Everson's eyes were wide with wonder, not just at seeing a place devoid of snow, but at the fact that he'd simply wished to be outside Ravenshold, and not ten minutes later, he was striding down a foreign street. He thought he'd gotten used to the quirks of the cottage, but being able to open his door outside a new city would take some time to digest.

Somewhat selfishly, he'd thought of wishing to go to Melodïgha to see Mira, but now wasn't the time for that—he hardly had time for this endeavor before Vastion and Druida's wedding, a mere two days away.

Besides, he didn't know if the cottage would go to Melodïgha; perhaps it only went to Wrestia and Ravenshold. He wouldn't lie, he was itching to experiment with the new magical development, but he'd have to save that for another time.

Fighting the Fen tucked securely in his satchel, he approached Ravenshold Library's gate. The building towered over him; two immense towers at the front of a long building with sharply pitched spires, all made of dark stone, stood silhouetted against the light gray morning clouds. Candlelight flickered from the gatehouse, and Everson cleared his throat as he approached.

An orc woman stepped out, glasses perched on her large nose, over which she peered at him. Her black hair was half up in a bun and half down, pointed green ears poking through the black curls that spilled across her shoulders.

"Yes?"

"I'm here to meet with the head librarian on urgent business."

"And what business would that be?" she said, eyes narrowing in her light green face.

"I run a library in Wrestia, and—"

"We've no record of a library in Wrestia," she interrupted, turning away, no doubt to return to her mug of Arcavian coffee Everson could smell from here.

"How would you know?" he shot back. "I only opened it a few weeks ago. And for your information, I'm here because I found a cure for the Fen flu."

She turned back, hands on her hips now as she drew herself up to full height, which was quite tall. "And what does that have to do with the head librarian? Or the library at all, for that matter?"

Everson swallowed a lump in his throat. He'd told himself he was done living in fear. Well, this was it. "That is for me and the head librarian to discuss."

As much as he wanted to pull out the journal as clear evidence, he didn't. He still wasn't entirely sure if the cottage created books out of nothing, or took them from real places, and he didn't want to be accused of stealing from Ravenshold Library.

A fang protruded from her lip as she gave him a wry grin. "You're talking to her. I'm Ithalia Stonecrusher, Head Librarian of the great Ravenshold Library. Don't make me ask again."

Fear slid down his throat. "Oh, I didn't—" At the look she gave him, he quickly returned to the topic in question. "Two things: one, I have the cure, which I'd like your help to spread the word across Viridia. And two, I found out about the cure through a book I know was sent here, with the intention of doing the same thing, twenty years ago."

The unsaid accusation hung in the early morning air between them like the almost invisible cloud of his breath. But with all the lives lost since then? He couldn't say nothing.

"And who are you?" she asked, arms crossed.

"Everson Wrestin, from the Library at the Edge of the Wood."

"Then what are we waiting for, Mister Wrestin? Come. We have much to do."

As they walked, the impossibly tall shelves peered down at the two of them as if in judgment. Everson unkindly wondered if perhaps this was where Overforth got his judgmental looks from, since he spent so much time here.

While she led him through the aisles, Ithalia Stonecrusher explained that being the first to arrive in the early mornings, she often took a shift at the gate before opening.

"*Fighting the Fallists... Fighting the...* Ah, here it is." Her low voice came out as an unmistakable growl. They were in a section marked *Personal Histories*. They had passed a dozen other sections as Ithalia had led him through the cavernous room, his own library titles few when compared to this robust collection. But if he was honest, he much preferred the company and atmosphere of his own library over this stuffy, judgmental one. Libraries should be welcoming; they were places of sharing knowledge, portals to other worlds and stories. He was suddenly glad he hadn't wasted his hard-earned coin on admission to Ravenshold University just to get a look at this place.

Everson held on tight to the book in his satchel. This was it. He was about to find out whether he'd been stealing books across the continent for the last month.

"*Fighting the Fen*? An original too. I've never read this one before."

It felt as if every fiber of his being melted like ice by a roaring fire, such was Everson's relief.

The head librarian opened up to the first page as if to start reading.

Everson couldn't help but blurt, "It's on the second to the last page."

She looked up at him over her glasses, then flipped to the end. He watched her eyes go back and forth as she scanned the page. The minutes ticked by painfully. "Interesting," she finally said. "And you say it worked? I'd like to send a healer to the dwarves in question to verify the results."

"They're, um, in Wrestia," he admitted. "I traveled here because I thought you could help the fastest. My stepbrother—Lord Vastion Wrestin—he's distributing the cure across Wrestia as we speak."

Her lips curled around her fangs in a thoughtful frown. "I've known many who've fallen to the Fen, and would do anything to help prevent that, if I could. I confess, I am new in the position of head librarian and wasn't here when this book arrived. I would have remembered it."

She pinned him with a look. "It's one thing for the nobles of Wrestia to make such claims in their own city. But I am not a noble. I'm a keeper of truth. I just can't use our channels all across Viridia to announce a cure that I don't know if it works without proof, you see?"

Everson's chest felt hot. "Then pass it along to the local healers, and see—or-or my friend Nod can tell you—"

"Nod Sawngrove? The carpenter?" she asked, her heavy brow furrowed.

"Oh, um, yes. The ones who were ill were his family, and he—er—" Everson's mind whirled as he tried to come up with something close to the truth. "I can bring him to you. He can tell you all about it."

"Yes, that would be acceptable," she admitted. "Tell him Ithalia Stonecrusher would love to see him."

I wish I were back in Wrestia, Everson thought, his back to the door. He was panting from the effort of getting the thing properly closed.

At first it hadn't worked, and he'd spent a good ten minutes panicking that his cottage was now trapped in Ravenshold, but eventually, he'd gotten the door closed tight enough.

"Now time to see if it worked," he muttered to Randalf, who had curled up on the chaise, not surprising Everson in the least. The blankets were due for another de-furring, but he'd get to that later.

He turned around and opened the door, peering outside. His face was hit with a biting wind, and he mumbled, "Yep, that's definitely Wrestia."

A figure was coming toward him, snowflakes whirling around the person from an errant snow cloud in the otherwise clear morning.

Uncle Overforth trudged up the porch, his hands stuffed in his pockets.

"Oh, hello," Everson managed through his surprise, opening the door farther.

"I don't know what in the Omens—" Overforth began, incensed. "Wandered 'round the wood three times before I found you!"

"Oh, no. The, uh, snow turn you around perhaps?"

"It wasn't the confounded snow," Overforth growled, stalking inside. He headed toward the shelves and scared Randalf into the loft. But instead of looking at the books, today, Overforth seemed more interested in the shelves themselves, running his hands up and down the wood.

Everson's eyes bulged as he thought back to Nod's curiosity about the wood of the bookshelves once he had learned about the magic. And Everson had just traveled to Ravenshold and back—had Overforth seen the cottage pop back into the wood just now?

No. Surely the man would have said something.

He couldn't let Overforth find out *anything* about the cottage. Though Everson now knew Vastion held no judgment for his mysterious heritage, Overforth would be livid. The man was always complaining about the strangeness of others—from pointing out a haircut that was a little too different to personal choices of a suspicious nature like a leading academic who decided to run away and join the Imminian army. Anything different or strange wasn't to be tolerated, particularly from someone related to him. Everson had endured many a lecture during his uncle's visits to the palace—from his "unnatural" love for books to his "improper" hiding away in his rooms. Even though Vastion had teased him about the very same things, the scathing judgment of Overforth's comments had nearly always brought Everson to tears, which he'd bottle up for his retreat to the solace of his rooms.

"Can I...offer you a cup of tea?" Everson said. He had hoped to go into town to retrieve Nod and bring him to Ithalia before the library opened at midday, but he'd be cutting it close if Overforth stayed much longer.

"Yes, Queen Gray, if you have it."

Everson made a soft noise of surprise and puttered about making the tea, hoping Overforth would get to the point about why he was here. He didn't seem particularly keen on checking out any books.

"Did the cure get distributed?" Everson asked, handing the teacup to Overforth who continued browsing.

"Yes, quite. Your brother called a meeting of the healers and gave them the recipe. They're pooling their resources to put the ingredients together, though your brother says you're going to acquire more through your... sources?"

Everson cleared his throat and nodded. "Mm-hmm, yes. Yes, I am." He took a sip of his own tea, which was almost too hot to drink. "Can I help you find a book, then? We're not open at the moment, and I wanted to run into town before we do."

He froze at the words that had come out of his mouth. They had been honest, but he'd never before dared speak so plainly to his uncle.

"I wondered if I might see the book on the Fen flu. I dabble in histories, you might say."

"Oh, um. I lent it to a friend," he lied. "They deal in —er—spices, so I thought maybe they could help acquire more ingredients." Of all the people he had lied to, it didn't bother him one bit about feeding untruths to Overforth. He *did* know a spice shop owner, and if push came to shove, he could likely get her to corroborate his story. But after his trip to Ravenshold Library, he suspected that the cottage had created a duplicate of *Fighting the Fen*, and Everson didn't want to lend such a thing to Overforth.

"I see," Overforth said. He set down the undrunk tea on the conversation table, and touched the brim of his cap. "Then I'm here to take back the rest of the ingredients to Wrestia—the healers will take over from here."

"Oh, that's perfect," Everson said.

In the firelight, Everson caught a glint of silver hair on the man's jaw. Everson reached up and touched his own face to make sure he'd shaved recently. Overforth, of course, was over sixty, so his silver hairs were earned, not bestowed upon him by the mysterious faerŭn. Everson's skin was smooth enough, though.

He found an old apple sack in the cupboard and packed up the ingredient jars.

Overforth took the sack, and to Everson's absolute dismay, he took out the lynchberry leaf tin. "This is... quite hard to come by. From Villikry, no less. We're going to need the information for your contact, so that we can acquire more. Wherever did you get the money for such a rare herb?"

Everson's shoulders had crept up toward his ears, and he dropped them as if in a shrug. "I've been saving to attend the university for a while," he rambled, "and I make a good profit on book deliveries."

"That is fortunate then," Overforth said slowly. Everson could hardly breathe. "There's been an outbreak in the west quarter—without this, I'm not sure how many would survive. The healers reported immediate results overnight in their current patients."

He found himself nodding, relieved that the conversation had veered away from Everson's ability to acquire expensive and rare herbs. "W-Will that be enough?" he blurted out. If the whole west quarter had broken out...

"We'll have to hope," Overforth said, putting the tin back. "I can't imagine your contact can move faster than the Fen."

Everson swallowed the lump in his throat. "Omens around us," he said in a hopeful blessing.

"Indeed," Overforth said, then cinched up the sack and made for the door. He paused longer than necessary, then grumbled, "You really should get this door fixed."

The crooked door slammed, leaving Everson alone with his thoughts.

An hour before the library was supposed to open, Everson heard the bray of a mule outside.

Since Overforth's departure, he had paced the cottage, mulling over what to do. And now six tins of ingredients sat on the counter in the kitchen nook.

Omens-be-cursed, he wasn't going to let innocent people succumb to the Fen if he could help it.

A cheerful knock came on the door. "Mister Everson, sir? It's me, Ferrace. I brought Princess."

Cold and hot washed over Everson; he was glad Ferrace had arrived, but only just now realizing he had intended to go get Nod to bring him to Ravenshold. He shook his head as he went to open the door. Ravenshold would have to wait.

Everson wrenched open the door, a smile bursting across his face when he saw Ferrace standing on the porch, threadbare mittens on his hands, which he was wringing before him. "I told you, no more '*sir*.' Just Everson."

"Sorry, Everson," Ferrace mumbled.

"Come on in, warm yourself up. Would you like some tea?"

Ferrace shook his head as he hesitated by the door. "Nah, s'alright. I've got Princess outside. Did you have book deliveries for me to bring into the city?"

"Sorry," Everson said, motioning for the man to wait by the fire. "I need to package them up still. Filgaria gave me a bunch yesterday, and I haven't had time to process them."

"Am I too early?"

"No, no this is perfect! I just had a strange morning is all. I'm so glad you're here. And I'm *starved*. I haven't eaten yet. I'm going to put on some porridge with chopped apples and walnuts—would you like any?"

"Oh, um, are you sure, si—Everson?" Ferrace said,

backing away from the hearth as Everson started bustling about.

"Positive," Everson said. "I always make too much."

By the time the two of them had eaten, the apples a little crunchy with the hasty cooking but a sweet contrast to the texture of the porridge, Everson had managed to wrap up his book orders, stamping each with his new stamps.

Ferrace had set his threadbare mittens on the stone hearth and was checking to see if they'd dried. Everson excused himself to the loft, where he summoned a couple of crates. Before he went down the ladder, he added, *I wish I had a new pair of warm mittens.*

He flung the curtain back and brought down a crate a little awkwardly. Ferrace bustled over to give him a hand, and they had the second one down in no time.

"Here," Everson said, handing over the mittens. "The library can't have its driver's hands getting too cold."

Ferrace's eyes lit up, but he didn't take them. "Everson, no, I can't, I—"

"Why not?" Everson said, tossing them into the crate Ferrace was still holding. "You need those fingers for handling books. I can't have you freezing them off on the sled. And I have something else for you to bring into town today too."

The tins of ingredients went into the second crate, and Everson nodded with finality. "Can you bring these to Adrilla the herbalist in the Winter Market? And give her this note." He quickly explained the need to deliver them to the healer's but said nothing of where he'd gotten them. If Overforth or anyone else traced the delivery back to him...well, he'd deal with that if it came to it.

"Will do."

"Oh, and Ferrace, can you do me another favor?"

"Anything, Everson."

Everson frowned, pulling out his coin purse. "This is kind of a personal errand, but when you're in the Winter Market, can you pick up some bread from the new baker, and if it's not too much trouble, more apples and carrots from the farmstands?"

"Of course! No trouble at all," Ferrace said with a grin, hitching up the crate and accepting the coins. Then he lowered his voice, "Everson, you could ask me to take the sled to every house in Wrestia for all I care, this is shaping up to be the best job I've ever had!"

Everson grinned back. "Ah, well, that's what I pay Filgaria for. The books should go to Hand to Hand Couriers—they'll take care of the rest. And maybe grab a dozen pastries from the baker while you're at it. You can join me for breakfast whenever you like."

Half a dozen patrons arrived at midday when he opened, and Everson put on a new pot of tea. Lyla and two of her friends from the book club sat on the chaise gushing about Bard Hour and comparing notes on how far they'd gotten in *Whirl of the World*.

Everson paced the cottage, feeling trapped for the first time ever while the library was open. He browsed the shelves and pulled books that weren't being read, although he'd have to make them disappear later, so he stacked them on his desk. He made another pot of tea but spilled the *jaalong* leaves all over the counter when he opened the tin.

Just as he was opening his ledger to double-check the list of books he was going to retire, someone shoved the door open, muttering, "Omens-cursed door."

Everson stood, chair scooting out from under him with an undignified groan. "Nod! Just the dwarf I wanted to see today!"

Nod ducked his head and removed his cap, stomping to knock the snow off his boots before coming inside. He jerked his thumb behind him. "Caught a ride from that nice lad of yours—Ferrace. He tells me he works for the library now, eh?"

"Indeed," Everson said, warmth filling his chest as he came over to clasp hands with Nod. The dwarf yanked him into a bone crushing hug and whispered, "Thank you, my boy."

"Y-You're welcome," Everson said, brushing the moisture away from where it had sprung to the corners of his eyes. "I'm glad I could help. Can I get you tea or anything?"

While Ferrace quietly unloaded the sacks of apples, carrots, bread, and pastries, Everson made them each a cup of the *jaalong* tea. It was a new tea, one that he'd read about in the herb book, and it had a tangy, almost grasslike flavor which was not unpleasant, followed by an aftertaste of jasmine. Nod sipped his reverently, closing his eyes briefly as he did.

"Any more deliveries today?" Ferrace asked after he'd tossed back his own tea.

Everson shook his head. "I'm afraid not. Would you mind sticking around until some of the patrons want a ride back to the city? Then you can just bring Princess back home. Which reminds me—Nod, how would you like a job building a little barn out in the woods while you're still in Wrestia?"

They fell to discussing particulars; Nod stroked his beard as he puzzled out a few dimensions, while Ferrace made suggestions for stowing the sled and tack. By the time the teapot was empty, they had a plan in place.

"About how much will that cost?" Everson asked.

"Oh...well..." Nod said evasively.

"Nod," Everson said firmly, "I *am* paying you."

"Fine," Nod gave in, throwing his hands up, and citing a number that sounded fair. Between his book deliveries and what was left of the donation box, he would still have plenty to live on.

"It's a deal, then!" Everson said. "Princess will finally be able to stay here."

Ferrace's face sank. "So does this mean, when you have the barn, you won't need..."

"Oh no. Of course not, Ferrace! I'll need you to run the sled to the city and back, maybe a few times a day! In fact, I believe we've got some patrons readying to leave now."

"Taking the Library Express, eh?" Nod said, elbowing Ferrace jovially.

Ferrace hitched up his smile and turned to the patrons standing beside Everson's desk waiting to check out their books. "Library sled's available, should anyone want a ride back into town!"

Everson processed their books, and the small crowd gathered by the door.

"I think I'll head back, myself," Lyla said. "You probably have a lot to do, Everson."

"Wh—"

"The wedding?" Lyla clarified with a wink. "You'll be part of the ceremony, won't you?"

Everson's stomach dropped, and he nodded. "Right, yes. You're right. Only two more days. I should see if they need help with anything else."

Nod clapped Everson on the back. "I think you've helped Wrestia plenty, Everson. Miss Lyla, did you hear that Everson found a cure for the Fen in one of these books of his?"

Lyla's expression melted into one of proud joy. "Oh, Everson, really? That's wonderful! I'd heard Hiron had fallen ill, and..."

"They're right as rain. Even my brother Raine," Nod added with a hearty guffaw.

"Vastion's managing the distribution, but we're keeping it quiet for now," Everson explained.

Lyla slipped her hand into Everson's and squeezed it. Her fingers were cold and smooth. "That's marvelous, Everson. You never know what you'll learn from a book. I think they all have the power to save lives. Even the stories about dragons and wizards and all that." She gave a knowing glance at Ferrace, who stood waiting by the door and fiddling with his new mittens, an easy smile on his face. She bid them good afternoon, and Everson's relief grew when he realized it was just him and the old dwarf left in the cottage.

"Nod, I went to Ravenshold this morning..."

"Is that so? Thinking of opening another branch of the library there?"

A chuckle burst from Everson. He slid a hand under his cap and itched his scalp, the relief twofold: he'd wanted to do that for an hour now, and since Nod knew his secret, he had nothing to fear.

"Omens, no," Everson said. "I can hardly keep track of all the secrets I'm keeping in *one* city, let alone two. No, I went to Ravenshold Library. Do you know Ithalia Stonecrusher?"

"Me and Ithalia go way back," Nod said with a low chuckle. "Think she owes me a drink, actually."

"Would you like to go to Ravenshold to see her?"

"Wouldn't say no to a pint. Could use one after all this Fen business."

LIZ DELTON

24

"And they're completely cured?" Ithalia Stonecrusher asked, looking over the top of her spectacles at Nod and Everson, her lips curled in thought around her protruding fangs. The noise level in the tavern around them allowed for a comfortable conversation.

"Completely," Nod said, lowering his pint, "if a bit tired. Hiron was running around the shop when I left, though, so clearly not *that* tired. Don't know where the boy gets the energy even when he's not recovering from a deadly illness," he added in a mutter.

"Garlic and silverleaf are easy enough to get," Ithalia mused, "but wherever did you acquire the lynchberry leaves the recipe references? Aren't those native to Villikry?"

Everson squirmed under the librarian's inquisitive gaze. He was reminded of Uncle Overforth's keen attention.

Nod finished his pint of ale and set it on the table

with a loud smack. "We can get more. Everson's got a connection."

Everson shot Nod a grateful look, although he felt bad that the dwarf was lying on his behalf. But technically the *cottage* was Everson's connection...

"Yep—ahem—yes," Everson said. "Yes, I can get you the lynchberry leaves from my connection. But I would like to ask something in return."

Ithalia tipped her chin down to peer at him. "Yes?"

"I-I want you to spread the word across Viridia. You have access to publishers and your own periodicals and... well... The journal shouldn't be hidden away in a private institution," he added, straightening his back.

Ithalia leaned back and took a pull of her dark stout. She belched impressively, never once losing her studious demeanor. "Aye, I'll do it. I read the rest of the journal last night. The author intended the library to share his knowledge, and yet, we hid it away." Her words turned harsh. "That's one of the reasons I fought my way to the head librarian position. Those who keep knowledge from others never have a good reason." She shook her head. "You're the right sort of person, Mr. Everson. But I'd also like a favor from you."

His heart thudding in his chest at her acceptance, he blurted out, "Of course. Anything!"

The orc slid the glasses off her nose and put them in a wooden case. "I want you to tell me exactly how your free library works." Her fangs framed a hearty grin.

"You mind if we stop at my workshop before we head back to Wrestia?" Nod asked as they left Rust & Raven, the pub Ithalia had chosen. The orc had retired early, explaining she had library duties to attend to in the morning. She'd promised to get in touch with her connections at the local printers to fund the journal's mass production and syndication around the country.

"Of course not," Everson said.

The sun had gone down behind the tall dark spires of the academy and library, and cheerful lanterns lit the streets as they headed toward the edge of the city.

Candlelight flickered in the lanterns outside Sawn with the Wind. "Oh, Helenia must still be in," Nod mused. "I hope she's not mad I left without saying anything."

"Nod, I don't know how *anyone* could ever be mad at you."

The old dwarf drew up short before the door and turned to Everson. "I could say the same about you, Everson. And hey, I know you feel like you need to keep your secrets from everyone—"

"But the library—"

"No, no, not the library. Not everyone should know you can ask for whatever you need or that you can go to Ravenshold on a whim. You'd never know a moment of peace! Trampled by patrons with requests every minute. No, no, I'm talking about your other secret."

Everson couldn't help his hand rising to check that his hat was on securely. Words froze in his chest.

Nod reached over and touched his arm gently. "You give so much, Everson. I hope you've realized by now that *you* are the best gift of all. Being what you are has shaped you—that's undeniable. But it's shaped you into the kindest, most generous, and most clever person I've ever met. I'd be proud to call you my own son, if I had one."

"I—I— Thank you, Nod," Everson said throatily. He wiped his eyes on the back of his sleeve.

"Now come on. Helenia loves putting my saws back in the wrong order to irritate me, and I'll need to find a couple to build your barn."

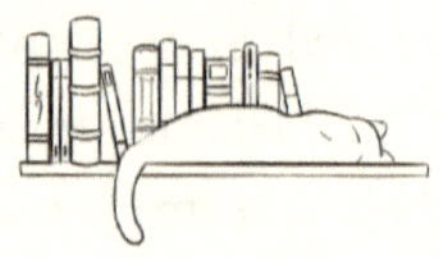

I wish I was in Melodïgha, Everson thought the next morning.

Everson's eyes were clamped shut as he waited a few seconds, unsure if it would work. Randalf meowed in annoyance by the chaise, and Everson's eyes fluttered open.

"Guess we'll find out, eh, Randalf?"

He fought with the door as usual, and when he finally got it open, he was hit with the delicious scent of warm spring air. The woods outside looked nothing like the Ingwood outside Ravenshold. Which meant the cottage really *did* go anywhere.

Early rays of sunlight peeked through the lush green foliage as he stepped out, adjusting his cap. He only had a few hours until the library opened, and tonight was the rehearsal dinner at the palace. This was his only chance to see Mira before the wedding.

The smell of chimney smoke and baking bread directed him to the city, which lay behind a light-colored stucco border wall. Hues of cream, white, and pinkish coral swathed the city, from the houses to their roof tiles to the well-tended gravel streets.

Soon he found himself wandering down the streets, passing large estate houses, quaint shops, and miniature gardens tended with care. He meandered until he found a cafe that was open this early. It had two small round tables in the street outside, each with a sunbrella giving shade to anyone seated there. Two elderly couples occupied the tables, sipping tiny cups of Arcavian coffee. Everson inhaled deeply and went inside the shop.

His gaze was immediately drawn to the *espresseaux* machine behind the counter, and his mouth watered as the scent of coffee and sweetbreads surrounded him.

"Morning to you," an old gnome chimed, his light magenta face wreathed in a cloud of white hair. "Care for a cuppa? Finest Arcavian beans this side of the Viridian sea."

"I don't doubt it," Everson said. "And yes, please, I'd love a cup. Can I also ask if you know of an art gallery opening? I'm trying to find a friend of mine. She apprentices under Master Raymyn."

The gnome got to work at the *espresseaux* machine, and Everson tried to watch him as he danced about, pressing buttons and pulling knobs. The sounds of grinding, clunking, and finally a deep burbling sound entranced him. "How'd you learn to use such a thing?" Everson blurted out.

"Arcavian born and bred," the gnome said, giving a thump of his chest. With another swift motion, he produced the most beautiful cup of coffee Everson had seen. Everson accepted the porcelain cup with reverence. It was filled to the brim, the coffee topped with foamed cream, and little lines of white and tan swirled across the top. "It can be taught easily enough, though. You're looking for a beautifully talented artist from Wrestia, did you say?"

"Ye—Wait, how do you—"

"Tortinigh," a familiar voice growled playfully.

"What?" the gnome squeaked. "It's true."

They turned to face the beautifully talented artist in question as Mira stepped out of the back room, tying an apron around her waist as she went. Her eyes were bright as her face broke out into a grin. "Everson, what in all of the Omens are you doing all the way down here?"

"Mira," Everson said, frozen as he stared at her.

"Well, yes?"

He shook himself. He'd forgotten how beautiful she was, with her golden honey skin and silky black hair. The way her smile lit up her whole face. And the flecks of paint on her fingers that never seemed to go away. "It's wonderful to see you."

Tortinigh hummed contentedly as he wiped down the *espresseaux* machine and headed into the back room.

"You should drink that while it's warm," Mira said, putting her elbows on the counter and leaning toward him. "Tortinigh makes an incredible *espresseaux*."

Everson complied wordlessly, compelled by more than just the scent of the delicious beverage. His eyes closed in bliss as it hit his tongue. "Gods and Omens, that tastes like it should be illegal."

Mira's lyrical laugh filled the cafe. She turned and busied herself at the *espresseaux* machine, going through the same grinding, clunking, and burbling motions as Tortinigh.

"So it can be taught then," Everson remarked. "How'd you learn all this so quickly?"

"Oh, I wandered in here on the first day we arrived in town—couldn't resist the smell after having some at the library. Master Raymyn gave me mornings off from gallery prep, and he sleeps in late anyway, so I figured I'd make a little extra money while I'm here." She shrugged as she returned to the counter with her own porcelain cup. The top of her drink was also covered in creamy foam, though she hadn't mastered the swirls on top as well as Tortinigh had.

"But how come you're here?" she asked, her eyes wide. "It's a long way from Wrestia just to—"

He leaned forward and touched her hand lightly. "The cottage," he whispered. "It has another quirk, you could say."

"No way," she breathed. *"No way."*

Everson nodded, taking another sip. "Omens, I'm jealous you get to drink this every day. My *espresseaux* machine hasn't arrived yet, but it should be there before the grand opening. I might need you to teach me how to use it."

A woman wearing an elaborate, flowy cream dress

sauntered into the cafe and spoke in a thick Melodïghan accent. "Miraluzana, my *dear*, the most gorgeous of mornings to you! And who is your friend here? He looks like another frosty Wrestian, if I'm not much mistaken?" She tossed her long blonde hair over her shoulder as she headed toward him. She was tall even without the white heels she wore, and she looked around fifty, her tanned face graced with only a few light wrinkles.

"Duchess Floratiño," Mira said, her face lighting up even more. "This is my friend Everson. He came to visit from Wrestia, yes."

"Oh, but this is wonderful! You're here to attend the gallery opening? You will be simply *overcome* at the special surprise our Miraluzana has been toiling over."

Everson swallowed. "Um—"

"I will have a ticket drawn up for you," she said, taking Everson's arm and leading him to one of the tables against the wall. "A guest of honor."

Duchess Floratiño waved her bony fingers at Mira, somehow indicating her drink order. Mira gave Everson an awkward smile and set to work at the machine.

The Duchess went on, "Mira and Master Raymyn have done a simply *marvelous* job setting up the gallery. You must be so proud of her, to travel all the way here from the frigid north." She gave a fake shiver, her long nails tapping on the table as she waited for her drink.

"I—yes, of course, I am quite proud of her. She's very talented."

"Talented?" Duchess Floratiño said. "Beyond talented! I am *delighted* she will have someone from home to attend the opening tomorrow."

"T-Tomorrow?" The wedding was tomorrow!

"Yes, of course. Shall I leave your ticket with Miraluzana?"

Mira walked over with a waxed-paper cup and handed it to the duchess, along with a paper bag that had some kind of lemon bread inside, from the aroma.

"That would be best, Duchess," Mira said, biting her lip. "Thank you so much for your generosity."

"Thank *you*, my dear. I'll see you at the gallery this afternoon. The flowers they set up are *all* wrong, and I want your artistic eye on them."

And with that, she swept out of the cafe, leaving a stunned Everson staring after her.

"But—the wedding is tomorrow," he finally managed.

Mira sank into the chair across from him. "I'm so sorry, Everson. She's like that *all* the time. It's hard to say no to anything she says." One corner of her mouth hitched up in half a smile.

A gentle pain throbbed in Everson's chest as he realized something. "But you're happy, aren't you? And... you've decided to stay." It was written all over her face, the joy, the guilt. Though his heart plummeted in his chest, he was still happy for her.

Mira ducked her head, running a hand through the flyaway hair beside her temples. "How could you tell? Yes...I... Master Raymyn has decided to stay here with all the attention from the duchess's gallery. He says the air here is better for him too. And so, I... It's wonderful, Everson. Everything I've ever wanted is here—"

He reached over and grabbed her hand, planting a

firm kiss on the back of it. "It's everything you deserve, Mira, and you deserve the best."

"I wanted to return to Wrestia," she explained, her eyes glistening. "I'm sorry—"

"There's nothing to apologize for," he said firmly. "And I'd love to come to the gallery opening, but it's the same day as the wedding. How long does it go for?"

As she described the duchess's plans in detail—the afternoon tea in the villa gardens, the musicians scheduled for the evening while guests viewed the artwork—the pain throbbing in his chest settled into a heavy, cold weight, like a block of ice.

She'd already decided not to return to Wrestia. Even if he could travel to Melodïgha on a whim whenever he wanted now, she hadn't known that when she'd made her decision. She must not want to be with him, not feel the same way he felt. He wondered if the kiss he'd planted on her hand earlier would be the last one he ever gave her.

"I think I can try and make it for the end. I'll do my best to slip away," Everson assured her. "I really am proud of you for following your dreams. And if this is the place you need to be for that, then I can't wait to see what you've done for the gallery."

"Thank you, Everson," she gushed, a sly smile curling over her lips. "It would mean so much to me to have you there."

"I wouldn't miss it for the world."

LIZ DELTON

25

"That sure is...a lot of rose petals," Ferrace remarked upon entering the cottage.

Six crates stood stacked in the middle of the cottage, each piled high with dozens of small silk bags filled with white rose petals. Everson had summoned them as soon as he'd returned from Melodïgha, throwing himself into the wedding preparations. The cottage magic had done little to ease the melancholy that had settled over him at Mira's decision to stay. Of course, he would do his best to attend the gallery opening tomorrow, but he wasn't sure how much Mira wanted him to visit.

"Yes, I just got them in," Everson said. "They're for Vastion's wedding. Oh! That reminds me. The library will be closed tomorrow, so you'll have the day off, all right?"

"I won't argue with that," Ferrace said with a grin. "And Glenda'll be ecstatic. I've got to build another little bunk bed and move Norrence out of the crib to make way for the new little one."

"And would you mind taking some of these pastries

home?" Everson said, handing the bag to Ferrace. "I don't think we'll eat them all before they go stale."

"Won't argue with that, neither! Thanks, Everson. Got any book deliveries today, or just the petals need to go into town?"

"Just the rose petals, if you wouldn't mind bringing them to the palace and coming straight back in case any patrons want a ride this afternoon. I'll ride back in with you at the end of the day—I have the rehearsal dinner to attend tonight."

"It's a plan, boss," Ferrace said, tipping his cap. "I'll get these petals loaded up on Princess, and we'll hoof it."

"Thanks, Ferrace," Everson said quietly, heading over to his desk to draw up a sign indicating the library would be closed tomorrow. He wouldn't bother posting it on the outside of the door, but he'd put up a few inside and be sure to let all the regulars know.

His favorite regular came in right at opening; Nod had Hiron bounding in at his heels.

The little dwarf boy skipped over to the children's section with a *whoop*.

"Hard to believe he had the Fen a few days ago," Nod said incredulously, heading over to Everson to give him a hearty handshake. "Can't thank ye enough, Everson. The entire west quarter's recovering already. I heard Adrilla gave all 'her' stock of lynchberry leaves to the healers, eh?"

"Oh, that's nice of her," Everson said mildly, then lowered his voice as Lyla and a few of her friends from the book club came in. "We'll have to make a quick trip to Ravenshold with their share of ingredients."

"Aye," Nod agreed, then cleared his throat. "Now, I've brought some of my tools, and I've already got a lumber order in for your barn. They'll be coming in a few days. Want to head outside and help me mark off where you'll want it? Saw a flyer about your grand opening—you'll probably want it up before then, right?"

Everson's brows creased. Ada had already made the flyers? That was fast. "If you can. Here, let me just finish this first." He slipped the *'closed tomorrow'* signs off his desk and tacked them up by the door for all to see.

Nod was busy digging in his satchel, and he waved Everson on. "Actually, I'll meet you outside. Go find the plot you want it on."

"All right," Everson said, quirking an eyebrow as he shrugged his coat on. Nod was glancing at the empty walls above the bookcases, holding a measuring tape and exchanging conspiratorial looks with Hiron.

The frigid temperatures had eased a little, so the snow on the ground sank a little with each step as Everson paced away from the cottage. He wandered a good distance and turned to study the place, hands on his hips. Having no idea exactly how the cottage traveled between places, he had a feeling they should place the barn far enough away that the magic didn't affect the new structure. Couldn't have the cottage magically breaking it down whenever it wanted, like it did with the door. He had begun to suspect that the brokenness of the door had something to do with the cottage's ability to travel.

He stepped deliberately in straight lines through the snow, marking what he thought would be a good outline for the barn. Finally, Nod joined him with no explanation of what the holdup had been.

"This is mighty fine," Nod said, indicating the rough shape Everson had made with his footprints. "And far enough away from the library..." He trailed off, making a vague hand gesture, perhaps to indicate the quirks of the cottage. "You'll have your Library Express up and running in no time."

Everson adjusted his hat one last time as he stood before the closed doors of the palace dining hall. Gentle conversation inside did nothing to entice him in, and he clenched his hands, suddenly wishing he'd invited Mira to the rehearsal dinner with him. But she was probably busy with last minute adjustments for the duchess. He brushed that thought aside. He just wished he had someone to hold his hand.

He squeezed his eyes shut and took a deep breath, then pushed one of the double doors open.

Vastion's laugh at something Druida had said filled the chamber. The long table was piled with food, Druida on one end and Vastion on the other. Overforth sat in the middle on one side, an open chair opposite him.

"Evening, brother!" Vastion said, standing to wave him in with his wine goblet.

"Everson, our hero!" Druida cried. "It's all thanks to

you there will even *be* a wedding tomorrow. These ridiculous traditions!"

Vastion's smile hitched even higher. "We've already drawn up a declaration to get rid of the rose petal tradition."

"Sooner would have been better," Druida said, sighing dramatically. "But Everson saved us."

"Yes," Overforth drawled. "That was quite a lot of petals to acquire so close to the wedding."

"Mm-hmm," Everson agreed, taking the chair that a servant pulled out for him and accepting a goblet of wine. He avoided Overforth's gaze.

"Where did they come from?" Overforth inquired politely, applying a pat of butter to the slice of bread before him with undue precision.

"I'm not really sure," Everson said, wishing he'd had a chance to tell Vastion and Druida the truth about the cottage. Then one of them could swoop in and rescue him from Overforth's questioning. "I'm just glad my connection could get them here so quickly."

"Indeed."

"I thought perhaps Ravenshold," Overforth commented, "as we do have quite a resourceful tea shop there. It's right by the library, you know."

"Oh?" Everson managed. He swallowed the lump in his throat before attempting to follow it with the bite of bread he'd just taken, but his mouth had suddenly become very dry. He'd *quite* forgotten Overforth had ties with the library.

"Yes, I stop in for a cup every morning before I visit

the library. I like to stay on top of the legal papers, you see."

"I see," Everson whispered, seizing his goblet of wine and taking a hearty sip. "Do you know the head librarian there? I've—er—corresponded with her recently."

"Ithalia Stonecrusher?" Overforth chuckled. "Of course, lad. Don't think she would have gotten the position without the help of the lawyer's consortium."

"In-Indeed," Everson said.

"I'll be returning to Ravenshold the day after the wedding," Overforth announced.

Instead of the relief he should feel over his uncle's impending departure, Everson felt sick to his stomach. If Ithalia knew Overforth so well, surely she'd mention Everson and Nod's visit, which Overforth would realize Everson couldn't realistically have done—traveling to Ravenshold and back before the wedding. Not without magic.

"The cleric will be here after dinner," Druida said, tactfully changing the subject, "to go over the ceremony expectations."

"Fabulous," Vastion said. "I can't wait til we're married. No more rose petals or full moon feasts."

"Or clerics," Vastion hissed silently to Everson, ducking his chin toward his brother. They had retired to the drawing room after dinner to meet with the cleric, who had instructed them through all the traditional words, ceremonies, and rites for tomorrow.

Everson set down the palm-sized crystal bowl he'd been given—tomorrow it would hold a sphere of ice—and grimaced. Vastion and Druida were right, there were *a lot* of traditions. A wedding should be about love and commitment, and that was it, in Everson's opinion.

"You're sure you don't want to stay here tonight?" Vastion asked Everson as they helped the cleric pack up all the artifacts.

"No, that's all right," Everson said. He was already dreaming about the warmth of his hearth and curling up with *Whirl of the World* in his reading nook. But first... "Let me take you out to celebrate, both of you."

"We'll be doing plenty of celebrating tomorrow—" Druida began.

"But *I* could never say no to more," Vastion chimed in. He put a hand on Druida's lower back. "You should get to bed, my dear. It's almost midnight."

"Another tradition?" Everson inquired.

Vastion chuckled. "No, no, Druida's just an early sleeper, so this is already *far* past her bedtime."

"And we all need to be well rested for tomorrow," Druida said, her hand on the door. "So don't keep him out too late."

Everson thought she was talking to him, but she pinned Vastion with a look. He chuckled and his gaze slid toward Overforth, who had picked up a book and was studiously ignoring them from his armchair by the fire.

"Come on," Everson said. "I think I know a place."

The Snowed-In Inn had a fine layer of snow on its three-storied gables, but no more than the surrounding buildings. A cheerful ruckus emanated from inside, and Everson shot an excited glance at Vastion.

Halmund trailed behind them at a respectful distance. Everson wasn't sure whether the orc normally guarded Vastion like this, or if Druida had instructed him to make sure the two of them didn't stay out too late. Though the wedding ceremony and feast didn't begin until tomorrow afternoon, plenty still needed to be done in the morning.

A young couple exiting the inn held the door open for them. Everson entered and was met with a wall of people. Suddenly he began to question his decision to take Vastion out. He shook his head and soldiered on through the crowd. It was his brother's wedding tomorrow, and Omens-be-cursed if he wasn't going to buy him a drink to celebrate. With the bar as his goal, he maneuvered through the chaos.

The sound of a lute struck a chord, and every face in the tavern turned toward the corner, where none other than Wren Malone had just settled onto a stool.

The singer's face lit up when she spotted Everson, who had seized the opportunity of everyone's pause to slip between two people to an opening at the bar. Wren waved enthusiastically, calling, "The librarian's here!"

A roar went up, and Everson's face turned hot. Looking around, he recognized a few faces from the library. He managed a small smile, and Vastion clapped him on the back, a hood over his head he didn't normally wear. Everson grinned back and leaned in to whisper in Vastion's ear, "Who's covering their head indoors now, eh?"

Vastion reached over to rustle Everson's cap slightly, and for the briefest of moments, Everson lived in terror that his brother would actually reveal his true identity. But Vastion's hand dropped from his head and slammed it on the bartop.

A burly dwarf bustled over, mopping up half a dozen rings of ale from the bar in front of them, which had been recently vacated. "What'll it be, gents?"

"An ale for me, please, and whatever my brother wants," Everson said with a grin.

"I'll take a Vehrgarde stout," Vastion said.

Everson left more silver than was necessary and turned to find somewhere more out of the way to sit, but the tavern had only gotten busier. Wren struck another chord on her lute and winked at Everson as she began to sing. Even after listening to her read for an hour, Everson couldn't believe how clear and strong her voice was. A hush came over the entire tavern as the sad melody wove around them.

> Snow drifts behind,
> The world, asleep.
> Lake's a'frozen and t'won't keep.

The ice, it glistens.
The ice, it calls.
The ice, it listens.
The ice, it falls.

Deep waters below,
The world awakes.
Sun's rays glitter 'cross all the lake.

The ice, it glistens.
The ice, it calls.
The ice, it listens.
The ice, it falls.

The melody petered out, and another musician joined in with the sudden jingling of a tambourine. Wren immediately launched into a new song. Everson blinked.

"That was something, wasn't it?" Vastion asked, taking a swig from his mug.

"It was," Everson said, remembering he was holding a drink.

"And she's quite pretty, eh?" Vastion asked, bumping his shoulder into Everson's. "I mean, for you. I've only got eyes for Druida."

Everson scoffed. "No, no, I'm not interested in Wren."

"You say that like you're interested in someone else."

"She was great at Bard Hour, though."

"And quite a success that was," someone interjected. Lyla slipped in between the people next to them, followed closely by Ferrace.

Everson's face lit up. "It's so good to see you two!"

Ferrace tipped his cap. "Got Princess all squared away, Everson, don't worry."

"I had no worry at all," he said with a grin.

"Glenda's been dying to meet you," he said, and produced a very pregnant woman from out of nowhere it seemed, which was quite a feat.

Glenda was shorter than Ferrace, with rosy round cheeks and flyaway hair that reminded him of Mira. Everson grinned. "I'm happy to meet you, Glenda. Oh, and I'd like you all to meet my brother, Vastion. Vastion, this is Lyla, one of our patrons, and Ferrace, who I've recently hired to be the sled driver for the library."

Ferrace's hand shot out and shook Vastion's heartily, pumping it up and down; he clearly recognized the noble. "What an honor to meet you, milord, Mister Wrestin, sir."

"No 'sir,' please," Vastion said, waving it away.

"Just like your brother, then," Ferrace said, grinning. "This here's Glenda, my beautiful wife. Neighbor's watching the little 'uns, since we're due any day now to have another."

Glenda smiled and shook hands with both Wrestins, but said little, her enigmatic smile and wide eyes taking in everything around her. Even without speaking, she conveyed the most complete sense of contentment. Ferrace hardly took his eyes off her for a second.

"A pleasure to meet all of you," Vastion said. "Friends of Everson's. I'm thrilled the library is truly going so well for you."

"Oh, yes," Lyla chimed in. "Everson's been ever so

kind. He let me start up a book club—we're discussing *Whirl of the World* in a couple of weeks! And we finally convinced Everson to hold a grand opening. *Everyone* in Wrestia should know about the library."

"*Grand* opening, did you say?" Vastion inquired.

"Don't get any fancy ideas," Everson muttered, earning a chuckle from his brother.

"*All* of my ideas are fancy, I regret to inform you," Vastion hissed in a stage whisper.

Wren finished up her song, and as the crowd cheered, she held up her hand to the bartender, who brought over a pitcher of water and a glass. The chatter grew louder, which somehow made it easier to listen to the cacophony of conversations around them. Everson sipped his ale and waited for the next song to begin, his brother beside him and his new friends by his side.

He didn't know what tomorrow would bring, but tonight, he would celebrate.

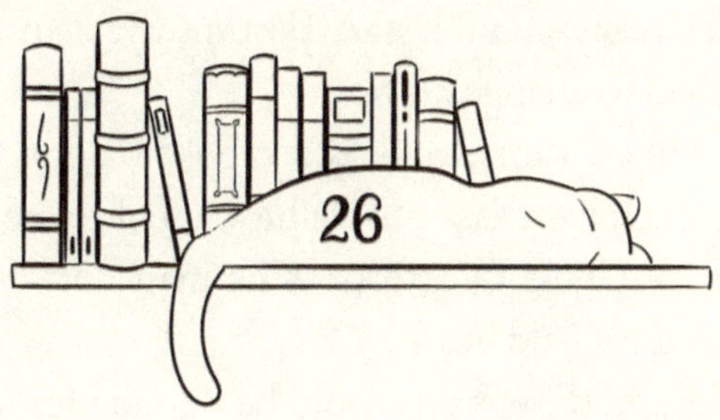

26

"How does this look?" Everson asked Randalf the Gray. He spun around, the sharp-cut blue coat furling out behind him.

Randalf meowed and rolled back over on the chaise.

Everson snorted. The library was closed, and he had hours yet until the wedding ceremony. He'd awoken early and enjoyed a cup of Queen Gray before asking the cottage for a new outfit for the occasion. Last night when they parted, he told Vastion he'd come to the palace early. He already had a couple of books tucked in his satchel, should he find any time to read while he was waiting for the ceremony to begin.

Since Randalf's input had been quite inadequate, Everson wished for a small mirror and looked over his appearance. His new hat—the one Vastion had ordered for him and forced him to deliver to the palace weeks ago —went over his slicked-back silver hair, covering his ears with its smooth felt. The material was thick, and though it wouldn't provide much warmth as he tromped through the snow, it would be formal enough to wear to the wedding. He nodded and set the mirror down, just as he heard footsteps on the porch. Everson suppressed a groan. He really should start posting flyers in the city when he had to change his hours.

The knock came, and the crooked door opened, revealing one of the last people he wanted to see gracing his cottage—Uncle Overforth. The man doffed his cap and revealed his bald head.

"Halmund thought it would be a good idea to send a sled," Overforth said with a sniff. "I find myself without anything worthy to devote myself to this morning, so I volunteered to come out."

"Oh," Everson said. "That's kind of you."

Overforth shrugged, looking around the library with his ever-keen eyes. "I do wish I had a warmer coat for this climate, I—"

A thick wool coat popped into existence on the floor in front of Overforth.

Everson's jaw dropped. "I—you—you—*what?*"

Overforth's eyes bulged as he stared daggers at the coat on the floor like it had insulted him.

Everything in Everson's chest hurt. All these weeks of running the library, and there hadn't been one awkward magical mishap, until now...

Except...he hadn't made any wishes. *Overforth* had. "You..." Everson began slowly. "You're not..."

Both Mira and Nod had tried unsuccessfully to make wishes when they'd discovered his secret. And both of them had concluded it must be something special about Everson, though Mira didn't know he was faerŭn.

Everson's gaze went to Overforth's bald head, which

showed no evidence of the cursed silver hair, but his ears... Overforth's ears were rounded. Well, rounded enough for his advanced age.

"Faerŭn?" Overforth whispered, his hands coming up to his face and covering his mouth.

"No," Everson said just as quietly. "It can't be."

Overforth reached a reluctant hand up to touch the tops of his ears, the gesture so familiar that Everson started to lift his own hands.

"H-How?" Everson demanded. "How is this possible?"

"So this *is* the place," Overforth said, not answering his question. "I'd heard tales of a cottage in the woods, of faerŭn magic, witches, tea shops..." It almost seemed like he spoke to himself.

"But you're—"

Overforth raised a silver-gray eyebrow. "Then so are you."

Everson's throat seemed to seize up, a massive lump forming. He shook his head. No. No. The last person he wanted to admit that to—

Overforth wandered away from the coat and Everson to inspect the bookshelves, as if he hadn't just admitted to being faerŭn after all these years. "I had a friend help me with—" He paused, gesturing to his ears. "A healer. The only person who ever knew. Besides my mother, of course."

Everson blanched, finally giving into the need to run his hands over his ears, but keeping his hat on all the same.

His step-uncle went on. "I was like you. Kept to my

rooms as much as I could. Started shaving my head as soon as I could hold a razor steady. Thought I could change the world to have more tolerant laws, so I studied up on that, went to Ravenshold University as early as I could."

Head spinning, Everson could picture it clearly; Overforth was practically describing his own childhood. The lonely rooms in the palace. Hiding—and finding—himself in books. But Everson had refused his inheritance, and the university had been out of reach.

"You've done more here than I ever could have," Overforth said, then fell silent for a long time.

The silence was like a snowflake, drifting high up in the sky on an updraft, and Everson had no desire to disturb it or bring it to the ground. Overforth? How could he possibly be faerŭn? He had always been so mean, so judgmental, so reserved...

"I never would have shared this cottage with anyone," Overforth said finally, his back still turned. "I would have kept it for myself and hidden away. But you turned it into something wonderful. Something that *gives*. Something not just for yourself. You're a better man than I ever will be."

Everson shook his head. "No, well, I just thought, the cottage gave me so much..."

Overforth turned around, and the bottom dropped out of his stomach as he realized he'd finally admitted something to the magic.

"That's why I wasn't so sure at first. I've traveled this way many times, and never seen this building, which was why I thought it could have been the place. But the books, freely given to the community—you even brought in someone to read to people... I thought surely if this place was full of magic, you would have kept it to yourself."

The pain in his chest was growing, but Everson didn't know what to say.

"Everson," Overforth said in a hoarse voice, "you deserve this place. But more than that, you deserve to be free in this world."

Everson bowed his head, acceptance washing over him as the pressure in his chest peaked and subsided.

Overforth shot a hand out and grabbed Everson's arm. "I never told my brother. My parents kept it hidden from everyone—they were ashamed. You still have that chance."

"I-I—He already knows. Druida and Vastion both. I finally told him just the other week."

An unfamiliar expression of joy swept across Overforth's face. "That's wonderful, Everson, just wonderful. Then, if you don't mind my asking, why do you still—" He gestured to Everson's ever-present hat.

Everson looked at his uncle—really looked at him. His weathered face, his bald head which was admittedly very clean-shaven even now to prevent anyone from seeing a slip of faerŭn silver. His ears... Oh, Omens, his ears. Everson had always thought of Overforth as just a cantankerous old man, displeased by everything in life, and taking it out on whomever he could. By the Omens, perhaps that *was* the case still. He'd kept his secrets to himself and hidden away, never letting anyone in.

"I..." Everson began. Then he lifted a hand to his

head and gripped the brim of the cap. "I think we have a wedding to get to."

He ripped off the cap and threw it on the floor.

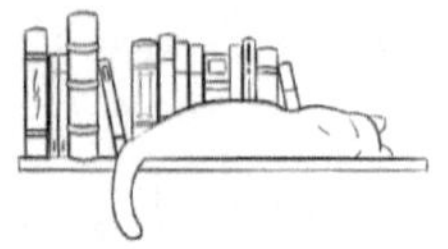

"And in the presence of all the Omens around us, Vastion Wrestin the Second and Lady Druida Glace, I now declare this union complete!" the cleric announced.

Joyous applause burst forth from the crowd assembled before them. Everson smiled, though his heart was still thundering as it had been all morning.

Everson gripped the crystal bowl, which he was supposed to keep in his hand until Vastion and Druida exited the garden. The ice sphere nestled inside was completely frozen in the frigid air, much like Everson's bare scalp.

He'd kept his gaze on the ice for most of the ceremony, occasionally sneaking glances at Vastion and Druida, but never once looking out at the crowd... until now.

To his ever-loving relief, all eyes were glued to Druida and Vastion, who had swept his bride into his arms and bent her back for a dramatic kiss. The crowd *oohed* and *aahed* as they kissed, and two fountains beside them began spurting water, an unusual feat outside the summer months, but possible by adding a small amount of salt to the water—or so Everson had been told.

A harp duet struck up at the back of the crowd,

causing everyone to turn toward the path to the ice gardens, where servants stood ready for the feast. A gentle chaos ensued as guests began heading for the small tents set up amid the ice carvings and servants circulated with trays of sparkling wine.

Everson turned to grin at the married couple, but they were still occupied with each other. He caught Overforth's eye on the other side of the garden dais instead. His uncle gave him a proud smile and bobbed his head.

There had been no rioting. No calls to run him out of town. No insults or looks of disgust. Nothing.

When he'd walked into the palace that morning with Overforth, his brother had simply smiled and said, "I like the hairstyle," then continued setting rose petal bags onto trays for the servants.

As the last of the guests filtered into the ice gardens, exhaustion quickly settled over Everson; all of the adrenaline from facing his greatest fear—revealing who he was in front of what felt like the entire city—had been spent, and all he wanted to do was go back to the cottage and settle in with a cup of tea and a book.

But he had duties to take care of, and right now, that meant holding onto this Omens-blasted ball of ice. Besides, there was no way he would abandon his brother during such a happy occasion.

After another minute, Druida and Vastion bowed to the cleric and made their way down the long garden path to the ice gardens. Everson watched them go, counting the seconds until he could put down the ice ball. As he watched the couple, he thought about the changes

Vastion and Druida would bring to Wrestia—particularly in favor of his own heritage. Simply "not rioting" at the presence of a faerŭn was a far cry from acceptance, he knew.

The cleric followed the happy couple, and Everson and Overforth were up next to wait their turn. They stood side by side—Overforth holding a chalice with seeds in it for some Omens-forsaken reason. Everson puffed out his chest.

"Your parents would be proud of you," Overforth said.

"Did you know I was...before?"

"No, no," Overforth said. "Had I known that, I would have realized for certain that the cottage was what it was. And perhaps would have been—" He paused and cleared his throat. "I would have been a little kinder. I think I saw too much of myself in you, the way you hid away as a child. But whether you were faerŭn or not, I should have..."

The cleric signaled for them to set down their artifacts and begin walking. Everson was looking forward to warming himself on one of the braziers they had set up under each tent in the ice gardens.

Overforth went on, "I should have treated you with more kindness. Shame...shame will do that."

"You have nothing to be ashamed of, Uncle—"

He let out a bark of a laugh. "Lecturing and mocking a mere child? Talking down to you as an adult, simply because I thought *I* was the only one handed the poor lot in life? And it's not as if I have many friends in Ravenshold, the way I speak to everyone. I have much to atone for.”

Everson shrugged. “We can only live the life we’ve been given. You had to hide who you were for so long, it’s no wonder...”

“It’s no wonder I turned out to be a cantankerous old man?” Overforth said with a snort.

Heat surged to Everson’s face. “No, I wasn’t—I was going to say it’s no wonder it was hard to find a way to deal with those feelings.”

Overforth clapped him on the back and chuckled. “I’m proud of you, Everson. Whether or not that means anything to you after how I’ve treated you all these years, I’m proud. And I think between you and your brother, perhaps you can change the fates of future faerŭn for the better. Prejudices are hard to break, though, so it won’t be easy.”

“I know.”

“I think I need to try a different tactic, myself,” Overforth said as they reached the ice gardens and passed a large carving of a stagicorn, the long horn on its head wreathed by an impressive display of antlers. “You know what they say; the lakes can’t make ice with hot air. Perhaps it’s time I moved back to Wrestia where I can make a difference.”

“You know, Uncle, there’s something else about the cottage you might not know.” Everson lowered his voice. “You could still visit Wrestia and live in Ravenshold with a wish.”

Overforth’s eyes widened. “So it’s true?” he said in a

hushed whisper. "No wonder I'd heard of it appearing in multiple locations."

Everson bowed his head. "I visited Ithalia Stonecrusher the other day and gave her the recipe for the Fen cure."

"I see," Overforth said. He stared ahead with glossy eyes as though seeing all the cottage's possibilities. "And that was how you came up with the cure in the first place, isn't it?"

"My friend, Nod—" Everson gasped, because the dwarf in question was barreling through the crowd straight for him.

"Everson, my boy!" Nod boomed, his arms out as he crashed into Everson and clamped him into a crushing hug, but not before Everson saw the joy and pride written all over the dwarf's face.

"It's good to see you," Everson managed, the corners of his eyes prickling.

Nod pulled away and grinned at him. "A beautiful ceremony, one I think all of Wrestia will remember for a dragon's age. Now, if you'll excuse me, I think I see some early maple candy on a tray of snow one of the servants is carrying—I'll see you at the grand opening, eh, Everson?"

"That's right. And maybe before then too?"

Hiron appeared out of nowhere, following his uncle's footsteps. Nod had tracked down the servant and gotten the sugary snack for each of them: maple syrup drizzled on fresh snow, freezing the sugary syrup into a semi-hard candy.

And though he was exhausted from the spent adrenaline and really just wanted to retreat into his cottage and a book, he found the table he had been assigned to, where Overforth had parked himself with a glass of sparkling wine—and no appearance of wanting to leave his seclusion. Everson found Vastion and Druida amid a gaggle of guests.

Vastion spotted him and took a step toward him, throwing an arm around Everson's shoulder. "My brother!"

"Congratulations, Vastion," Everson said, putting his own arm around him and clapping him on the back. "I couldn't think of a happier marriage for you."

"And you," Vastion said. "I'm so glad..."

Everson shook his head with a small smile. Though he'd done the impossible, he wasn't quite ready to talk about it with so many people around. He had noticed a few curious glances and wasn't sure how things would go *after* such a happy event as the lord of Wrestia's wedding, but Everson would rather enjoy the moment now. He didn't want to think about what the library would be like after he'd pulled such a stunt.

"Oh, that reminds me, I wanted to invite you to the grand opening of the library, a week from Sylsday before our book club. I should have—"

"We'll be there!" Druida burst in, pulling herself away from an enamored guest and lunging into the conversation with a glass in hand.

Everson chuckled. "You don't even know what I was going to say!"

"Let's see, a library's grand opening. You'll have... books?" Vastion guessed, a roguish grin on his face.

"*No,*" Everson drawled good-naturedly. Then he

frowned. "Well...erm...yes, the books will still be there. But we'll also have our *espresseaux* machine by then! I ordered one from Arcavia weeks ago, and I have..." he trailed off. "I have someone who might be able to teach me how to use it."

His joy evaporated a little into melancholy as he remembered the other event he'd been invited to today. And even though he wasn't sure where he stood with Mira, he had said he'd make it, and so he would.

After chatting with Druida and Vastion about the delights of Arcavian coffee, he let them return to the other guests. He knew the wedding feast was just as important a tradition as all the others, and the couple was required to be there for the entire thing, although Everson felt happily detached as he flitted through the crowd toward the food tables.

He didn't run into any other patrons from the library, and he wasn't sure whether that was a good or a bad sign. The crowd was large, and many guests wandered around the ice sculptures or availed themselves of the delicacies at the food tables. Everson selected a plate of cold cheese to nibble on, then went to the end of the food table where guests were roasting prepared skewers of meat over braziers. He selected a kabob with finely marbled steak paired with chopped onions and—after eyeing everyone else using the braziers to see how they were doing it—found a comfortable place to stand where he could hold it over the heat to cook. He underestimated how long it would take, but he had committed to it, and all the finished skewers looked mouthwatering.

"A fine wedding indeed," an old woman said, coming

to stand next to him and hold her own skewer over the small flames.

Everson swallowed, keenly aware of his bare head. "M-Ms. Francesca. A pleasure to see you here."

"And you, Everson," she said primly, rotating her skewer evenly over the brazier. The meat she had chosen looked like chicken, covered in a virleek and rosemary herb marinade. The mingled aromas formed an intoxicating cloud of deliciousness, making him wonder if he'd chosen the wrong flavor.

Ms. Francesca cocked her head toward him, and he could see her gaze sweep over his ears and silver slicked-back hair. She nodded. "You know, I quite enjoyed those last few *Dragon Lord's Queen* books," she said in a voice that was louder than he was expecting. "It's my favorite book series. I'm so glad the library was able to get them."

"O-Oh," Everson said in surprise. "I'm happy to help." He couldn't think of anything else to say, the shock at her admitting to liking the spicy fantasy book in front of the wedding guests mingling around them left him frozen to the spot. What had finally gotten her over her reluctance to admit such a thing?

The woman roasting two steak kabobs across from them said, "*Dragon Lord's Queen*, did you say? Have you gotten to book six yet?" Her eyes lit up with a delighted fervor.

Ms. Francesca grinned maniacally. "Oh, dearie, have I! Everson's got the whole series at the library—have you been yet?"

Stunned, Everson listened to them discuss the books and the library until he realized his kabob was almost overdone, and he hastily pulled it from the fire. He wasn't sure what had gotten into Ms. Francesca, but he was proud she had finally overcome her spiky embarrassment and even found a new friend to discuss theories with over the next book. Ms. Francesca's new friend Delilah, in turn, promised to attend the grand opening next week, and Everson decided to take his kabob and go. He really should be getting back to the cottage to try and make some of the gallery opening.

As dusk settled around them, he sought out Druida and Vastion to say a proper goodbye, but the crowd gathered around to give them well-wishes was six-deep, so Everson shrugged and slipped away toward the ice garden gates. Now that the sun had gone down, night would sink in fast, and he wasn't sure how long Mira's gallery opening would last.

He passed under the gate and set a hand on the cold stone archway. Scanning the crowd in the ice gardens, his thoughts trailed to his mother and how happy she and Vastion the First would have been today. A small smile lifted the corner of his mouth, and he struck out for the cottage and Melodïgha.

LIZ DELTON

LIZ DELTON

Music cascaded around Everson as he entered the duchess's garden. People in elegant colored suits and dresses of cream, coral, and tan mingled throughout the garden; others wandered through the large doorway to the gallery, where a pianist was playing an entrancing tune, luring people inside like a siren. The delicious temperate air was like a balm after his frosty walk back to the cottage, and it felt odd to put aside his heavy coat.

It felt even stranger to be walking into a new place without his cap. It was currently stuffed in his pocket.

But he held his back straight and headed for the art gallery. Whether or not it was due to his buoyed spirits after the wedding, he wasn't sure, but he knew he couldn't hide any longer. Mira deserved to know *all* the truth, and even if she never spoke to him again, he had to do this. She had already decided to stay in Melodïgha anyway, so what did it matter?

He pulled on his collar to straighten it before he got to the door.

"Everson, is that you?" Mira's melodic voice called. He turned, his heart in his throat.

She was dashing toward him on heels not dissimilar to those the duchess had worn the previous day, and by all the gods and Omens, her face lit up at the sight of him.

Suddenly he couldn't breathe. She clacked toward him, and her hands reached up to grasp his arms. "Everson! You made it!"

All he could do was nod.

She brushed a strand of hair away from her face and the two of them stood there looking at each other.

"Say something," he breathed when he couldn't take it any longer.

Her lips curved into a smile, and she leaned in. "You look dashing, Everson. I'm glad to finally meet the real you. I *thought* you had another secret hiding in there." She poked him in the chest playfully.

He bowed his head and ran a reluctant hand over his slicked-back hair, the tips of his ear catching on his hand. "I'm sorry. I've kept it from everyone until recently—I hadn't even told my brother."

"Oh, Everson," Mira said, leaning in and squeezing him in a hug, "I'm so glad you came." Her long black hair felt like silk under his fingertips, and he leaned in closer to rest his head on her shoulder.

"I am too."

"And I'm sorry I...I'm sorry I didn't send you a letter or anything about moving to Melodïgha, I really wanted —Well, I think it's better if you see—" She halted, and pulled away, taking his hand and guiding him toward the gallery.

The moment he walked through the door, his gaze was drawn to the artwork hanging on the stone walls around the airy room. Everson's jaw dropped as his steps slowed, the piano's melody fully submerging him in what almost seemed a dream of beauty.

It was all Mira's art. He knew because it was mostly paintings of the library. She must have done them in Master Raymyn's studio or at home, because he'd never seen any of them before. Randalf dozing on the chaise by the fire. Hiron and his friend excitedly poring over a book they were holding, the dwarf boy's expression captured perfectly in swaths of paint. Then there were other portraits, land-scapes, and still lifes of flowers. The simplicity of the strokes and colors bringing everything to life.

Everson turned in place, looking at the rest. Hanging directly over the door where he'd come in was the largest of all, a painting of...himself.

His mouth popped open slightly. In the portrait, he was sitting at his desk in thought, with a small smile on his face. He, of course, wore a cap on his head and had a steaming cup of tea on the desk before him. He glanced at Mira and back at the portrait.

"Say something," Mira begged.

"They look *dashing*," he said, grinning. "I can't believe you would paint...me. They're *incredible*. When did you even do all of these? I thought the gallery opening was for Master Raymyn's art?"

She twisted her hands, a happy smile on her face

nonetheless. "Well, you know how the gallery opening got moved up early? It was because Master Raymyn wrote to the duchess to ask her to feature *my* artwork instead; he'd seen my studio paintings. They're going to do another gallery night for Master Raymyn's as intended, but he thought mine were good enough so he put my name forward... And then the duchess loved them too and..."

"They're wonderful. Incredible. Mira the Master Artist." He reached over and squeezed her arm.

"Everson the Magical Librarian," Mira whispered, leaning closer. "You must know, I never wanted to leave Wrestia. Or you, for that matter. I'm sorry."

He bowed his head. "Mira, you don't have to apologize for chasing your dreams. Not to yourself or anyone else."

"But with the cottage...?" she asked tentatively, her gaze lifting through her thick lashes up at him.

"With the cottage, you can have both," he replied with a grin.

"Both it is," she said with a nod. Then she gave a mischievous look out of the corner of her eye and before he knew what she was doing, she'd leaned forward and kissed him. Her lips met his, and everything around them disappeared.

LIZ DELTON

EPILOGUE

"Sorry, again, Everson," Ferrace said as the two of them got into the sled. "But I think we'll still make the grand opening in time."

Everson looked across the snowy expanse between Wrestia and the wood and nodded. "It's fine, Ferrace. We have plenty of time. Mira and I got everything else ready last night, anyway, and she already knows how to use the machine."

The *espresseaux* machine was carefully strapped to the sled. The reason they were leaving the city so late was that Ferrace had forgotten the straps he'd promised to bring. When they'd gotten the package from Hand to Hand, Filgaria said she didn't have any either. So, they'd had to go back to Ferrace's house, where Everson had gotten waylaid by Glenda, who'd heaped a bag of cookies on him for the grand opening. Ferrace's neighbor was going to bring their kids by later so Glenda could have a nap in a quiet house during the goings-on.

He'd retrieved Mira from Melodïgha yesterday, and after she'd helped him with his preparations, she decided to spend the night in Wrestia so she'd be close by. The gallery opening had been a hit; she'd sold a few paintings and received several portrait commissions. Over the last week, she had very slowly moved her belongings to Melodïgha with the help of the cottage. So he'd walked her home and gone to the palace afterward for dinner with Druida and Vastion. Dinner had turned into drinks and virnolz in the drawing room, and he'd spent the night in his palace rooms, waking in time for a glorious palace breakfast, which had delayed his return to the cottage as much as Ferrace's detour.

Princess trotted across the snowy field, Everson's heart jangling along with the mule's harness. Though Vastion's wedding had been a week ago, and the library had been open since then, today felt different.

When they got to the library, Everson grinned at the sight of the barn in the woods. Nod had finished it the day before, and Princess belonged to Everson now. She had her own place to stay, and he and Nod had already tested out moving the cottage to make sure nothing strange happened to the barn. Ferrace came by every morning to care for Princess, and to run any errands with the sled, ferrying patrons back and forth to the city during opening hours.

Nod stood next to the barn; he appeared to be inspecting something on the trim of the side door where they kept Princess's sled and tack. "Oh, hey there, Everson! We're a bit early. Hiron's already gone inside."

"Good to see you, Nod," Everson said, hopping off the sled the second it stopped moving.

Ferrace set to work unstrapping the *espresseaux*

machine crate while Nod clapped Everson on the back and they headed for the cottage.

"Got something to show you," Nod said, puffing out his chest.

"Oh?" Everson asked. They got to the porch and Everson swept his cap off his head with a grin as Nod yanked on the door.

As Everson stepped inside, he immediately noticed the new, dark—and empty—shelves high on the walls above the children's and histories sections.

"What...?" he whispered in wonder. Then he turned his head back to Nod. "You didn't."

"I did," Nod said, grinning proudly and twirling a finger to indicate the rest of the cottage.

Everson turned to see Mira on a rolling ladder in the corner behind the door, stocking books on the new shelves Nod had built. "Y-You even did the ladder?"

"Better fetch a chair—I think he's going to faint," Mira said with a grin.

"How did you even have time to...?"

Ferrace walked in with the crate and grinned guiltily at him. "Sorry, Everson."

He stared at the shelves, which added half as much more storage space to his collection. He wouldn't have to remove books as often, and he could spend some time looking for new titles... "I need a cup of tea."

"I've got one right here," Lyla said, coming over with a fresh cup of Queen Gray. The familiar scent of bergamot clouded his stunned senses.

Another sled pulled up outside, and someone

bounded up onto the porch and through the door. "Was he surprised?" Vastion cried.

Everson scoffed after his sip of tea, "What, you were in on it too?"

"'Course. Can't have you running out of bookshelves with how valuable you are to the community."

"And we *did* really want to see you for dinner," Druida said, coming in on Vastion's heels.

"Mm-hmm," Everson said, setting down his cup and finally taking off his coat. "Well, we've got some more work to do then, I hope all of you know. We can't have bare shelves for our grand opening."

"It was worth it," Nod said, picking up a stack of books next to Everson's desk.

"And I have something else for the walls," Mira said, hopping down from the ladder.

Hiron's sly grin wasn't missed by anyone as he nabbed the ladder while it was still moving and hopped on for a joy ride. Everson chuckled as he turned to see what Mira was retrieving from under a piece of fabric she had leaning in the kitchen nook.

It was a painting of Randalf on the chaise. Everson's heart lifted and he strode over to her. "Miraluzana the Generous," he murmured. "You didn't have to..."

"I insisted. I told the duchess I would paint one of her to replace it, and she was perfectly happy with that."

"Then I'll have to thank the duchess as well," he said.

"Give it here," Nod said, reaching for the hammer hanging from a loop on his trousers. "The mantle all right? Think that's the only place."

Everson watched as Nod hung up the painting, then turned to the cat. "What do you think, Randalf the Gray?" The cat meowed lazily and rolled back to continue his nap. Everson nodded. "Now, who has book requests?"

Those gathered seemed to inch closer to Everson as he gave them a nervous grin. He'd told each and every one of them in the last week, from Ferrace to his brother and Druida to Lyla, who now bustled over, tying an apron over her dress and pulling out a small notepad. "We could use some more children's adventures. Now that the Fen is cured, the kids are back in lessons and are hungrier than ever for something that's not dry history."

"A perfect assessment from my new assistant," Everson said. Lyla grinned. He'd asked if she wanted to work part-time for the library when she'd come in the day after the wedding. He wanted the extra help and was looking forward to taking days off from running the library to do something thoroughly non-bookish. "I wish we had a dozen new children's adventure books."

Everyone seemed to hold their breath as a dozen books appeared on the floor before him, and he said, "Great. Let's get to work."

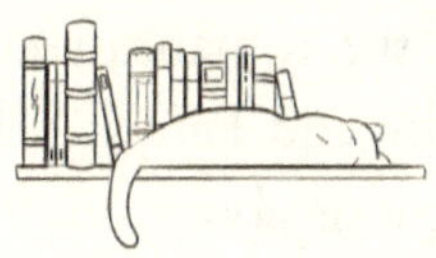

An hour later, the cottage was filled with voices as Everson hid in a corner of the kitchen nook and snagged a glass of Melodïgha wine from the tray there. The palace had donated plenty of food and drink that had been left-over from the wedding—so much that Everson would have leftovers for weeks if it kept.

"Is it ready yet?" Filgaria asked as she came up to him.

Everson shook his head, biting his lip.

"I swear, this is the same one I have at the cafe," Mira complained, giving the *espresseaux* machine on the counter a not-very gentle smack on the side. "But I can't—"

"May I take a look?" Geminigh said, appearing beside Filgaria. "I think I had a similar problem when mine arrived..."

The gnome got to work while Filgaria watched with interest over his shoulder. Mira simply drew back, shaking her head. She busied herself with the bag of Arcavian coffee beans Everson had ordered instead. He'd wanted to test them against what he could summon with the cottage, but that experiment would have to wait until after the grand opening.

Everson sipped his sparkling wine and looked over the crowd that had come to celebrate the library. Lyla was busy talking to her friends from the book club, and Ferrace had his small children underfoot while his neighbor browsed the romance section. Ms. Francesca was standing nearby and launched into a conversation with Ferrace's neighbor about one of the books on the shelf—Everson had a suspicion he knew what book series it was. He grinned.

The portrait of Randalf hung above the hearth, while

the cat himself hid upstairs in the loft, away from the commotion. Everson didn't blame him.

Halmund arrived next, the orc hard to miss as he came through the door that they'd left open. With so many people crammed inside, and the fire going, there was plenty of warmth to not have to deal with the crooked door.

"Everson!" Halmund roared. "The place is marvelous!"

Everson grinned, then furrowed his eyebrows at yet another orc entering the library. Ithalia Stonecrusher.

Curious, he gave Mira a pat on the arm and pushed himself off the kitchen counter to make his way through the crowd.

"Ithalia, it's nice to see you—" he began as he reached her.

"Mr. Wrestin," she said. "Quite the library you have here. Nod sent me an invitation to your grand opening."

"Oh, yes, of course! I'm so glad you could make it. I hope the journey wasn't too long." He bit his lip.

She waved a hand. "It's the least I could do. I'm staying in Wrestia for a couple nights, took some days off from the library so I could get to know yours better, if you don't mind."

"Not at all," he said, bobbing his head. "We're actually having a book club meeting after the party, if you want to stick around."

Her eyes lit up, and she gave him a fang-studded grin. "I would love that."

Halmund turned to introduce himself to Ithalia,

who gave him a toothy smile. Then they got to talking about Everson of all things, so he made himself scarce.

"Oh, sorry," Everson said, bumping into Uncle Overforth.

"That's all right," Overforth assured him, testing the balance of his sparkling wine glass to make sure it hadn't spilled. "Congratulations, Everson."

"Thank you. For...everything."

"You have nothing to thank me for," Overforth said, his expression turning disheartened, as if remembering their history.

"I have everything. I never would have been able to show my true self to all these people if it wasn't for...for our discussion."

Overforth nodded, his lips pressed tight, then he clapped Everson on the back. "You're a good lad, Everson. You'll do great things here—you already have. Is that Ithalia I see?"

Everson nodded, "Came all the way from Ravenshold."

"Then I think I need to have a word with her about the work she's going to do on the Fen journal—I'd like to see what I can do from the lawyer's consortium."

"Well," Everson lowered his voice, "keep the copy I gave you to yourself until they start publishing more, all right?"

"Of course," Overforth assured him, one hand over his heart.

A cheer went up in the kitchen nook, and Everson turned to see Mira triumphantly brewing a cup of coffee.

Soon the enigmatic scent bathed the cottage, and voices dropped to murmurs as everyone watched.

"The first cup for our librarian!" Mira called. "Get over here."

Everson's face warmed, and the crowd parted so he could retrieve the cup. Last night, he and Mira had arranged all the cups and glasses that he'd asked the cottage for.

"Did I mention you look quite dashing?" Mira murmured as she handed it to him.

"I could say the same to you." She smiled, red lips curving up enticingly. He leaned in and kissed her quickly on the cheek.

Ooohs burst from the crowd, and Everson called, "Now, now, the romance section is over there!" He pointed, his face even hotter than before. That earned him a chuckle from those assembled, and the general discussions picked back up.

He brought the cup to his lips and moaned. "Mira, are you sure you don't want to give up your life of artistry and make coffee for the library forever?"

She leaned over and returned his cheek kiss, making his heart leap in his chest. Or that might have been the coffee, he wasn't sure. "I think I can do a little of both," she said.

Indeed, Mira was engulfed in coffee requests for the rest of the party, with Geminigh giving her a hand. Everson shook hands, gave book recommendations, and even filled out a few library cards for some new patrons who'd filtered in and out during the party.

Soon the sun was low in the sky, and most everyone had left except for the book club and the two orcs. Halmund was having a deep discussion with Ithalia and showed no signs of leaving, even when Vastion offered his sled home.

Everson clapped his hands to get everyone's attention and said, "Are we ready for the book club? There's nothing better than discussing books with friends."

THE END

ACKNOWLEDGMENTS

What a wonderful experience this book has been! I couldn't have done it if it wasn't for the success of The Witch at the Edge of the Wood, so thank you to everyone who supported and loved that book!

Thank you to my husband Jeff, and to our two boys, who still call book one "The witch at the **end** of the wood", and claimed a copy for themselves even though they're four and seven. They're still trying to get me to give them one of the gold versions...

I also want to thank the Indie Fantasy Addicts group on Facebook, a delightful corner of the internet I help run, for showing such support for this series!

Thank you to all my artists for bringing the magic to life: Amy Marchant, Amber Finnegan, Mirela Pilko, and J.P. Misslecrow. Thank you to our audiobook narrator, Charles Linshaw, for voicing the story!

And the biggest thanks of all, to the 401 backers who supported the Library Kickstarter campaign! The amount of love and excitement for this story just blew me away!

Thank you:

A. E. Richardson

A. Vogel

A.A. Jankiewicz

Adam Kosakowski

Adam Robinson

Aisha Froese

AJ Nadolsky

AJ Snodgrass

Alexander Hale

Alexandra Corrsin

Alexandra G

Alexis W

Alicia Spangler

Allison Culley

Amanda Arand

Amanda Balter

Amanda Bean

Amanda Cummings

Amanda Tallon

Amber G

Amenda Wong

Amsel

Ana Lewis

Andrew Godecke

Andy McAllister

Angela Tucker

Angie Torres

Anna Beth Harrison

Anna L

Annarose Willhite

Anne Mollova

Anneli

Anthony Atthowe

Antoinetta Aquila

Arianne Hartsell-Gundy

Arthur Wilson

Ashleigh Lindsay

Ashleigh Lowry

Ashley M. Orndorff

Ashley M. Todt

Barbara Meijsen

Belinda Kroll

Ben M.

Bet Zyx

Bex Godby

Billye Herndon

Bob Eddy

Bonnie Solomon

Boris Veytsman

Brenna Greenfield

Brianna P.

Bridgette Findley

Brittany Watson

Brodie Smith

Brooke Chatelain

Brynn Rabinowitz

Caitlin Millsaps

Caitlin Pollastro

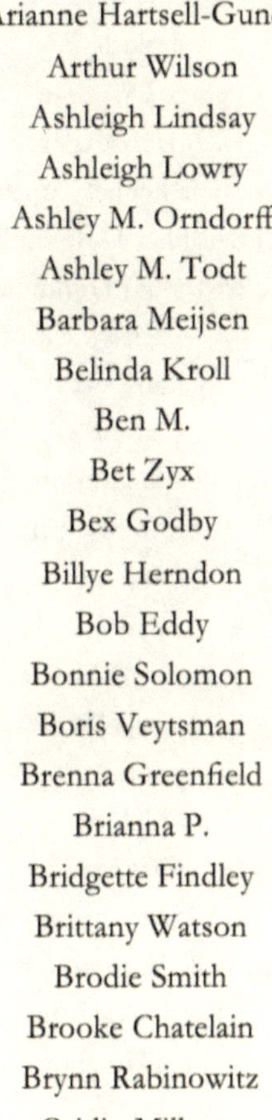

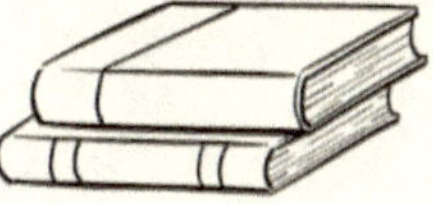

Caleb G.

Carol MacLennan-Gonzales

Catarina H.

Catherine Holmes

Cathrine Bonham

Charlotte P.

Cheryl Wildner

Chris Roeszler

Christina Schlickenmeyer

Christopher D Shramko

Christopher Dunnbier

Christy S

Chumyshka

Claire B.

Claude Baridon

Clayton Mytych

Codey Aker

Cody Jones

Cortney Babcock

Costa W

Cyann Ava

D. Marie

Dakota

Dan Kenner

Danielle Katherine Bird

David DeHaan

David Holzborn

David Turner

Dawn Marie

Dayna C.

Dean Lambert

Deann Fox

Debby M.

DebMarie Gilmore

Denise P

Denise R.

Dustbound

Edward and Hannah Jurina

Efrain Montalvo

Eileen Halecki

Elisabeth Brown

Elizabeth N. Carrillo

Elizabeth W.

Elizabeth Willems

Émilie Roy

Emma Flaws

Enalia T

Erik Kandefer

Eris

Finley Ymir

Frost

Gianna Christopher

Gwen

Halcran

Hannah Cole Orsag

Hannah H

Hazel Thompson

Heather H.

Heather Morikone

Heather S

Hillary C. Warren
Hollie Dance
Ilana Costello
Inka York
Irene Davis
Iris Juylyenne
J.A. Andrews
J.R. Johnson
Jack Oskay
Jaimie Smith
Jamie Brott
Jasper H.
Jaxon Charlton
Jay Roberts
Jeanna Stay
Jenn Oramous, PhD
Jenna Minick
Jennifer Greive
Jennifer Talbert
Jesper Holm Knudsen
Jess Harris
Jessica H
Jessica Kurnas
Jessica Retherford-Lattimore
Jessica Tucker
Jessica Wilbert
Jessie Marston
Jesslyn Wijaya
Jo Anderson
Joanna Masters

John Fritz
John Idlor
John P Curtin
JojoRose
Josh MacDonald
Joshua Gerdes
Julia Benson-Slaughter
K MacLeod
K.D.Brogdon
K.Low
K.Q. Kimler
Kaarin B.
Kaitlin Voor
Karen Monticello
Karina Krogh
Kat Vroman
Katalin Laczina
Kate Healey
Katelyn Mason
Katharine Wibell
Katherine Crowe
Katherine Malloy
Katrhiana Bauer
Katrina Eurell
Keith Edwards
Kel P
Kelly Knight
Kelly S. Castañeda Corona
Kelsey
Ken A. Baker

Kenyon Wensing
Kimberly Gonzalez
Kiwi Kuro
Kris Guthrie
Kristina Meschi
Krys Galvez
Krystal Bohannan
L. J. Lamotte
Lance Krautlarger
Lara H
Lark Cunningham
Lesley Jones
Leticia Henriksen
Lex Ransom
Lia Winnard
Liana
Lindsay Cunningham
Liz Semkiu
LN Emmert
Lorien Cord
Lou Dakin
Lucy
Luke Golding
LunarMoth
M. H. Woodscourt
Magda
Mallory
Marcee Brightenstine
Margaret A. Menzies
Margit Hofmann

Maria Bossard
Marie O' Keeffe
Mark Goodfellow
Marvin Travon Turner
Mayer Zsuzsanna
Megan Sanborn
Melanie Stark
Meow
Meredith Lowe Prather
Michelle Glover
Michelle Holloway
Michelle LaCrosse
Michelle Lynne Brenner
Michelle White
MichelleG
Mickey Spencer
Mike Dubost
Mike E.
miss pepita
Natalie Munford
Natasha Flerova
Natasha Savoie
Nery S.
Nick Lambert
Nicole Klem
Nicole Pfau
Nicole Sanders
Niki Kuhlman
Nikki Gibson
Nikki P

Nirkatze
Nord
Olia B.
Pamela Franson
Patty Abelt
Patty R
Peter "Tonour" Basak
Phi
Piotrek Kloda
Polinchka
R Wood
Ray Esterheld
Rebecca
Rebecca O'Neill
Rebecca P
Rebecca Winsdale-Floyd
Ren D
Ricardo Monascal
Richard Osborne
Rick Parker
Risa Scranton
RLS
Robert J Perez
Rosa Thill
Rosalie Weyer
Rosemaiden
Rowan Stone
Ruth Crook
Ruth Sanderson
S. C. Eston

S.L. Rowland
Sabrina Christina
Sally Lane
Samantha
Samantha Landström
Samantha Newberry
Sara Lawson
Sara Liming
Sarah E.
Sarah Faith
Sarah L Lawrence
Sarah Maier
Sarah Metcalf
Sarah R.
Sarah Rogers
Sarolta
Scarlett Luna Strange
Sebastian Stephens-Young
Shay Dinur
Sheldon Albertson
Sherry Cammer
Simon Mark de Wolfe
Sonia Munoz
Sophie Lovelock
Soras
Stacey Sturgis Andrews
Stefani Stewart
Stefke Leuhery
Stella Nussenbaum
Sue-Rae Rosenfeld

Suzy Kehret
Tabitha Mashburn
Terry Steinke
The Owlbear Enclave
The Pergola Family
The Sagers
The Tinsleys
Therese Marie Edman
Tiffany
Tony Hamlin
Tracy Lee
Trista R. Whitaker
ValerieAnne
Vanessa Villarreal
Ven
Vidi Castañeda
Wineke Sloos
Winnie L
Zephyr Mini
Zilla
ZombieOfBerlin

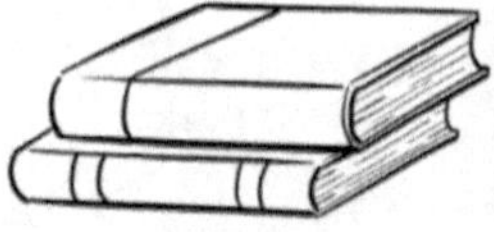

LIZ DELTON

Liz Delton writes and lives in New England, with her husband and sons. She studied Theater Management at the University of the Arts in Philly, always having enjoyed the backstage life of storytelling.

World-building is her favorite part of writing, and she is always dreaming up new fantastic places.

She loves drinking tea and traveling. When she's not writing or reading, you can find her baking in the kitchen or out in the garden making valiant attempts at keeping her plants alive.

Visit her website at **LizDelton.com**

ALSO BY LIZ DELTON

<u>COZY COTTAGE SERIES</u>

The Witch at the Edge of the Wood

The Library at the Edge of the Wood

The Tea Shop at the Edge of the Wood (2026)

<u>LEGENDS OF GOLD AND SILVER</u>

Flames of Gold

Echoes of Silver

Gods of Obsidian (2026)

<u>REALM OF CAMELLIA</u>

The Starless Girl

The Storm King

The Gray Mage

The Starlight Dragon

The Fall of Azurite

Realm of Camellia Omnibus

<u>SEASONS OF SOLDARK</u>

Spectacle of the Spring Queen

The Mechanical Masquerade

All Hallows Airship

The Clockwork Ice Dragon

Seasons of Soldark Novella Collection

<u>EVERTURN CHRONICLES</u>

The Alchemyst's Mirror

<u>FOUR CITIES OF ARCERA</u>

Meadowcity

The Fifth City

A Rift Between Cities

Sylvia in the Wilds

The Four Cities of Arcera Omnibus

<u>WRITER'S NOTEBOOKS</u>

Writer's Notebook

Teen Writer's Notebook

Guided Writer's Notebook

Shop **LizDelton.com**

for direct ebooks & audiobooks, signed books, merch, and
exclusive bundles.